THINKWAVE

CAMPBELL, WARP THE WAVE!

R Duncan Williams

Book II: Through the Phantasian

R DUNCAN WILLIAMS

ISBN: 1530450004
ISBN 13: 9781530450008
Library of Congress Control Number: 2016904383
CreateSpace Independent Publishing Platform
North Charleston, South Carolina

Thinkwave, Through the Phantasian is dedicated to my father, David Williams, who always believed I could accomplish whatever I set my mind to.

ACKNOWLEDGEMENTS

Like the first installment, completing this book would not have been possible without the help of others. I would like to thank the following for their help and support:

My dear friends and colleagues, Paul Schultz and Scott Moneyhon, whose encouragement feeds my spirit, and whose shenanigans feed my soul; the Morgan family, my first and finest fans; Sarah Scott, for her excellent advice and editorial assistance; Margie Morgan, for being the best fine-tooth-comber around; my sons, Aidan and Duncan, for being my heroes; and finally, my wife, Terri Michelle, for helping shape this story and those of her three boys.

PROLOGUE

Though encased by a mineralized shroud, he still heard every spoken word. Through the eyes of the hound, he had seen. He knew the boy's name and would recognize his face, if only he were free. There was still hope for his resurrection from the petrified sarcophagus. With enough time, they would figure out a way to free him. Unfortunately, time had all but expired. His wisdom was essential. There would be no going back without it, and without going back, the lights and life of Ecclon would fail.

GNARL

1

The clouds of Ecclon were nothing more than faintly glowing embers. No longer nourished by the thought energy of earth's inhabitants, the golden vibrancy of the orbs, which had nourished life on Ecclon for centuries, had cooled to a listless orange. Soon they would gray, then blacken, then dissipate altogether.

It had been two days since the Flurn Council had asked Harvey to warp to an unspecified time in earth's past. Unfortunately, the writings of the petrified Gnarl the Deep had proved fruitless regarding time travel. Consequently, Flurn and human had been frantically working, trying to figure out how to either revive or resurrect Gnarl the Deep.

Like wood-boring insects, fear and anxiety had begun to tunnel their way into Harvey's heart. His momentary victory over Nezraut had inflated his confidence enough for him to quickly agree to warp back into an adventure that had nearly taken his life. But now, with the Kreen nectar almost out of his system, and the reality of what was before, or rather behind him, he began to have second thoughts.

A cool breeze brushed Harvey's body and face. The layer of moving air interrupted his thinking. He tightly wrapped his arms around his body and rolled from his side onto his back.

Harvey had slept under the leafy branch-arms of Bellock, using Fromp's warm and furry belly as a pillow. Erratic movements of the warp-hound an hour earlier had awoken Harvey. Once he was jolted awake, he realized that Fromp was in the middle of an active dream, perhaps replaying his vicious tangle with Sköll, the leader of Nezraut's Volkin Wolves. Fromp's legs were sporadically extending and contracting. Muted whines, low growls, and shallow barks wound their way into the open air through teeth and gum.

Harvey's movements roused the warp-hound. Once awake, Fromp stretched his belly like an accordion and yawned gapingly wide. He turned to face Harvey. His baggy, watery eyes, still far from being awake, met those of the young human. Emerging from between his jaws like an eel from an underwater cave, Fromp's pink tongue painted a streak of slobber across Harvey's right cheek.

"Hey there, boy," Harvey said as he scratched Fromp under the chin.

Fromp responded by thumping his lengthy tail upon the ground. The blades of grass around Harvey lightly vibrated. A tiny tremble spiraled up through Bellock's trunk and spread to the tips of his branches. A leaf detached and slowly drifted downward.

Still lying on his back, Harvey was transfixed by its meandering glide. The leaf gently touched down on the bridge of his nose. He grabbed the stem and lifted it off of his face. He was just about to toss into the breeze, when a flash of color caught his eye. On the outer edges of the leaf was a line of orange and yellow. It was no more than a sixteenth of an inch wide, but it was clear and distinct.

Harvey stood up and looked into Bellock's eyes. Bellock had been in deep thought for the previous hours, sifting through possible ways to revive Gnarl the Deep. Harvey held the leaf out, breaking his gaze. Turning his attention to Harvey, Bellock said, "It is not the first one, nor will it be the last."

"How many?" asked Harvey.

"Five or so, similar to the one you are holding now."

"But there will be others and with more color?"

"Undoubtedly. We Flurn have always been adorned with leaves of verdant green. Never in the history of Ecclon have we worn plumage of red, yellow, and orange. I am certain that my appearance will be quite stunning. Too bad it will portend my death," Bellock said with a hint of a smile.

"We'll find a way to stop it. We'll find a way back."

"Let us hope so, and let us hope that it will be soon. I can feel the chlorophyll departing. Without it in my leaves, I will soon be unable to absorb what little light remains. Trees of your planet, color, shed, and sleep until awoken. It is a process which always begins with dimming sunlight and cooler days. For Ecclon, the weakening orb clouds are ushering in such a change. The first autumn of Ecclon is now upon us, though for us it will be different. Once we fall asleep, we will never again awaken."

The shock on Harvey's face was obvious. Up until this point, the threat to Ecclon had seemed distant and remote, but now, seeing the effects on Bellock, it felt real and personal.

"How much time before you lose them all?"

"Not enough to waste it fretting about how much of it I have left," Bellock said with the same flicker of a grin.

Just then, Salix, the wispy and often crotchety Flurn, interrupted their conversation.

"Bellock," Salix said with a jagged edge, "Merum's warp-hound has found something."

"Something?"

Already exasperated, Salix replied, "Do not make me waste words with explanations what seeing can accomplish more readily!"

Harvey did his best to repress a smile. The more time he spent around Salix, the more he had come to realize that the gruffness of his words was primarily bluster with very little storm.

Bellock obliged, and with Harvey and Fromp in tow, walked over to where ten other Flurn were gathered around the trunk of Gnarl the Petrified. As they approached, they could see that the focused attention of the Flurn was on a warp-hound that was gnawing at one of the exposed, petrified roots.

Merum turned to Bellock and began, "He has been gnawing on the same spot since we first gathered here today."

"Do you have any idea what has so captivated Tivit's snout and tongue?"

"It appears to be sap. Blue Flurn sap to be precise, oozing from a crack in the stone root. You know what this could mean, Bellock – living wood, somewhere inside. Gnarl the Deep, or at least some part of him, might still be alive."

"Sap does not necessarily indicate life," Bellock cautiously replied. "You know as well as I do that Flurn can excrete sap for years after they have been gathered to the plains of the Unseen."

"I understand, Bellock, but the fact that it was not oozing yesterday sets leaves to flutter."

"Leaves to flutter?" questioned Salix. "What in the name of Ecclon are you implying, Merum?"

"That it is significant."

"Balderdash! What manner of nonsense are you speaking? I agree with Bellock. I have seen sap drip from the most robust and vibrant Flurn to the deadest of the dead. Sap means nothing! Nothing but nonsense, including this ridiculous plan to somehow bring a dead Flurn to sprout and flower again!"

"Salix," Merum replied, "you should know me well enough to realize that I have little use for nonsense, the one exception being my tolerance for you, of course."

With this remark, Merum glanced over at Salix, who responded with a grunt and a humph. Bellock asked Merum to resume speaking.

"As I was in the process of explaining, yesterday, when we gathered around Gnarl the Petrified, my warp-hound, Tivit, accompanied me . . . "

"Of what matter is that?" barked Salix. "My warp-hound accompanies me wherever I go, as does every warp-hound of every Flurn on Ecclon! What does this have to do with there being a shred of the 'Deep' still dwelling within the 'Petrified'?"

By the time Salix finished with his last question, he was gesticulating wildly with his rootlet hands. Merum stared squarely at Salix, each of his leaves lightly quaking.

"Why it matters will be evident to you, old friend, if you will allow me to continue," Merum countered, more than a bit perturbed.

"You need not ask my permission. In fact, I am growing quite impatient waiting for you to do so."

Merum raised his mossy eyebrows, sighed, and with a forced smile, continued. "Once again, as I was explaining, Tivit was with me here yesterday. I recall him sniffing around Gnarl's trunk, but never once did he pause on the spot where we find the sap oozing today."

"Maybe something cracked the root. Couldn't the weight of a Flurn stepping on it crack it?" Harvey asked.

"It is possible, Harvey, but I do not believe very probable. It would take a significant amount of force, directed at exactly the right spot to crack a petrified root so thick. Futhermore, I don't recall any of us being close enough to the trunk to step on it."

"What then?"

"What then to be sure, my young friend. I believe it to be a type of distress signal sent from Gnarl the Deep, letting us know that he is alive and listening."

"Merum, I think your brain is as petrified as Gnarl's trunk," Salix said. "You see nothing but a dab of sap on a tree root and then deduce that it is a Flurn distress call. All of this is wasting what little time we have left. We should be using it for strengthening our defenses against Nezraut and not on some wild Zuit chase!"

"Our defenses are as formidable as possible," Bellock sternly replied. "But if we cannot establish a way to send Harvey back, all the defenses in our universe will do little to keep Ecclon from failing and falling."

"For argument's sake," said Salix, "let us suppose that Merum's notion that Gnarl is not completely petrified is true. What difference does it make? If he is alive, he is imprisoned in solid stone. The likelihood of freeing him seems relatively low, if not impossible."

"Could we not break away the surrounding stone?" asked Ukroon, an elderly, wide-trunked Flurn with gray moss hanging loosely from his branch-arms.

"It could conceivably work," replied Merum, "but the time required to remove it is precisely what we lack. We would have to chisel the stone away slowly and carefully, for we have no idea where inside we would cut into Gnarl's living wood, assuming that there is any. If he is buried deeply, then by the time we reach him, Ecclon will have been overrun by Nezraurt and his horde of Volkin Wolves."

2

Suddenly, a faint flutter of flapping leather echoed in the air above. A wispy shadow hurriedly fled over grass and rock. Harvey looked to Bellock to see if he had observed it. The Flurn leader's eyes, like those of the others, were transfixed on the trail of the now vanished shadow. Bellock then directed his gaze above and about.

"Aerial scouts," said Bellock, clearly alarmed. "Insips I suspect. It appears that Volkin Wolves are not the only new arrivals on Ecclon."

"Insips?" questioned Sheef, who walked up to the gathering with Jules and Joust, the two sleek and silver female warphounds flanking him. He and the girls had been gone for hours collecting Kreen fruit. After their battle with the enemy, Sheef's Kreen nectar supply needed to be replenished.

He slung down an overly stuffed backpack. It was straining at its seams with more than three dozen pieces of Kreen fruit. Fromp excitedly greeted the girls with his usual sniff, lick, and tail wag.

"Insips?" Sheef asked again. "How so? They're invisible to normal sight, and invisible objects don't typically cast shadows. Yeah, I saw it, too."

"Invisible on Earth," Bellock replied, "but Ecclon orbits in a different dimension, one that resonates and reflects the Unseen's realm noticeably more. We should not be surprised that what is completely hidden on Earth is only partially so on Ecclon."

"Well," Sheef commented, "if you're right, and those were Insips, I can tell you one thing, they weren't just out scouting."

"What do you mean?" asked Merum.

"What I mean is that I've spent more time than I care to recall around those flying weasels to know that if one's close by, it's there to listen. I guarantee you it wasn't just some fly-over reconnaissance. They were probably lurking behind a boulder or bush, eavesdropping on every word you've been chatting about, which by the way, wouldn't be very difficult to do. I could hear Salix shouting over a mile away."

"I was simply making a point," said Salix, now clearly embarrassed.

Harvey looked curiously to see if Flurns blushed when embarrassed.

"Well, maybe next time your point could be made with a little less racket."

Merum snickered.

"How long do you believe they were listening?" asked Salix, partially because he wanted to know, but mostly to redirect the unflattering attention away from himself.

"No way to know with any certainty," replied Sheef, "but I can promise that it was long enough for them to learn what we're up to. And it won't be long until Nezraut knows of our plan to send Harvey back and before."

"Then do we change the plan?" asked Harvey.

"No," said Bellock decidedly, "we adhere to the original plan, but if we do find a way back through time, it is likely that you and Sheef will not be traveling alone. You can rest assured that if Nezrarut learns what you are about, he and his hounds will be in close pursuit where and whenever you go."

"Then I guess it's a good thing that we've got plenty of Kreen," Sheef said with a chuckle. "If the enemy's breathing down our necks, it will make matters a whole lot easier if we can see him."

A flutter to flight from behind a nearby shrub interrupted Sheef. Attention was redirected to the sound. Bellock led the noise with his eyes and targeted his voice on the sound's projected trajectory.

In a rumbling baritone he fired his words. "We are creatures of the Unseen! You cannot endure His truth and power! I command you to cease in your machinations and reveal yourself!"

Apparently, whatever was flying over their heads clearly heard the words and understood, for a shifting, semi-transparent blur suddenly materialized into opaqueness and froze in the air. Twenty feet above the ground, a visible but paralyzed Insip struggled to remain airborne.

Stunned by Bellock's words, it was unable to flap its leathery wings. A panic-stricken realization flashed in its beady eyes just before it plummeted to the ground. It never hit. Before it had the chance to, Joust, Jules, Fromp, and Tivit latched onto either its wing or leg. The Insip's muscle and sinew were no match for the tugging ferocity of the four warp-hounds pulling in opposite directions. Within seconds, each of the hounds was shaking and gnawing their own play chunk.

"Must've been a straggler," said Sheef, "that failed to take off with the others. Probably hoped to listen in on one more tasty tidbit which it could offer to its Vapid Lord."

"Unfortunately," Bellock said, "the others heard, escaped, and by now have reported, which means it is imperative that we extricate Gnarl immediately."

"Demanding that we figure out a solution does little in the way of helping, Bellock," said Salix. "Gnarl is lost to us forever! A solution is not apparent to us Flurn because of the very fact that a solution does not exist, and demanding immediacy will not change this. The sooner you accept this reality, the sooner we can formulate a sensible strategy for protecting our planet."

Surprisingly, Bellock wasn't in the least bit perturbed by Salix's rude criticism. Instead of being agitated, Bellock's countenance warmed luminescent, sparked by two of Salix's words.

Bellock turned to Harvey as he addressed the entire group. "Salix," he said as excitedly as a dignified Flurn is capable of, "a word which you spoke has cleared the mist that has hung heavily in my mind ever since we endeavored to discover a method of freeing Gnarl the Deep from his petrified enclosure. The reason, which I now clearly comprehend, that we have not been able to discover a solution is that our resource of discovery has been entirely too dependent on 'we', rather than on 'he'. We Flurn have been relying solely on our wisdom and have failed to ask Harvey for his."

Without even looking, Bellock knew that Salix was on the cusp of interrupting with yet another ornery remark. But rather than letting him insert one of his characteristically rude, pithy comments, Bellock quickly closed the conversational gap by accelerating to his next statement.

"Harvey, I must apologize for not asking for your input. Since your return from Earth, numerous ideas have been proposed for somehow releasing Gnarl, but never once did any member of the Flurn Council think of inquiring of your thoughts."

"That's all right, Bellock," Harvey offered, becoming uncomfortable with the direction of the conversation. "I mean, what would I know about bringing a Flurn back to life?"

"No less than we do," replied Bellock, "for it has never been done."

"Never?" asked Harvey surprised. "But I thought at least at some point . . . some time ago . . . it must've occurred."

"No. Never. There was never a time when such an event was warranted. You must realize that your ideas, if you have any, are no less valid than anyone else's."

Bellock stopped speaking but continued staring at Harvey. Ten seconds of dead air crawled by as the rest of the Flurn Council, including Salix, turned their appraising eyes on him.

"Well?" Bellock finally asked.

"Well what?" replied Harvey, knowing full and well what Bellock had meant, but instinctively played dumb to buy time to generate an idea.

"Do you have any ideas you would like to contribute?"

Nothing. Harvey had absolutely nothing. For days, while the Council members launched, juggled, debated, and jettisoned ideas, Harvey had racked his brain, trying to come up with something, anything to suggest. And now, while withering under the heated gaze of expectant Flurn eyes, he still had nothing.

The last time he was in a situation for which he had no immediate answer – Sheef about to fall to his death, daggling precariously from a canyon wall hundreds of feet above the ground – he had turned to fruit, Kreen nectar to be precise. And now, faced with a situation for which he had no good response, he once again did the same.

"Kreen . . . what about giving him some Kreen nectar?" asked Harvey hesitantly. "It healed a deep gash in Sheef's leg, and basically made me into a super hero... at least temporarily."

"A what?" asked Salix.

Not wanting to explain a comic book super hero and why he temporarily behaved like one to a sentient tree, Harvey, with a wave of his hand said, "It doesn't matter, but giving Gnarl some Kreen might do something. It at least would be better than standing around doing nothing."

Sheef was the first to speak. "Kreen might actually work if we could somehow get it to the living part, if it exists, of Gnarl. But we can't very well give him the nectar to drink, and other than doing that, I don't see any other way of introducing it into his system. It's good thinking, Harvey, but . . . "

The fuzzy, static-laden cloud, which had dulled Harvey's imagination, suddenly vanished. In the clear, fresh air of his mind's eye, a sharp image glistened: his mother in a hospital bed with an IV needle in her left arm. At any other time, the image would've been unwelcome and quickly deleted, but in this desperate moment, he let the picture linger.

"What about something like an IV?" Harvey interjected.

"A what?" asked Merum.

"An IV," said Sheef. "Intravenous therapy. In our hospitals patients are given fluids, medicine, and even blood by inserting a needle directly into a vein. It's the easiest way to quickly introduce these into the body.

"I fail to see how this wonder of human medicine has any relevance to our present situation," snapped Salix sarcastically. "I do not suppose either of you have the implements necessary for the utilization of one of these IVs of yours?"

With no response from Harvey or Sheef, Salix continued. "I did not think so. And even if you did, I cannot imagine how you would manage to break through Gnarl's petrified exterior in order to deliver the Kreen nectar to his fictitious living part."

Completely ignoring Salix's remarks, Sheef turned to Harvey and asked, "Harvey, what exactly do you have in mind? Why did you bring up the IV?"

"I don't know. The image of my mom with an IV in her arm just came to me out of nowhere. It flashed in my mind like a photograph."

Bellock eyed Harvey critically and said, "Sudden, vivid images, such as this one of your mother, are seldom random and never meaningless. It seems that once again the proximity of the Unseen to you is made evident. And after everything you have experienced, this should come as no surprise to you."

Logically, it shouldn't have come as a surprise, but to Harvey, it did. He was still having difficulty wrapping his brain around the notion of the Unseen taking such a particular interest in a very average teenage boy.

Sheef was studying Harvey with a searching expression. In an instant, the search was over. His face pulsed with light like an Ecclonian orb cloud.

"Bellock's right," said Sheef, "the way things have been happening around you, Harvey, I wouldn't doubt the significance of one of your burps, and I think I might know why you were given the IV image. Gnarl may not have an exposed vein, and we may not have a needle, but we do have a crack, and an oozing one at that."

"Why of course, the crack! How could we have not seen it? It appears that our understanding has been as dense as Gnarl's trunk," Merum said with a chuckle of self-deprecating humor. "If the sap is actually flowing from the living wood of Gnarl, then what flows out must also flow in."

"My thoughts exactly," said Sheef. "If the sap is coming from him, then maybe it will behave like a vein and carry the Kreen nectar back to wherever he's trapped."

Sheef reached down and picked up the backpack of Kreen fruit and pulled out a small, empty bottle from his pants pocket.

"We've got no shortage of fruit, and I figure we can use the eye dropper from the bottle to drip the nectar into the crack. Don't know how much of this stuff it will take, or how long, or even if it will do anything at all, but it looks like the only shot we've got."

An hour later, Sheef had rigged up a makeshift drip mechanism. He had asked for one of Ukroon's long strands of moss which hung plentifully from his arms. He tied one end of the moss to Gnarl's petrified branch-arm directly above the root crack, and the other end to a piece of Kreen fruit. In the bottom of the fruit, he inserted the glass eyedropper. Its tip hovered less than an inch above the crack.

Everyone watched with rapt attention as the first drop of nectar emerged at tube's tip. The seconds sluggishly passed as Flurn and human impatiently waited for the first droplet to grow large enough to detach.

When it finally did let loose and fall, the luminous drop wobbled downward. The turquoise blue sap was still slowly flowing from the root crack when the droplet hit. Tiny yellow spheres rested atop the sap until small fissures opened up, and the nectar rolled in and disappeared.

3

They all stared expectantly at the now vanished Kreen nectar. The seconds fell into one another, dominoes collapsing in pre-arranged order, and yet, nothing. No change was observed. No signs of life from Gnarl-the-Apparently-Still-Petrified.

"Well, you really didn't expect anything to happen with just one drop, did you?" asked Sheef. "It'll take time to reach to wherever Gnarl's hiding in there. And how much nectar will be required? Who knows? But I don't think there's any reason to worry yet."

"'Who knows' is quite right, Sheef," said Merum while laughing to himself. "I realize that our situation is dire to say the least, but you must also admit that all of us intently gazing upon a sappy root, enthusiastically waiting for Gnarl to magically materialize after such a modicum of nectar has been dropped, is ridiculous."

"I am glad that you can make light of our potential demise and find humor in it," said Salix with patronizing condemnation.

"Oh come now, Salix," replied Merum, "we have little to do now but patiently wait, and we can either choose to do it as enjoyably or as miserably as possible. Of course, I have no doubt as to which choice you shall make."

Salix turned and walked away in a huff, leaving his words trailing in his wake. "If we are to wait for the inevitable 'nothing' to occur, then I suppose I can perform it alone and away from overly assertive Flurns who desire to impose their erroneously optimistic emotive state on others who would like their emotions to be respected and unmolested!"

The smidge of a smile worn by Merum grew wide and tall at Salix's tone and topic. Eventually, however, everyone else followed Salix's lead and drifted away from Gnarl in pairs and groups. And as the dim Ecclonian orbs sailed overhead, the steady cadence of nectar dropping onto the sap continued.

Bellock moved over to the edge of Council Gorge and burrowed the rootlet toes of his feet into the sandy soil. He invited Harvey and Sheef to come and rest under his branch-arms.

They both happily obliged. The view from the edge of the gorge was spectacular, but due to their recent slide and suspension from a similar elevation back on Earth, Harvey and Sheef elected to sit on Bellock's less scenic side.

Sheef cut a small piece of Kreen fruit in half with his pocket knife and gave one of the halves to Harvey. They both took just one bite, which was more than enough to satiate their hunger and thirst for the entire day. Harvey savored the flowery, citrus flavor.

Harvey looked at the orange orb clouds expand, contract, and reshape in the manner of boiling water as they drifted silently overhead. When his eyes began to blur, he imagined the floating clouds to be campfire sparks, snapping airborne into an evening sky. Soon his mind, too, was adrift, wandering into unconsciousness.

In his dream, someone was chasing him while cracking a large whip. Harvey was on foot, running as quickly as his feet would carry him, but with each step, his legs grew heavier, as if he was running through thickening concrete.

He looked back at his pursuer, who was rapidly closing the gap. Riding atop a carriage of twisted branches and black thorns was Nezraut, furiously snapping his whip on the backs of four massive Volkin Wolves that pulled the carriage. The pupils of their green eyes were dilated in a frenzy of hatred. Foam bubbled and trailed from their snarling jaws.

Harvey strove with every muscle to run faster, but the more energy he expended, the more leaden his legs became. In a matter of seconds, he had slowed to a trot. He turned his head for a final look, just in time to see one of the Volkin Wolves leap, its razor-jagged mouth mere inches from his calf. The teeth penetrated skin and muscle.

He tripped and fell, hitting the ground hard. The wolf held tightly, violently shaking his leg. Harvey flailed wildly, trying to free himself from the animal's tenacious bite as he let fly a blood-curdling scream.

"Harvey! Harvey, wake up!"

Sheef shook Harvey's leg as he continued trying to shout him awake. On the fifth "Harvey", the shutters of his eyes flung wide.

"It's got my leg! Get it off!"

"Harvey, calm down! There's nothing on your leg but my hand! You're having a nightmare. Come on, kid, wake up!"

Harvey's terrified eyes, which seemed to be fixed on some faraway vision, suddenly blinked and averted their attention to Sheef. It took him a few minutes to get his bearings. With the three-dimensionality of the nightmare fading back into the two-dimensionality of the dream world, Harvey finally calmed down enough to speak.

"Sheef, it was just a dream? But it was so real. I swear I felt it bite me."

"Felt what bite you?"

"A Volkin Wolf. Nezraut was riding on a black carriage covered with thorns. It was being pulled by these massive Volkin Wolves, and he was cracking a long leather whip on their backs. I was on foot, running as fast as I could, but the faster I tried to run, the slower I went. They caught up to me easily, and then one of the wolves lunged forward and latched onto my leg."

"That cracking sound you heard in your dream, you weren't making it up. We all heard it."

"What? You mean Nezraut's really here?" Harvey asked in a panic.

"Physically . . . thankfully, no. I, at least, haven't seen that putrid, two-mouthed, sewer spirit. And I would've, too. Just before you dozed off, I placed a drop of Kreen in both eyes. After the incident with the Insip, I wanted to be on my guard. No, the cracks came from Gnarl the Petrified. Sounds like the nectar might be working its magic. Why don't we get up and take a look."

Sheef extended a hand to Harvey, but as he stood to his feet, a searing pain shot through his leg. When he reached down to investigate, his fingers encountered a tepid, slippery liquid. He looked over at Sheef's right hand, the one he shook Harvey's leg with. It was splotched red.

"Sheef, your hand!" Harvey shouted. "There's blood all over it!"

Sheef looked down. He slowly raised his hand, rolling the fluid between the tips of his fingers.

"I told you it felt real," said Harvey. His eyes widening again.

"This is more than just a feeling, Harvey," said Sheef, his voice cutting more seriously.

"What do you mean?"

"I mean that feelings don't rip the skin off a leg and draw blood."

"Then what did? Do you think it could've really been Nezraut? Here on Ecclon?"

Sheef inhaled deeply, momentarily held his breath, and then measuredly released it through his nose before replying. "Not physically. That much is obvious. Like I said, I put Kreen in my eyes. Besides, even without the nectar, I would've seen something. Remember what Bellock said? Ecclon is more attuned with the resonance of the Unseen. Evil, for lack of a better word, 'sticks' out here. If we were able to easily spot an Insip, then you can rest assured that old sewer mouth would stand out like a flamingo at a crow convention."

"Then what was it? Something bit me. That blood came from a wound that wasn't there before I fell asleep."

Harvey was becoming visibly agitated. Sheef lowered the volume and treble of his voice before responding.

"Harvey, remember that the field upon which the Vapid and Insips wage their warfare is primarily in the mind, and when a powerful Vapid Lord like Nezraut has probed and manipulated your thoughts, he's had the opportunity to learn what makes you tick: your desires, fears, weaknesses, and blind spots."

"Like how he deceived me by twisting my desire for a normal family?"

"Exactly. But it doesn't end there. Whenever the enemy spends time poking around in your mind, trying to bend and contort your thoughts, he also establishes a sort of connection or link with it, and the stronger the enemy is, the more intense the connection."

"So you're saying that it was Nezraut's thoughts that did this to my leg?"

"No, I don't think they were Nezraut's thoughts at all. I think they were yours."

"What?" asked Harvey incredulously. "That's insane. I would never do that to myself!"

"Settle down, kid. I know you wouldn't knowingly or intentionally harm yourself, but consider this for a moment. What if Nezraut were to use your fear of him as a weapon against you? Recall what Bellock told you about how human thoughts and words have the capability to alter reality. Since we are created in the image of the One whose thoughts and words alter the physical realm when He expresses them, the same holds true for us. And if you don't remember that, I guarantee you that you can recall what you did to Nezraut and his Volkin Wolves back at his canyon lair."

Harvey grinned at the recollection, enjoying the image of Nezraut's serrated teeth shattering.

"But, Sheef, there was a huge amount of Kreen in my system."

"True, but the Kreen nectar only amplified what was already there. It was your thoughts that altered the physical realm, enabling you to battle Nezraut. And today, he used your very own thoughts to injure you."

"But how's that even possible?"

"While you were napping, Nezraut played a little horror movie in your mind, and he made it so intense that your fear of him was fully aroused, a fear which he used against you."

"You're saying that it was my own fear that bit my leg?"

"I know it sounds crazy, but that's exactly what I'm saying. Your thoughts, the same type that knocked Insips from the air and shattered teeth, today took on a life of their own and physically harmed you. "

Harvey's face blanched as he nervously rubbed his hands together.

"The news seems to be getting worse and worse."

"Unfortunately, that's typically the way things go when you're in the middle of a war."

"How do you know all this?"

"Come on, by now you should be able to answer that one on your own. My story? I willingly gave myself over to Nezraut for a matter of months. Remember? And even though it's improving and they're becoming less frequent, there are still nights when he tries to pay my dreams a visit."

"But what can I do? How can I defend myself when I'm asleep?"

"The same way you do when you're awake. It doesn't matter which world you're in: Earth, Ecclon, or Dream, you battle using the same weapon."

"Same weapon?"

"Hit him right between the eyes with the truth. The same weapon you used back on Earth. When you become skilled using this weapon in the dream world, dark forces will tire of being bruised and beaten, and they'll look for easier prey."

Sheef's words were followed by another jarring crack that rattled the atmosphere. Both Harvey and Sheef looked to where the Flurn were gathered around the glowing trunk of Gnarl the Petrified. It appeared that someone might finally be waking.

4

Harvey and Sheef hurried over to where the Flurn Elders were huddled together. Gathered as they were, they resembled a small grove of trees, a fiery glow outlined their branches, trunks, and leaves.

Bellock and Merum were standing next to each other. When they heard Harvey and Sheef's approach, they stepped aside, allowing the two humans to view what was occurring.

Harvey had seen film footage in school of molten lava bubbling and oozing forth from an active volcano. What lay before him was strikingly similar.

The petrified rock exterior of Gnarl had been liquefied, apparently by intense internal heat. Layer upon layer of his melting trunk slid down upon the ground where it set flame to grass and plant.

Harvey and Sheef were at least forty feet away, but the radiating heat had already singed their eyebrows and reddened their cheeks.

"We better back away before our faces begin to blister," cautioned Sheef.

Harvey nodded and stepped backward.

"Sheef, what's happening?"

"Can't say for sure, but something's cooking in there."

"I guess the Kreen worked."

"That just might be the understatement of the year, kid. 'Guess the Kreen worked'," Sheef said in a mocking voice while playfully slapping Harvey on the back.

There was no time to react to the explosion and blinding flash. Flurn and human were blown back and over. If Bellock and Merum hadn't moved aside moments earlier, Harvey and Sheef would have been crushed to death by twenty-foot Flurns toppling backward. Man and teenager hit flat on their backs, and a second later, Bellock and Merum landed with ground-quaking thumps on either side of them.

Sheef grimaced in pain from the grapefruit-sized rock that he had landed on. Having the wind knocked out of him, Harvey had to wait a full minute before he could manage to say anything.

"I think . . . Gnarl's either free . . . or there's nothing left of him," Harvey wheezed.

"Agreed," grunted Sheef.

A billowing cloud of dark grey smoke obscured whatever remained of the ancient sage. Without a wisp of wind, the smoke stubbornly hovered in the same spot, a theater curtain hiding the next act of the play.

Bellock turned towards Council Gorge. He closed his eyes, created a particular thought, and then released it into the gorge.

Moments later, a gust of wind leapt over the cliff's edge and hurried over to where the smoke cloud was still loitering. The wind gust flung the curtain aside, revealing a living, breathing Gnarl the Deep.

5

Harvey was finding it difficult to comprehend what was before him. He had expected that if they found a way to bring Gnarl back to life, his appearance would resemble what it had been when he became lost in his thoughts and was petrified. But instead of his bark being gnarled and twisted like the wrinkly contours of an elderly face, his trunk and branch-arms were smooth and vibrantly green. New leaves were unfurling and spreading wide.

A fluorescent gleam shimmered in the air surrounding the highly esteemed Flurn. Everyone took a tentative step closer. Two eyes suddenly opened and knowingly panned from left to right, narrowing briefly before becoming welcomingly large.

"Greetings, friends and fellow sproutlings of the Unseen." Gnarl's voice was neither weak and trembling nor deep and seasoned, characteristics one would expect from a Flurn of his age and understanding. On the contrary, his voice was bulging with excitement, similar to a child's narrative of his first visit to the ocean or amusement park.

"Come closer, my friends," said Gnarl invitingly. "There is no reason for creatures of one mind and heart to stand with a stranger's gap betwixt them."

Flurn and human accepted the invitation and moved to a conversational proximity around Gnarl's slender trunk. All heads were respectfully tilted downward out of respect for Ecclon's most revered Flurn. The more prominent leaders gathered in front. Harvey stood half hiding behind Merum.

"Bellock," said Gnarl, "it has been many growths since I last talked with you; you were not much more than a sapling. I doubt that you remember the words I shared with you."

"I was young, but your words I have never forgotten. You laid your hand upon my trunk and declared, 'Deep roots to great heights, then you shall lead them well.' I recited it often as a young Flurn."

Bellock then knelt before Gnarl in an attitude of humility, his large branch-arms sweeping the ground, and said, "It is an honor, and the utmost privilege, to by graced by the living presence of Ecclon's most eminent Flurn."

"Nonsense, Bellock, do not subjugate yourself to me," replied Gnarl. "We are all equal in the eyes of the Unseen. Rise, and let us converse on level ground as friends." Bellock slowly rose to his feet, feeling slightly embarrassed.

"And now, where is our young Harvey?" asked Gnarl turning to his right. I see Sheef . . . but not the boy." Gnarl nodded to Sheef, a gesture which was reciprocated. Harvey, meanwhile, slowly stepped out from behind Merum's trunk.

"Ah, there you are, my young friend" said Gnarl with a gleaming smile. There is absolutely no reason for you to be timid,

Harvey, especially in light of your courageous exploits against the Insips and that detestable Vapid Lord back on Earth."

Gnarl's words stunned Harvey more than the Flurn's youthful appearance. "How," asked Harvey in a tenuous voice, "do you even know my name? And how could you know anything about my battle with Nezraut? I mean . . . you've been trapped and petrified. You couldn't possibly know anything about me."

"I understand how baffling my words must sound to you, but do not assume that my encasement in rock rendered me deaf and dumb to what was occurring on Ecclon and Earth. I was neither asleep nor unaware."

"But you couldn't hear or see anything in there . . . could you?"

"Perhaps if I explain the circumstances surrounding the stillness which lead to my petrification, you will be able to understand how it was possible for me to apprehend certain events that transpired on both planets. This will also explain, which I suspect each one of you is wondering, why I appear to be so young.

"My assumption is that all of you gathered here have heard, and possibly offered your own speculation, as to why I remained motionless in one location for such a long duration, a period of time so long, as you know, that my body eventually succumbed to the forces petrification."

Everyone nodded. For decades a favorite topic of conversation amongst Flurn, both young and old, was the cause of Gnarl's transformation to stone.

Gnarl began again. "Now I believe that two of the more popular notions are that I was either chasing down a perplexing thought or trying to unknot a maddening enigma, both of which are utter nonsense, because they are so far removed from the actual truth."

Gnarl paused, letting this revelation be absorbed before proceeding. "What I was actually engaged in was meditation upon the goodness of the Unseen. I was plumbing the depths, ascending the heights, and exploring the girth of this most alluring part of His nature. The experience was . . . well, it is actually very difficult to put words to. Exhilarating, fulfilling, freeing . . . I could continue with modifiers indefinitely in order to describe what it was like, but words become but weak and inadequate symbols in conveying such a sublime experience.

"I was enjoying the process of losing myself – falling into Him might be a more apt way of describing it – so much that I lost my grip on time. You must understand that His goodness has no ceiling, floor, or walls. The deeper you dig, the richer the soil. The higher you fly, the more brilliant the lights. It was the greatest pleasure of my life, and so I let go of time in order to allow the current of His presence to carry me away into even richer places.

"Before I knew it, decades upon decades of your earth years, Harvey, had passed. The only reason that I became aware of myself and time was because the Unseen instructed me that I was needed to watch and listen for what was unfolding on Ecclon and Earth."

"But I still don't understand," asked Harvey, "how you were able to see and hear what was going on outside, especially what was occurring on another planet, in another universe, and in another dimension?"

"A very good question, Harvey, but before I answer it, I would like you to consider with whom I was communing."

"The Unseen, right?"

"Correct, the Unseen . . . the omnipresent and omniscient One. Since I was communing with an all-knowing being, I had access to events occurring beyond my own sight and hearing. Through His revelations, I was able to closely follow certain events and individuals on Ecclon and Earth, including you, Harvey. I have been observing you, through the Unseen, since you were a young boy, and you also, Sheef, beginning with your first warp to Ecclon."

For the first time since they met, Sheef appeared more stunned than Harvey.

"You should also understand that I was never imprisoned by rock, but rather captivated by His presence, and I would have gladly stayed where I was indefinitely. The rock exterior only fell away now because my time of observation had come to an end, and you required my assistance. The thought to infuse my sap with Kreen nectar was, incidentally, planted by the hand of the Unseen."

"But what about your appearance?" asked Sheef.

"Yes, yes, thank you for reminding me. It would seem logical that I would emerge from my petrification looking older than when I entered. And honestly," Gnarl remarked while laughing to himself, "I was not the most wooing and winsome wood to gaze upon, especially in my later days. My skin-bark was quite aged and weathered, gnarl upon gnarl upon gnarl covered my trunk and arms. I was also quite ponderous – wide trunk, you know. It occurs to all Flurn as they age, and I was over seven hundred years old when I fell into meditating upon the Unseen.

"But carefully consider, my friends, the ramifications of any creature soaking his roots deeply into the goodness of the Unseen for the duration of time that I did. If the Unseen is the source of vibrant, pulsating life, then does it not logically follow that one who absorbed the richness of His presence would not age in mind and body, but instead, grow younger?"

Harvey and Sheef nodded, showing Gnarl that they were still within sight of his train of thought.

"And what I have come to realize," he said as he continued, "is that time is not the sole culprit responsible for aging. The distance that a creature places between itself and the Unseen has a much more significant effect. Those who seek independence from Him become like orphans. But those who tenaciously cling to Him are at peace, for they know that they are His children. A sense of security flows from such an understanding, revitalizing the mind, body, and soul. Independence ages. Dependence rejuvenates.

"But enough about this. Time is rapidly eroding away, exposing our roots more perilously by the hour. We must be about the business of sending Harvey and Sheef back."

"Then you know how to do it," asked Sheef, "sending us back in time?"

"How to? Yes. Exactly when and where? No. But there are others who can help where I cannot."

"We won't have to break them out, too, will we?" asked Harvey.

"Certainly not, my young friend," replied Gnarl with a grin.

"Do you at least know," asked Bellock, "the event which occurred that began turning so many humans away from the thought energy of the Unseen?"

"Yes I do, but it was not, and is still not, an event. It is an object."

"An object?" interjected Merum. "Like the book the Vapid created?"

"Similar, but this object long predates their book. In fact, this particular item is quite ancient, and its origin is not of Earth . . . but Ecclon."

"From Ecclon?" asked Salix incredulously. "How could that even be possible?"

"It was stolen," replied Gnarl in a much more serious tone, "and taken to Earth. It is an object of incredible power, fashioned by skilled Lacit artisans centuries ago and . . ."

At the mention of the name "Lacit" Harvey's forehead furrowed. Gnarl's perceptive eyes observed this, and he paused with his explanation.

"Harvey, is there something that I said which has confused you? It appears that your countenance has clouded quizzical."

"I'm sorry, Gnarl sir, but I don't have any idea who the Lacit are."

Now it was Gnarl's turn for his smooth skin bark to wrinkle in confusion. "Not familiar with that word, but how can this be? Surely Bellock told you about the Lacit, considering that you and your – "

Bellock halted what Gnarl was about to say with a blustery interruption. "We have not the time for an anthropological lesson about a certain people group. Please, Gnarl, tell us what the object is, what it does, and most importantly, where we might locate it."

Gnarl responded to Bellock with a knowing look. "You did not tell him, did you? The boy has no idea who he is, no idea as to the true identity of his parents. Bellock, why? You should have informed him by now. It is Harvey's right to know the truth."

Harvey looked at Bellock, confusion already wrinkling the skin of his brow. His body swayed slightly back and forth, as if a small earthquake had shifted the ground under his feet.

Bellock rubbed the bark above his eyes with one of his rootlet hands. "I know . . . I should have informed him by now, but I felt that with all the burdens already placed on his young shoulders, the truth about his family might have been too much to bear. I was waiting for the opportune moment."

Harvey felt as if he had just been simultaneously whacked in the side of the head and punched in the stomach. Blood drained from his face as his extremities began to tingle.

"Bellock," Harvey said with a tinge of hurt in his voice, "what are you saying? What haven't you told me? And what does Gnarl mean by my parents' true identity?"

"Harvey, I never meant to hurt you. On the contrary, I was making, as I see it now, a feeble attempt at protecting . . ."

Bellock stopped speaking. The leaves on his arm stood upright. The breeze which had been lightly blowing for the last ten minutes abruptly stilled. The temperature plummeted from warm to frigid. Something other than Flurn and human had arrived.

6

The razor-sharp howling of thousands of wolves pierced the atmosphere. Echoes ricocheted through the hollowness of the gorge. The sound was initially faint, but intensified as the source of the howling drew closer.

"Volkin Wolves!" shouted Sheef.

"We may only have minutes before they arrive," said Bellock, trying to remain calm, "and with all that howling, their numbers will likely prove too much. Sheef, you and Harvey must warp back to Earth before they arrive. And Gnarl, you need to tell us as quickly as you can, where and when they are to warp!"

Gnarl gazed directly at Harvey as he said, "Your mother holds the key to . . ."

Gnarl's words were cut short by black clouds materializing around them. Sheef turned a circle and saw at least twenty oily-looking formations.

"Warp holes!" yelled Sheef. "And they don't look like friendlies!"

Bellock shot Fromp a thought. "Open a warp hole on the edge of the gorge to the Shellow Plain. Warp directly into the Shellow leading to Earth. Focus on Harvey's home. Now!"

During his first visit to Ecclon, Harvey learned from Bellock that warp-hounds can only open warp holes to Ecclon. In order to exit the planet and travel to another world or dimension, a Shellow must be accessed. Millions of them were arranged like constellations on the vast Shellow Plain of Ecclon.

Fromp streaked between two of the oily clouds. When he reached the gorge, he initiated the opening of the warp hole by speedily spinning in circles.

Meanwhile, the gaseous shapes surrounding the group began to rotate in a clockwise direction, slowly at first, but the rotations rapidly increased until they resembled many sucking whirlpools.

"Here they come! Brace yourselves!" commanded Bellock.

Twenty-three Vapid Lords stepped from their separate warp holes, each accompanied by a large, snarling Volkin Wolf. But for one, the yellow eyes set deeply in their skeletal faces were glaring menacingly at the gathered group. The one exception was pleasantly smiling, as if he were being reunited with dear friends after a prolonged absence.

A jolt of fear scurried up Harvey's spine. The teeth of the creature's double mouths were greatly damaged. Sheef's face paled. Nezraut had arrived.

In precisely the same amiable voice with which he had spoken to Harvey back on Earth, Nezraut addressed the gathering. "So . . . this is Ecclon," he said as he looked about. "For years

I have had one very pressing desire: to travel here, the gateway planet to all other worlds. And today, before Vapid and Flurn witnesses, this long-awaited desire has become a reality." He chuckled to himself as he clapped his hands together.

"And who, might I ask, are in attendance as delegates of the welcoming party for myself and my fellow Vapid Lords?" Nezraut asked with pleasant condescension as his dark companions tightened the circle around the group.

"Ah," said Nezraut as he stopped less than a foot from Bellock, "You must be the legendary Bellock of whom I have heard so much about. Lord of the Flurn! It is quite the honor to make your acquaintance." Nezraut's tone was sarcastic but coated with a cheap veneer of amiable politeness. "I must confess, though, that you have engendered in me a feeling of embarrassment. Merely your presence alone, Bellock, would have been more than propriety requires, but look at all these Flurn!" Nezraut remarked, waving his arms about the group.

"I have no doubt," the Vapid Lord continued, "that each one is very notable in his own right. Much more than was necessary, but nonetheless, I do appreciate the gesture." With this last sentence, Nezraut performed an exaggerated bow. Flurn and human remained riveted to the ground, immobilized by the present threat and bleak future that the Vapid's presence signified.

"I hope you realize that my Vapid Lords and I would have travelled here much sooner if not for the light. Do not mistake what I am saying. We are, by no means, sensitive to all light, only certain types. The one that radiates from your orb clouds is really quite offensive to our senses. I am not quite certain what it is about this particular light that irritates us so. Perhaps we are merely allergic to its source," Nezraut said sarcastically.

"But with the light of the orb clouds nearly extinguished, the environment of your planet now seems to agree with me, and . . . well . . . here I am!" Nezraut stretched his hands wide in mock anticipation of a hug as he turned himself around."

"I can assure you," seethed Bellock, "that no one here welcomes your games or sarcasm. What is your business here?"

Before Nezraut could reply, thousands of Volkin Wolves wildly burst into the gathering. They jostled against each other, forming enormous clusters of saliva, pants, and snarls.

"Quiet, my pets," said Nezraut as if addressing young children. "I know that you are all eager to play, but you must be patient. Soon enough, you shall be released for hours of fun with our hosts."

Bellock shot a swift glance to the gorge. Fromp had opened the warp hole and dragged it off the edge. The top of it was visible, horizontally rotating in midair . . . hovering . . . waiting. The warp-hound lay flat behind a large boulder, his eyes and snout the only features visible.

Bellock gave an almost imperceptible nod to Sheef. Sheef, who was standing next to Harvey, nudged him lightly and directed his eyes to the gorge. Harvey didn't know exactly what he was being told to do, but decided to follow Sheef's lead whenever he made his move.

"And, Sheef," whispered Nezruat, turning to face him. "How long has it been? Far too long for my taste, my friend." Nezraut walked over and stopped in front of Sheef. The Vapid Lord leaned down, so that his face was only inches from that of Sheef's. Sheef couldn't help but inhale the vile exhalations from the double mouths. His stomach turned, and he felt that at any moment he might vomit into Nezruat's smarmy face. The Vapid Lord lifted one of his elongated, skeletal fingers, slowly dragging its nail down Sheef's cheek.

"Do you not miss it, Sheef, doing my bidding? The hate, anger, and all that power. I know you remember the power. It could be yours once again, old friend. You need but ask, and it is yours for the taking."

Sheef's face and limbs began shaking uncontrollably, and though it was difficult to get the words out, through chattering teeth, he said, "Never again, you putrid piece of dung!" The last word was enunciated with such intensity that a fair amount of spittle accompanied it.

Nezraut's smile vanished, replaced by a sneering contempt. His hand dropped down to Sheef's neck, where his skeletal fingers wrapped tightly. He lifted Sheef two feet off the ground. And like the smile, the soft, pleasant voice hardened into viciousness.

"Just remember, Sheef, when you are suffering, tortured by the unfathomable darkness of my thoughts, that I gave you a chance."

"A chance," Sheef gasped, "to be a slave again to your deceptions? Not on your life."

"Correct, Sheef," Nezraut said with a sneer, "it will not be on my life, but yours."

Without warning, Nezraut whipped his head in the direction of Harvey.

"And do not think, young Harvey, that I have forgotten about you. We have a bit of unfinished business to tend to."

Nezraut flung Sheef backwards. He flew at least forty feet before landing atop a large Kreen bush. He staggered to his feet while rubbing his throat. Limping back to the gathering, he soon rejoined Harvey.

"Bellock," said Nezraut, the pleasantry once again drizzling his words, "you asked a moment ago what my business was. The answer, which may surprise you, has nothing to do with you. The destruction of the Flurn, you see, was never my ultimate goal. It is, and has always been, controlling Ecclon."

"We will never allow you to take it," replied Bellock.

"Oh, my dear Bellock," laughed Nezraut, "for someone reputed as being the very paragon of wisdom, you have responded with the words of a fool. Do you not realize? Can you not see? Ecclon is already mine. You are surrounded by my most powerful Vapid Lords, not to mention thousands of ferocious Volkin Wolves. It appears that too many of those humans you care so much about on Earth have turned away from the thought energy of your beloved Unseen. The lights of Ecclon are nearly out, as are you and your fellow Flurn."

Nezraut drew a deep breath before continuing. "Well, I believe that is enough chitchat for now. The time has arrived for my Vapid Lords and Volkin Wolves to decimate our new Flurnish friends, and for me to acquaint Sheef and young Harvey with the ramifications of defiance."

Bellock knew that if he didn't act immediately, it would be too late. He needed to create a momentary distraction that would allow Harvey and Sheef to make a run for the hovering warp hole.

Nezraut was in the process of redirecting his attention to the entire group when Bellock swung long and wide with his right branch-arm. The inertia of the traveling wooden arm collided with Nezraut's head, tumbling him backward. His acrobatics were halted by the dense trunk of an ever-pink tree. The diversion worked. The other Vapid Lords descended on Bellock, leaving an open path to the gorge.

Sheef smacked Harvey on the back. "That's our cue! Time to make an exit!" And with that, Sheef took off running towards the gorge. Harvey followed on his heels, sprinting as fast as his feet would carry him. Out ahead, Sheef showed no signs of slowing down. When he reached the edge, he leapt out into thin air, dropping down and out of sight.

Because Sheef had proved to Harvey time and again that he was trustworthy, Harvey followed his friend and mentor's bizarre lead without hesitation.

When he jumped, he quickly glanced back at the gathering. Nezraut stood directly over Bellock who was on the ground, being bitten on all sides by a pack of raging Volkin Wolves. As he fell into the warp-hole, he heard the distant words of Gnarl: "Remember, she holds the key!"

1

Harvey and Sheef were warped directly into the Shellow leading back to Earth. And like he experienced before, Harvey was flattened and twisted as his body was vacuumed up into the seashell shaped object, coiling tightly around its circling innards before vanishing.

They emerged back on Earth, ten feet off the ground, whereupon they were violently pulled down by an abusive gravity. Their flesh and bones absorbed the impact. If this wasn't bad enough, Fromp made the situation far worse and more painful when he dropped onto their backs only seconds later.

"Fromp, get off me!" yelled Sheef. "I wish we didn't have to take that Shellow ride. It doesn't matter how many times you go through one of those, you never get used to being twisted up like a pretzel."

Sheef did a cursory examination of his body and then brushed a bit of dirt off his shirt. "I don't believe anything's broken, but I'm going to be sore for the next two weeks! Harvey, you okay?"

"Yeah, I'm okay," Harvey said as he sat up. After a long, wordless pause, with a quiver in his voice, he continued, "Sheef, when I jumped for the warp hole, I glanced back. Bellock was being attacked by a pack of Volkin Wolves while Nezraut glared down at him. Do you think that he's . . . you know . . ."

"I really couldn't say, kid."

Sheef could see the tears pooling in the corners of Harvey's eyes. He couldn't imagine how Bellock might have survived, and he knew that Harvey was probably thinking along these very same lines as well.

"Harvey, Bellock knew what he was doing, and if anyone could escape from old sewer mouth's clutches, it was him. But I can tell you this, if he didn't make it, and I'm not saying that's what happened, he did it to save you and me. So we'd better be about the business of making our lives count."

Harvey sniffed and wiped his nose with the back of his hand. "You're right, Sheef, even if he didn't make it, he wouldn't want me to sit here wasting time and feeling sorry for him, or for myself for that matter."

Sheef could tell by the broken manner in which Harvey spoke that they were forced words, devoid of the emotions which they feigned. He also knew that before Harvey's true feelings returned and overwhelmed him, he needed to distract him and get him focused on the task before them.

"I figure the first thing we need to do," said Sheef as he stood, "is to determine where exactly we are."

"That's an easy one, Sheef," said Harvey as he stood to his feet. "We're in my backyard."

"Your backyard? Why in the world would Bellock send us here?"

"It must've been what Gnarl said."

Sheef looked at Harvey with a blank expression.

"Didn't you hear what Gnarl said about my mom?"

"Sorry, kid, when Nezraut showed up, I was a little overwhelmed at seeing him again."

"But Gnarl said it before the Vapid even arrived."

"That might be true, but I felt Nezraut's approach before the warp holes opened. You forget that I was connected to him for months. If he gets anywhere close to me, I'm able to sense him long before anyone else can."

Harvey observed that Sheef's face was losing its color again. Apparently, he wasn't the only one who needed to be distracted.

"I think you spit in his face."

"Whose face?"

"Nezraut's. When he lifted you off the ground and was squeezing your neck, you said, 'Never again you something piece of dung.'"

"Putrid"

"What?"

"I called him a putrid piece of dung."

"Oh, yeah . . . anyway, when you said the last word, you spit in his face."

"Are you serious? I was so scared. I had no idea what I was doing. I can't believe what I said. And then I really spit in his face?" Sheef laughed to himself as his color returned.

Joining in with his own laughter, Harvey replied, "Yeah, and I think right in his eye."

Once the disbelief and humor subsided, Sheef asked, "So what did Gnarl say about your mom?"

"He said that she was the key."

"The key? The key to what? And your mom? What does she have to do with any of this?"

"That's exactly what I want to know. Gnarl didn't get to finish because Bellock interrupted him, and I think Bellock was about to explain something about it to me when the Vapid Lords showed up. He also said the word 'Lacit' and then acted like I should already be familiar with it. "

"Lacit?"

"Have you ever heard of it?"

"That's a new one to me. But you know, if your mom is the key, then maybe we should go and ask her about it. See what she knows."

"Are you crazy? If I go in there and begin telling her about talking trees and other planets, she'll think I'm on drugs! Besides, how do I explain who you are and why I suddenly have an enormous purple dog with me?"

"You're right, it would sound crazy, but there must be a reason that Gnarl said what he did, and since we don't have any other leads about where and when we're supposed to go, not to mention what we're looking for, I don't see that we really have much of a choice. You agree?"

"Yeah, I guess, but don't say anything. Let me do the talking."

"The mic's all yours. Do you think she's home?"

"Trust me. She's home. My mom's really sick. She never leaves the house except to go to see her doctors, but she hardly goes to see them anymore. They couldn't figure out what's wrong with her, so they've pretty much given up. She can barely get out of bed, and that's probably where she is right now, sleeping or watching another one of her classic movies. I bet she hasn't even realized that I've been gone," Harvey said dejectedly.

Sheef could sense the deep hurt behind Harvey's words and immediately felt compassion for him.

"I'm sorry, Harvey. That's rough. No one, especially someone your age, should have to deal with something like that."

"Thanks." It was the only word Harvey was able to respond with. He was fighting back emerging tears. Ever since he had been whisked away to Ecclon, things had happened so quickly that he had little to no time to think about his mom and dad, much less to miss them. Now, however, with the return of familiar sights and thoughts, the old emotions came rushing back. He had no idea how powerful they were until he had distanced himself from them by another universe and dimension and then returned home.

Harvey climbed the stairs to the deck. Sheef and Fromp followed a number of feet back. As they walked across the deck to the backdoor, Harvey looked down at his grandfather's old rocking chair. It was from there, while gnawing on a pickle, that he first saw Fromp, who had apprehended him by tail and whisked him away into the unimaginable. It seemed so long ago, another life time, in fact. Harvey wondered where he would be a month from now. "Still alive, I hope," he thought to himself.

He reached down, turned the door knob, and entered into the next act of his adventure, wondering if it would prove to be as unbelievable as the last.

LACIT

8

The house was still and lifeless as usual. Everything appeared to be in exactly the same place as when Harvey was last here. It was silent, like a historic home in which visitors are permitted to look but not touch.

Fromp scent-hunted for any dropped morsels of food. As fine wine is to humans, so too, is dropped human food to warp-hounds, the older the better. The flavor of cheese, meat, and other tasty vittles deepens and becomes more complex with time. Unfortunately for Fromp, there were no such scents to satisfy his sniffer.

When Harvey reached his mother's bedroom door, he could hear muffled whimpers inside. It sounded as if someone was softly crying. He slowly pushed the door open.

Surprisingly, the television wasn't on, and his mother wasn't asleep. Instead, she was propped up on a pillow. Used tissues were scattered about the bed. Her bloodshot, baggy eyes indicated that both tears and insomnia had been frequent visitors of late.

It took a moment for her glassy, watery eyes to focus and then recognize who had entered the room, but when she did, her deafening shriek was powerful enough to shatter glass.

"Harvey!" she screamed, "You're back! Thank heavens you're okay! You've no idea how worried I've been. I haven't been able to sleep for weeks. But now you're back, right here in my room! Oh please, come and let me hug you."

Harvey walked over to the side of the bed and sat down. Sheef, feeling awkward in the presence of such intimate emotion, reversed it a few steps back into the hall.

Harvey's mother embraced her son tightly, burying her face into his shoulder. He could feel the run-off from her nose seeping through his shirt. She held him for more than two minutes. Her mixed cries and laughter created a bubbling sound like a cat purring underwater. When she finally surfaced, she sat back against her pillow, wiped her eyes, blew her nose, and did her best to pull herself together.

Astonishment blanketed Harvey's face. For someone who had assumed that he hadn't been missed, the reception from his mother knocked his unprepared emotions off their feet. Tears ran unchecked down his cheeks.

Through sniffles and tears she said, "Oh, son, just look at you. You've changed. I can tell. There's something very different about you. You've matured into a young man, and I've a fair idea as to what might've brought it about."

"What on earth is she saying?" Harvey thought to himself. "How could she have any idea of what I've been through?"

"And who is this with you, Harvey?" asked his mother. "Please come in," she motioned to Sheef. "It's quite all right. Any friend of Harvey is welcome here."

Sheef tentatively stepped forward. Fromp stretched his boxy, curious head and neck around Sheef's chest and peered into the room.

"Harvey," his mother said excitedly, "you have a warp-hound! But of course you would. How silly of me." Her eyes grew suddenly wide in recognition. "Sweetie, your hound must be one of Clesia's pups. She had the most lovely coloration of any warp-hound I've ever seen. Beautiful indigo, just like your warp-hound. There's no doubt in my mind, definitely Clesia's offspring."

Harvey turned back to Sheef and whispered, "Sheef, how does my mom know about warp-hounds?"

"I'm as in the dark as you are."

"What's his name, son?"

"Uh . . ." Harvey was so befuddled because of his mother's behavior that he couldn't find the words. "Um . . . uh . . . Fromp. Fromp's his name."

"Fromp. What a wonderful name. Suits him perfectly. I love it," she said excitedly as she patted the top of her mattress. "Come here, Fromp. It's okay. Come and see me."

Fromp didn't need to be asked a third time. Tongue flapping loosely from the side of his mouth, he bounded twice before launching himself onto the bed. Unfortunately for the bed, the wooden slats supporting the box spring and mattress were no match for Fromp's solid "kerplunk". The wooden slats snapped, the bed crashed down, and Harvey's mom laughed like she hadn't in years.

"I guess it's a good thing that I moved over to hug you Harvey. If not, Fromp's landing might have done me in."

Fromp's enormous tongue began bathing Harvey's mother's right ear.

"It's so nice to be loved on by a warp-hound again! I've forgotten how affectionate they can be. It must be close to twelve years since I last saw one."

Harvey ran his fingers through his hair before slowly sliding his hand down his face, stretching his eyes and mouth. "Mom, what are you talking about? How can you possibly have an idea what a warp-hound is? Unless . . ."

"Unless what, sweetie?"

"Unless you've been there yourself."

"Do you mean Ecclon?" his mother asked with a coy smile.

"Sheef, what's happening here? Please tell me you know what's going on. How does she know the name of that planet?"

"Like I said before, I'm in the dark. I've got nothing. Why don't you just ask her?"

"That's a marvelous idea," said Harvey's mother, her voice reminding Harvey that she could hear everything that he and Sheef had just said. "But before you ask me anything, shouldn't you introduce me to your friend?"

"Uh . . . yeah . . . sorry. This is John Sheefer," Harvey said as he motioned towards Sheef, "but he prefers to be called 'Sheef'."

"Sheef . . . yes, I've heard of you. You're the one that went after the book the Flurn suspected the Vapid were creating."

"Okay . . ." said Sheef, "this is getting really weird now."

"It's not weird at all, Sheef. Before I left Ecclon for Earth, I recall Bellock mentioning your name."

"Before you left for Earth!" Harvey blurted out. "Mom, what are you saying! I really need to sit down."

"Sweetie, you're already sitting down."

"Oh, yeah. Then maybe I need to stand up." Harvey stood up and began nervously pacing around the room.

"Son, come sit back down next to me, and I'll explain everything."

Harvey nodded and sat down once again on the edge of the bed. Sheef pulled up a chair from the corner of the room. Fromp, meanwhile, rested his head on Harvey's mother's lap and received an ear massage.

"Harvey, before I begin, I need to apologize for not telling you sooner," she said as she reached up and gently stroked his cheek. "The reason I kept it from you is because I just didn't think you were ready to learn the truth about our family. I want you to know that I love you more than anything, and that I only withheld what I'm about to tell you for your own good."

Harvey simply nodded, tears once again welling up in his eyes."

"Okay then . . . well, for starters, our family isn't human. We're Ecclonian, Lacit to be precise."

"I'm not human?" Harvey asked with saucer eyes.

No you're not, but Lacit are very similar to humans. In fact, other than a slightly enlarged lung capacity and two hearts, the anatomy of the two species is nearly indistinguishable.

"Two hearts!"

"Settle down, sweetie. There's no reason to panic," she said while lightly patting his hand. "Your second heart is directly behind your first. That's why it doesn't appear on any x-rays. It's likely that it was dormant and didn't begin pumping until you warped to Ecclon. The change in gravity and atmosphere probably awakened it. Have you felt stronger and more energetic since spending time on Ecclon?"

"Are you kidding? I've felt stronger, faster, and more energetic than I've ever felt in my life. But I thought it was because of the Kreen nectar."

"Kreen would definitely be a contributing factor, but that second heart of yours is also feeding every cell in your body with twice the amount of oxygen."

Harvey placed his hand on his chest and moved it about, doing his best to detect a second heartbeat.

"You've got to be kidding me," Sheef whispered under his breath.

"Not at all, Sheef," said Harvey's mother smiling again. "Yes, I heard you. Lacit also have more sensitive hearing than humans."

"Oh . . . good to know," said Sheef, clearly embarrassed.

"I didn't know," said a dumbfounded Harvey, "that there was anything else besides the Flurn on Ecclon. I just thought . . ."

"You assumed, and rightfully so, son. If no one informed you otherwise, as Bellock obviously didn't, why would you think any differently? So, you and I, Harvey, are Lacit."

"But not just any old Lacit," said a booming voice preceding its source into the bedroom. "Interesting family discussion we appear to be having. Seems as if someone has returned seeking the truth."

"Dad," said Harvey, "you're home! Wait, what did you say?"

"Well, it's Friday," he replied, ignoring Harvey's question. "Pulled into the driveway minutes ago. But as I was saying, your mom's not your average Lacit. She's Ecclonian royalty."

"Like a princess?" gasped Harvey incredulously.

"Actually, more like a queen. Although that's not official quite yet. Your mother's father passed away shortly after we left for Earth. Your mom's next in line, but, like I said, it's not official yet, not until the coronation. That is if she ever returns, and from what I've been hearing lately, there may not be anything to return to."

"Then does that make me a . . ." mumbled a pale and dazed thirteen year old.

"It certainly does. Prince Harvey. Has a nice ring to it doesn't it?"

"Then that must make you the King."

"Oh no. In order for that to be the case, I would have to be your father."

As on Ecclon, so now on Earth, this was too much revelation at once. Dizzy to black. Sitting to slide. Faint to floor. And Harvey was out for the count.

9

The sweet aroma of breakfast rustled Harvey awake. After he fainted, someone had moved him to the couch in the living room. When he opened his eyes, he could see Sheef wearing an apron, milling about the kitchen.

"Hey, look who's decided to rejoin the land of the living," said Sheef while flipping something over in a pan. "Harvey, do you want an omelet? They're delicious and made to order."

Harvey's mother and father, or whoever he was, were already eating at the kitchen table. Fromp had maneuvered himself strategically near the stove, waiting for any flavorful discards to drop.

As Sheef turned to transfer his omelet to a plate on the kitchen table, he tripped over Fromp's legs and paws, which extended outward like the exposed roots of an adult oak tree.

Sheef was able to locate and retrieve his balance before he fell to the floor, but the jarring motion sent the omelet airborne, directly into the gaping, slobbery jaws of a certain warp-hound.

"Fromp, you oversized fleabag!" yelled Sheef. "You were just waiting for an opportunity like that, weren't you? Actually, on second thought, I'll bet you created your own little opportunity, placing those tree-trunk legs right in my path."

Fromp licked his chops and then sheepishly placed his boxy head on the floor between his enormous paws.

"Oh no, don't you dare try to play innocent with me. I'm onto you and your schemes."

Harvey's mother was laughing so hard that the orange juice she was drinking threatened to blow right out of her nose. "Sheef, don't be too hard on him," she said while giggling. "He has to eat, too."

"I already gave the space-mutt three pounds of ground beef. I suppose next time I should go ahead and put it in an omelet for him. So, Harvey, you want one?'

"Sure, I guess," was his groggy response.

"Harvey," said his mother, "would you please come over here and sit with us?"

Harvey reluctantly slunk over to the kitchen table and sat down.

"Sweetie," said his mother while placing her hand on his, "I'm so sorry it came out like it did. I can't imagine what a shock it must be. Believe me when I tell you that it's not at all the way I wanted you to learn that Thurngood is not your father."

"Thurngood?"

"Yes, his real name is Thurngood, not Henry George. He is the captain of the Lacit Royal Guard."

"So our last name 'George' was made up?" asked Harvey both dubious and hurt.

"It was one of the first names we came in contact with," said Thurngood, "and we needed an alias. We read it on the paper currency."

"Are you telling me that you got our last name from George Washington? You've got to be joking."

"Not at all, son," said Harvey's mother.

"So, I suppose the whole toilet paper salesman job was a lie as well."

"No," replied Thurngood, "that's actually true. I really did sell toilet paper. When your father disappeared, I had to find a way to make money while your mother continued her search. I also needed a cover while here on Earth. Believe it or not, I actually began to enjoy the job. That said, I hope we can keep this our little secret. If and when we ever make it back to Ecclon, I can only imagine what the soldiers under my command would think and say if they learned what I was selling on Earth."

"What did you say about my father? Disappeared? Where? I mean how and when?" The words were flying out of Harvey's mouth so rapidly that they were becoming tangled and tumbling over themselves.

"Slow down, son" said his mother in a mollifying tone. "Why don't I back up and begin again. What I have to tell you will explain what happened to your father. Is that all right?"

"I suppose," replied Harvey while rubbing his forehead.

"Let's see, before you fainted, you heard me say that you and I are Lacit, and more specifically, of the royal line."

Harvey nodded.

"Twelve years ago, just after you were born, your father, Arrick, I, and you of course, warped to Earth in order to search, and hopefully retrieve, an extremely powerful artifact that we determined had been stolen and taken to Earth decades earlier."

"We heard Gnarl say something about that," said Sheef.

"But I thought he was petrified?" asked Thurngood.

"Don't ask about that one right now. I'm not even sure if I understand what happened to him," replied Sheef.

"Anyway," continued Harvey's mother, "your father, like Thurngood, is a member of the royal guard, in addition to being in charge of Ecclon's Hall of Artifacts. Thirteen years ago, when the hall of artifacts was being repaired, we took advantage of the situation to reorganize and inventory the thousands of artifacts which were housed in the hall. During the process, much to our dismay, we learned that an artifact known as the Narciss Glass was missing."

"Never heard of it," replied Sheef.

Very few living souls have, and for good reason. It was crafted over eight-hundred earth years ago by Ecclonian artisans. It was intended to be an instrument of punishment for the universes' worst criminals, specifically the tyrannical ones bent on oppressing and subduing others in order to feed their lust for ever-increasing power."

"The Narciss Glass was created," interjected Thurngood, "to give these power-hungry tyrants precisely what they so desired, which in the end, would be the worst possible punishment of all."

"How so?" asked Sheef.

"Let me answer this one, Thurngood," said Harvey's mother.

"As you wish."

Harvey's mother took a sip of coffee before launching into long elucidation, beginning with two rhetorical questions: "Why are tyrants so consumed with the acquisition of power, and what is it about power that proves so addictively intoxicating? The answer to both of these questions is one's self. Every tyrant, dictator, or absolute ruler is enthralled, even consumed, with his self, and he will do everything and anything to acquire additional power in order to feed his growing selfishness. Even a little bit of power, however, can be a dangerous thing, for it is highly addictive. Commanding the attention, adoration, and at times, the worship of people is very intoxicating, more so than any drug.

"And how do tyrants and dictators go about compelling people to give them more of this drug? They accomplish it through the use of fear, intimidation, force, violence, bribery, and so on. When you peel back the surface layer of their actions, though, what you find lying beneath is nothing but utter selfishness, a black sucking hole, if you will.

"And once someone becomes addicted to the power drug, his addiction can never be satisfied. He becomes a parasitic power leech, feeding off of the lives of those he conquers and subdues, all the while bending more and more inward upon himself. This internal bending eventually distorts reality so much that he falls victim to unimaginable deception."

"You make it sound like Hell," remarked Sheef.

"It is," said Harvey's mother gravely. "In the end, the pursuit of power becomes a self-imposed hell."

"But how does the Narciss Glass tie into this?" asked Harvey.

Thurngood sat down at the table after retrieving a second cup of coffee, and as he did so, a thunderhead moved in front of the afternoon sun, darkening the atmosphere of the kitchen. He lowered his voice and spoke in quiet tones, as if he was sharing a ghost story.

"The Narciss Glass is named after Narcissus from earth's own Greek mythology. He was the one who fell in love with his own reflection. Ecclon and Earth share many of the same myths, which is a story for an entirely different conversation. The Narciss Glass is nothing more than a hand-held mirror. But the purity of the glass and the way in which the skilled craftsmen shaped it, refracts the image of anyone peering into it, and reflects it back in such a way that the person is immediately enthralled and infatuated with his own reflection."

Thurngood dropped his voice even lower, almost to a whisper. The room darkened another shade. "If he continues to peer into the mirror, his awareness of the outside world rapidly fades. Soon, he and he alone is all that matters. He becomes increasingly captivated by his own beauty and magnificence, which eventually leads to irrationality. He becomes aggressive, even to the point of murder, towards anyone who ventures too close to the mirror. Before long, he shuns everyone, feeling hatred for all creatures, even the well-meaning ones who only want to help him.

"Ultimately, he is left completely isolated. He becomes a puny god, ruling his own personal, tiny universe. And he is so engrossed with himself that he soon loses his appetite and thirst, and thus, eventually withers and dies, becoming mere dust that, ironically, no one grieves or remembers."

When Thurngood finished speaking, Harvey and Sheef, and even Fromp, were staring at him, wearing fresh, stupefied expressions.

"That's an awfully horrific punishment," commented Sheef.

"Precisely, and that's why it was reserved for only the worst of tyrants, and why, incidentally, it was only used once before being archived away," said Thurngood.

"And that's the object" asked a shocked Harvey, "that was stolen?"

Harvey's mother nodded.

"Do you have any idea who might have taken it?" asked Sheef.

"We do," responded Thurngood. "Once we realized it was missing, we began to scrutinize the records of anyone who worked in the Hall of Artifacts, starting with the present clerks and filers, and then painstakingly working backwards. We searched for the minutest of clues that would shed light on the person who might have taken it. We went back decades, sixty years, and still found nothing out of the ordinary, not a single anomaly. We were on the verge of giving up when we came across what police detectives refer to as a smoking gun: a major piece of evidence pointing directly to the guilty party."

Thurngood paused for dramatic effect, which is understandable, given the fact that he had not been able to tell this tale to anyone new for over a decade and was relishing sharing every detail.

"What was it?" Harvey asked, breaking the dramatic pause.

"The smoking gun," said Harvey's mother, stealing the thunder from Thurngood, "was the sudden disappearance of a disgruntled Hall of Artifacts clerk many years before I was born. His name was Millud, and from what I've been able to gather, he was a weasel . . . slippery, always wiggling his way in and out of conversations and situations that he didn't belong in, continually hunting for leverage, looking for opportunities to promote himself. Soon after he disappeared, a number of small, rather insignificant items were found missing. At the time, however, the

Narciss Glass wasn't missed, due to the fact that practically no one knew of its existence."

"How's that possible?" asked Sheef. "The most powerful Ecclonian artifact and nobody knew the story behind it."

Harvey's mother responded. "As Thurngood told you, the Narciss Glass was only used as a means of punishment on one individual. The Lacit Council was horrified when they learned the details of what the Narciss Glass did to this individual. The process of him slowly, over many years, collapsing into himself was determined by the Council to be excessively cruel. Thus, after only one use, it was officially banned and stored away in a nondescript container on the lowest level of the Hall of Artifacts. Written on the label affixed to the outside of the container were the words 'damaged' and 'valueless'."

"More importantly," she continued, "all information regarding its existence, purpose, and power was officially censored. Everyone who had any knowledge of it was sworn to secrecy for the good of Ecclon's future. And so, in time, those who knew of the Narciss Glass passed on, and with them, all knowledge of its existence. This is why when it disappeared, no one missed it, and why we only learned that it was gone when we took inventory of everything in the Hall of Artifacts. The records indicated that we were missing the box, and it was only after much digging and research did we learn what was inside it."

"Okay, that makes sense, but how do you know with any certainty that it was this Millud character who took it, and why do you believe he fled to Earth?" asked Sheef.

"Luckily for us," began Thurngood, "There was an elderly Lacit who had been an archivist at the Hall of Artifacts his entire adult life. What was his name?"

"Clivell," offered Harvey's mother.

"What?" asked Thurngood.

"The old Lacit's name. It was Clivell."

"That's right, Clivell. Anyway, Clivell apparently knew Millud when they were both young men. He shared with us that Millud felt underappreciated. And right before he disappeared, Millud told Clivell that he had stumbled upon an object of incredible power, and that he would soon be taking it to a planet where he would be recognized for his talents. The most logical place for him to go to was Earth because of the similarity between Lacits and humans. Somehow he must have made it all the way to the Shellow Plain without being detected by the Flurn, no doubt a testimony to his slippery ways."

"Do you have an idea when this all occurred?" asked Harvey.

"Our best guess would be earth's early 1930's."

"Once we figured that much out, things stared to make sense," Harvey's mother said as she rose and walked over to the couch in order to lie down.

"I'm sorry, everyone, but you'll have to excuse me. In my sickly condition, it takes very little to fatigue me. I can't seem to sit upright for very long without becoming tired. If you don't mind, I would like to continue our conversation in the living room so that I might rest on the couch."

Everyone nodded and followed her into the living room. She positioned herself, took a deep breath, and continued. "A decade and a half ago, the Flurn Council informed my father, the leader of the Lacit, that they had observed a significant change in the luminosity of Ecclon's orb clouds. Since, as you all know, the intensity of the clouds is directly linked to how attuned humans are to the thoughts of the Unseen, any reduction of the orb clouds' light could only mean one thing: humans were, for some reason, turning away from the Unseen in rather large numbers.

"Bellock and the Flurn Council suspected that a book containing powerful human deceptions was being created by the Vapid. They feared, and rightly so, that this book could be used to further blind humans to the truth of the Unseen and turn even more away, diminishing the light of Ecclon's orb clouds."

"Trust me when I tell you that we know all about the book. Don't we, Harvey," said Sheef with a wink.

"More than I care to remember," responded Harvey with a sigh.

"Your father believed," resumed Harvey's mother, "that there had to be some underlying cause or event that was turning so many people away from the Unseen. It wasn't long after this that we discovered everything about Millud and the Narciss Glass. Your father, being trained as a soldier and historian, immediately wanted to go on the hunt for the object. He was always one for adventure, especially if it involved anything from the past. A warrior who knows his history, that's your dad, the man I love."

Harvey smiled and said sarcastically, "Beats selling toilet paper for a living."

"Hey, kid, don't knock what put food on the table for you for years," said Thurngood good-naturedly. "Remember what I used to say? It's a necessity that man can't live without."

"Yeah, I remember you saying that about a thousand times," Harvey said, still reeling from the revelation that Thurngood wasn't his real father. His emotions were all over the place. Mixed together were feelings of hurt at being deceived, comfort in the knowledge that his mother knew what he was going through, excitement about possibly meeting his real father, and anger at a situation that wouldn't allow him the time to sort through it all.

"Harvey," his mother continued, "your father and I felt confident that in some way the Narciss Glass was playing a major role in humans turning from the Unseen, the creation of the book, and the dimming of the orb clouds on Ecclon. We shared our thoughts about there possibly being an underlying cause with the Flurn Council. We didn't specifically tell them about the Narciss Glass at that time. Even so, they were quite skeptical."

"I'll bet I can guess which one was the most skeptical," said Sheef, glancing over at Harvey.

"I gather that you've met Salix," said Thurngood smirking.

"Bellock discussed the matter with your father," Harvey's mother said. "In the end, it was decided that Bellock and the Flurn would attempt to locate and destroy the book, while your father, Thurngood, and I went in search of a possible underlying cause."

"The Narciss Glass," said Harvey.

"Yes, son, the Narciss Glass."

"Well, it makes perfect sense to me," said Sheef. "Somehow the Narciss Glass has been affecting, not one, but thousands, probably more like millions, of people, turning them away from the thoughts of the Unseen. This has led to them collectively believing and uttering deceptions about being alone in the universe, and thus, masters of their own destinies. These thoughts and declarations have manifested themselves on the pages of the book, or books as Harvey recently discovered. As the Vapid read these deceptions over the human race, the blindness and wandering from the Unseen increased exponentially. The consequence for Ecclon has been the weakening of her orb clouds. And as we all know, once the orb clouds cease to shine, all life on Ecclon, including the Flurn and Lacit, will perish."

"And let's not forget about Nezraut and the Vapid's ultimate goal," said Harvey. "With the dying orb clouds, the Vapid can now tolerate the once Unseen-infused atmosphere. And since Ecclon is the gateway planet to every other world, it won't be long until they control and dominate every creature in every universe in every dimension."

"It's even worse than I feared then," Harvey's mom whispered to herself while staring unblinkingly at the other side of her room. It took her a few minutes to absorb the shock of her son's words before she was able to continue.

"It seems that you know a great deal more than I do about the current state of Ecclon. I want to hear all about what you've experienced that has grown you from boy to man in such a short amount of time. But first, I need to retire to my room and rest. The news of my planet's demise has sapped what little energy I had."

Thurngood helped Harvey's mother off the couch and into her bedroom. A few minutes later he exited the room, quietly closed the door, and rejoined the others.

"She's getting weaker by the day," said Thurngood in a low voice.

"The doctors haven't discovered anything new?" Harvey asked, concerned.

"No, and I don't believe they ever will. Your mother and I now feel very confident that the reason for her worsening condition has nothing to do with any disease from this planet."

"It's Ecclon's orb clouds, isn't it?" asked Harvey. "She's connected to them."

"Yes. Your mother's health is somehow intertwined with the fate of Ecclon's orb clouds. You, Harvey, and I seem to be unaffected. I don't know why this is the case. My only guess is that your mother, as emerging queen of Ecclon, is directly connected to the health of the planet. My point is, as the orb clouds weaken, so does she."

"Which means . . ." Harvey started but couldn't finish.

"That she doesn't have much time," said Sheef somberly.

Thurngood silently nodded.

"Sheef, we have to go. We have to find the Narciss Glass. My mom, I can't . . . She's . . ."

Harvey was in a near state of hysterics. He had risen out of his seat and was nervously pacing around the living room. Sheef stood up and grabbed hold of him, embracing his quivering body.

"Listen to me, Harvey. Calm down. We're not going to let your mom die. We'll do whatever it takes. We'll find this Narciss Glass and change things, but I can't do it alone."

Sheef pushed Harvey back so that he could look him in the eye as he finished his remarks. "I need an intrepid young man who knows how to save a guy hanging off the side of a cliff and a warrior who doesn't back down from Vapid Lords."

"Don't worry, Sheef, I'm in. I'm definitely in." Harvey took a huge breath and slowly exhaled. "And you're right. We're going to save my mom and Ecclon. And if I have the chance, destroy that doubled-mouthed Vapid once and for all."

"That's the Harvey I know and need!" Sheef said as he playfully punched Harvey on the shoulder.

Thurngood was on the verge of volunteering his services, when a massive crashing sound erupted from above.

"What was that noise?" Sheef asked clearly rattled.

"Sheef," said Harvey nervously, "the last time we heard sounds on a roof was just before your cabin was ripped apart."

"Dark Flurn," said Sheef.

Harvey nodded in response.

"Dark Flurn?" asked Thurngood.

"One of Nezraut's little botanical experiments," sighed Sheef. "Dark Flurn are vicious and single-mindedly obedient to Nezraut. They don't appear to be very bright, but they are extremely strong and are covered with razor-sharp thorns. A small forest of them ripped apart my cabin and nearly killed Harvey and me."

"Oh, well that makes me feel better. For a minute there, I thought they might be something to worry about," said Thurngood sarcastically. "So what's the plan?"

"If there really are dark Flurn on the roof, it's much safer to stay within these walls," answered Sheef. "Thurngood, do you have any weapons in the house?"

Thurngood smiled from ear to ear. "I thought you'd never ask. Would the captain of the Lacit Royal Guard travel to Earth without being properly armed? I've got much more than rolls of toilet paper in my arsenal."

"Arm us with anything you have, and then we'll give whatever has decided to drop in on us a proper greeting."

10

Thurngood returned minutes later with three swords in his hands. The blades were short, about two feet long, and composed of a semi-transparent blue stone.

"Dad, I mean Thurngood, where have you been keeping those?"

"Hanging on the back of the water heater in the garage. I made sure to have weaponry on hand in every room in the house. It's not difficult. You just have to be good at hiding them, that's all."

"Weapons in every room of the house," Harvey bewilderingly thought to himself. He was still having a very difficult time processing all the new information. It seemed that whenever he was able to wrap his brain around a new revelation and become comfortable with it, another one would bubble up and burst, flinging him over again into a stupefied disorientation.

He had watched actors in movies and on television impersonating drunken people. They would stagger and bump into things, but after downing a pot of coffee, they seemed to sober up and find their equilibrium. Ever since Ecclon, Harvey had felt like such a person. Only with him, the cycle never seemed to end. It was as if he took one powerful drink after another, with very little time in between to sober up: nabbed by a warp-hound; transported to a different planet in another universe and dimension; educated by a talking tree; learned of glowing clouds dying; informed that he was the great hope; attacked by Insips and Vapids; flirted with death; and shocked by the revelation that the guy who sells toilet paper, who he thought was his dad, turns out not to be, but rather is the leader of a group of sword-toting warriors. Not to mention that his entire family is royalty! It was a little much to take in, to say the least.

With growing exasperation and while staring blankly, Harvey said, "This entire time I thought that my dad was nothing more than a salesman, but then I find out that I've never actually met him, at least not that I can remember, and not only that, but he's not even from this planet."

With no good response to Harvey's comments, Sheef changed the subject. "Thurngood, the blades of the swords. Haven't I seen that material somewhere before?"

"I'm sure you have if you've ever been to Council Gorge. The entire place is coated with the blue rock. It's called Querreck. Hardness like that of one of your diamonds. When it's fashioned by skilled hands, there's nothing sharper."

Thurngood handed both Sheef and Harvey one of the swords. They were significantly lighter than they appeared. Harvey felt completely foolish. He had never held a sword in his life. It dangled loosely in his hand.

Thurngood nodded to everyone and took a step towards the hall which led to the attic, as Sheef reached into his backpack.

"Before we investigate whatever's lurking in the attic, I suggest that we all open our eyes and ears to that other dimensional world. I didn't have time to squeeze the nectar into any bottles when we were back on Ecclon, so we'll have to get it straight from the source."

As he said this, Sheef pulled out a piece of Kreen fruit. He sliced it into thirds, handing one to both Thurngood and Harvey.

"Squeeze a drop in your ears and eyes. Probably a good idea to take a bite of it, too. It will give us additional strength to face whatever's up there."

All three squeezed, dripped, and squinted. Harvey took a medium-sized bite of the fruit, and like times past, felt an immediate flush of energy. Strength rippled through every nerve and muscle fiber in his body, and without even being conscious of what he was doing, he gripped the sword tightly in his hand, deftly flicked the blade 360 degrees, and cut a blue speed-blurred "S" in the air, all before twirling the sword over his head and catching it adroitly by the handle.

Thurngood and Sheef looked at Harvey and then at each other with astonished expressions.

"Harvey," said Sheef, "What exactly was that?"

"I don't know," said Harvey, clearly perplexed while looking down at his sword. "As soon as I swallowed my bite of Kreen, it's like my muscles and reflexes took on a life of their own. I wasn't even thinking about the sword."

"I've trained many a soldier in the art of sword tactics," said Thurngood, "and the quickness and control which you just displayed takes years to master. When and how did you learn to do that?"

"Nowhere. I didn't. Learn it, I mean. It just happened. I've never even held a sword before today."

Thurngood gave Harvey a scrutinizing stare while stepping closer to him, as if zooming in would help him find an answer. "Harvey, who are you?"

"I'm not sure what you mean."

"I'll tell you who he is," said Sheef. "He's the one chosen by the Unseen for such a time as this."

"Okay then," said Thurngood, stretching long each syllable. "Good to know. And to think we've been living under the same roof for all these years."

"My thoughts exactly," replied Harvey bitterly.

Thurngood took the lead, walking lightly as possible down the hallway. The attic hatchway was in the ceiling in front of Harvey's bedroom.

Thurngood held his sword offensively in front of him. He motioned to Sheef to pull on the string which was hanging from the attic hatch. It yawned open slowly. The springs of the hatch groaned loudly, as if annoyed and reluctant to be roused from their slumber.

The noise, which was amplified by everyone's silence, startled Sheef. He stopped pulling on the string. The hatch and its folded stairs ceased moving.

All three looked at each other, waiting, straining to hear any sound of movement. A loud thump thudded against wood. Nobody moved. A few seconds later, the same thud was heard, and then again and again.

"What do you think's making that sound?" whispered Harvey.

"Only one way to find out," said Sheef as he opened the hatch all the way and quickly unfolded the stairs. They ascended the stairs, swords in hand and at the ready, bracing for combat with whatever secret the darkness above was hiding.

Fromp, who had followed the three down the hallway, pawed at the narrow staircase. After whining a half dozen times in frustration, he made an attempt to climb up, and though the warphound was extremely agile for a creature his size, the steps were just too small and his paws too large for the rickety staircase. He made it all the way to the sixth step before his front right paw slipped off. His snout slammed down hard.

When he attempted to stand back up, he lost his footing for a second time. He hit the stairs with his belly, his four legs splayed outwards. He thumped and bumped on his belly back to ground level.

For an animal with the capability of opening up trans-dimensional warp holes and gracefully transporting himself through them, being humiliated by a set of folding attic stairs was just too much. He took his anger out on the stairway with a vicious, snarling bite into the third wooden step. A quick head flick to the left tore off a large chunk of wood. He then flung it into the hallway wall. With the stairway now soundly defeated, Fromp lay down at the foot of the stairs, licking his paws and gnawing away at his nails.

Thurngood's head was the first to surface into the stale and musty attic air. The rhythmic cadence of the thumping continued, but the sound was now echoing loudly in the enclosed space.

The light from the downstairs hallway drifted up and through the opening, awaking the darkness to gray shadow. Thurngood flipped on a light switch with the tip of his sword. It was wired to a solitary, bare bulb affixed to one of the attic rafters. The flip did nothing.

The hatchway was located in the middle of the attic. On one side was the air conditioning and heating unit, on the other was the floored storage area, filled with a mishmash of old yard equipment, picture frames, outdated electronic equipment, and stacks of boxes of every shape and size.

Thurngood took slow and deliberate steps towards the storage area and the thumping sound. He motioned for Harvey and Sheef to follow. On his fifth step, Thurngood felt and heard the crunching of broken glass under foot. He stopped and lifted his shoe, understanding then why the light had failed to turn on.

Harvey and Sheef crept up beside him.

"Do you see anything?" whispered Sheef.

"No, but something shattered the light bulb," replied Thurngood, pointing up at the light socket. "The noise sounds like it's coming from behind the boxes. Let's edge around the side. And be ready."

"For what?" whispered Harvey.

"Anything."

Thurngood and Sheef took a step towards the boxes. Harvey was preparing to follow when he froze. On the ceiling, to the left of the boxes, the shadow of a very large arm raced across the rafters and plywood of the ceiling and back again. A few seconds later, the shadow moved in exactly the same fashion.

"Thurngood, Sheef," Harvey whispered.

They looked back to Harvey who was pointing at the ceiling. A second later, they saw the moving shadow for themselves.

"Dark Flurn," mouthed Sheef.

"Thurngood nodded and then whispered, "Let's not wait for it to attack. On 'three', we rush around and hack it to toothpicks."

Harvey and Sheef agreed. Harvey noticed that the knuckles on Thurngood's sword hand suddenly turned white. Thurngood nodded and then mouthed the first three numbers.

The attic air shuddered from the bellowing war whoops of two men and a young teen as they quickly cornered the stack of boxes and entered into bewilderment.

It was a Flurn all right, just not the orientation or the version they were expecting. Hanging and swinging like an inverted metronome from a hole in the ceiling, was the top half of Gnarl the Deep.

11

"Is that who I think it is?" asked Sheef.

"I think so," replied Harvey. "At least the top of him."

"Who are you talking about?" asked Thurngood with an edge of annoyance in his voice.

"The recently freed Gnarl the Deep," replied Sheef.

"That can't be Gnarl," said Thurngood. "I've seen him before. He was all twisted and contorted with old age."

"I know," said Sheef, "but when he broke free from his petrification, he emerged as a green-wooded Flurn."

"But how is that possible?"

"I think it would be best if I let him explain it to you. That's if he's still alive."

"Of course I am still alive," said a groggy, somewhat confused voice. "Though my head is certain to ache for many a day after hitting the roof at the velocity that I did."

It was easy now to see what was causing the thumping sound. Gnarl's large rootlet feet were sticking out of the roof in opposite directions, allowing him to hang downward through the hole like a bat.

He was attempting to free his feet from the hole by swinging back and forth. Every time he swung to the left, he pushed hard against one of the attic's vertical wooden beams, making a loud thump.

Once Sheef, Thurngood, and Harvey realized that there was no threat in the attic, and that Gnarl wasn't seriously injured, the humor of the situation budded and flowered.

Upside down and swaying side to side, attempting to extricate himself, Gnarl looked like a green wind chime dangling in the breeze.

As Gnarl swung by, he observed three faces frowning at him, which he would have actually seen as stupid grins if he were standing right-side up.

In a tone heavily glazed with sarcasm, Gnarl said, "I am exceedingly pleased that my crash into a terrestrial home and subsequent entanglement in its wooden covering are serving as a means of entertainment to you all, but if I might be so bold as to interrupt your amusement for only a moment, would it be too much to ask to find it in your good natures to possibly get me down and turned around?"

Sorry, Gnarl," said Thurngood snickering. "Right away."

It didn't take long to free Gnarl from his inverted entanglement. Thurngood and Sheef climbed the roof and set to hacking and sawing with their swords. The sharpness of the blades easily cut through the roof and soon there was a hole large enough to release Gnarl. The final attic thump occurred when Gnarl's head made contact with the plywood floor.

Shafts of sunlight shone in through the hole, creating standing columns of light and swirling dust. Two silhouetted heads bobbed in the large opening. Harvey, who was still in the attic, knelt down next to Gnarl.

"Harvey," shouted one of the bobbing heads, "is he okay?"

"I am," wheezed Gnarl in a tone which seemed to contradict his self-assessment. "Being a Flurn does have its advantages. Our heads being composed of extremely dense wood is the one which I am most cognizant and grateful for at this particular moment. If my wood was aged and dried, though, as it was in the days prior to my petrification, such a fall and blow might have resulted in a crack, but now with it being young and green, it is able to flex and bend. It appears that being Gnarl the young and green has unforeseen advantages."

By the time Gnarl had finished speaking, both his tone and attitude had somewhat recovered.

"Harvey," said Gnarl, "help me to my feet and please lead me out of this confining wooden cavern."

"It's an attic."

"Yes then, lead me from this attic, as you say, and into what I hope are more spacious levels of this abode. And let us do it with haste. I must speak to all of you immediately. Events on Ecclon have shadowed even darker, and I now fear for the very lives of my fellow Flurn."

Harvey's face paled as he tried to raise a question, but it was cut short by Gnarl. "Harvey, let us depart the attic first, and then I will explain and you may ask."

It was fortunate that the young and green Gnarl was only eight feet in height. If he had been the twenty plus, which he had towered to when he was petrified, he never would have fit into the attic or any of the rooms in the house. Actually, if he had been his previous size, the impact of such a large object on the house would have left few, if any, rooms intact.

Harvey led Gnarl down the folding stairway and into the hall. Though not twenty plus, eight feet was still a tight fit. Consequently, everyone thought it best to gather outside on the deck. Harvey's mother, who was jolted awake by the crash, was helped outside by Thurngood and set down on a lawn chair.

It wasn't until Harvey was on the deck that he noticed he was still carrying the sword Thurngood had given him. When he had realized that there was no danger lurking in the attic, he had placed the sword blade in between his belt and jeans as a make-shift scabbard. Now on the deck, he attempted to hand it back to Thurngood.

"Hold on to it, Harvey. I have a feeling we're going to need every weapon at our disposal for what is coming, but we'll have to fix you up with a proper scabbard. Until then, why don't you just lay it on the table there. Wouldn't want you to accidently slice your leg open before all the fun begins."

"And by the way, Harvey," continued Thurngood in a quieter tone, "I'm really sorry that I didn't tell you the truth sooner, but your mom and I just thought that it was easier for me to go on pretending that I was your dad. I mean, what are the chances you would've believed us before you saw Ecclon for yourself? And why tell you about your dad if there was a fair chance that he might never return?"

"Because I'm his son and deserve to know," Harvey shot back in a resentful tone.

"You're right. We should've told you sooner. But I want you to know that I've always loved you like you were my own son."

"Well, you sure didn't act like it. You were hardly ever home. Always on the road stocking and selling toilet paper."

"Yeah, I was. I had to pay for all your mom's medical bills, which was a complete waste now that we know the reason for her illness. But that's not the only reason. I guess deep down there was the glimmer of hope that your dad might one day walk on through the front door and pick up where he left off. I just didn't want to take his place."

Thurngood reached over and tousled Harvey's hair. "I hope you can forgive your mom and me for not telling you the truth sooner. We never meant to hurt you."

Harvey's chin quivered and a tear fell overboard and rolled down his cheek. He knew he should have nodded his head at that moment. He knew he should have forgiven, but the wound was too fresh, and he did not want the healing to begin just yet. He decided to hold on to the offense for a little while longer. Let it fester a bit. Coddle and enjoy it. He would forgive and release soon enough, or so he thought.

A squirrel emerged from the canopy of one of the oak trees in the backyard. Half way down the trunk it stopped and flicked its head a few times, scenting something in the air. It looked directly at Harvey, chattered menacingly, and then shot back up the trunk, disappearing in the branches and leaves.

Gnarl was the only one besides Harvey who observed the strange behavior of the squirrel. He glanced briefly at Harvey with a look of penetrating inquiry before turning back to address the group.

12

When everyone had positioned him or herself in relative comfort somewhere on the back deck, Gnarl looked to where Harvey's mom was lying down and began speaking.

"Princess Dwen, it is an honor to make your acquaintance, though I do wish that it were under more pleasurable and peaceful conditions."

"Dwen?" whispered Harvey to Sheef. Who's Gnarl referring to? My mom's name is Mary Anne, not Dwen."

"Apparently she's not Mary Anne on Ecclon. And, kid, I think it's a pretty safe bet to assume your real name is something other than Harvey."

"With the way things are going today, that wouldn't surprise me at all."

"The honor is all mine," said Harvey's mother. "In my wildest dreams, I never thought that I would be blessed by your actual living presence. Ever since I was a little girl, I have heard tales of Ecclon's most sagacious Flurn, and I have memorized countless proverbs which you uttered long before I was born. You are legendary to me, and very seldom does one actually have the opportunity to converse with a legend. But I must confess, I am somewhat bewildered by your . . . um . . ."

"Appearance? Your confusion is understandable, but you are only baffled, and please do not take offense to what I am about to say, for you know not the benefits of sinking one's roots deeply and continually into the flavorful waters of the Unseen's goodness. How I wish we had the time for me to converse more about this, elucidating to you about my transformation by the Unseen, but unfortunately, the tint of my words must now darken."

Here Gnarl turned to face Sheef and Harvey. "Your warping escape from Ecclon unleashed Nezraut's fury. Eluding his grasp, once again, when he was confident of your decimation was humiliating for one so powerful. In a sense, he was defeated for a second time by a thirteen year old. If I had not been present to witness what followed next, I might not have believed it, for I had no conception whatsoever that Flurn were capable of such destructive behavior."

"Destructive behavior? Sounds like you had a run in with some dark Flurn," remarked Sheef.

"Yes, they were dark and hideously twisted in trunk and branch. They appeared by the hundreds and were accompanied by additional Volkin Wolves. Within moments of their arrival, they closed their ranks, forming a tight circle around Bellock, Merum, Salix, and the other Flurn Elders. But what is strange is that they completely ignored me. Nezraut, in fact, acted as though I did not even exist. Perhaps, because of my youthful appearance and diminished size, he assumed that I was unimportant."

"He didn't do anything to you?" asked Harvey.

"No, he did not, but he did say something to me. He looked directly into my eyes, a malevolent grin besmearing his face, and said, 'Young Flurn, tell the others of your planet what you are about to witness, and let them know that they would be wise to not resist me. If they do, the same fate as that of the Flurn Elders will befall them.'"

"What did he do to the Elders, to Bellock and Merum?" asked Harvey worriedly.

"Please, Harvey, try to calm yourself that I might finish explaining what occurred. Nezraut and his Vapid Lords receded back behind the encircling dark Flurn. It was from there that he spoke. The trapped Flurn Elders were unable to see Nezraut, but his hollow, insidiously refined voice wound its way through the twisted, thorny branches of the dark Flurn and into their hearing.

"I am not certain," said Gnarl, "that these are Nezraut's exact words, but if not, they are very close: 'There are quite often unpleasant consequences for the thoughtless actions of others. Unfortunately, when those who performed the thoughtless actions are not present to suffer the consequences, others must take their place. In our present situation, Ecclon's most illustrious Flurn shall fulfill that role.'"

"With these words," Gnarl continued, "Nezraut closed his eyes, whispered something with his double mouths, and then nodded his head. The circle of dark Flurn in front of him extended their thorn-encrusted rootlet hands toward the Flurn Elders. With their palms facing up, cracks emerged from fingertip to wrist on each of their hands. A brown steaming sap oozed forth from the cracks. Soon, every dark Flurn held two spheres of hot, gelatinous sap.

"Nezrarut inhaled deeply and then released a foul, pungent column of streaming vapor into the atmosphere. It snaked its way over the heads of the dark Flurn, resting atop one of the sap spheres.

"A violent snapping of Nezraut's fragmented teeth created a small spark. When he opened his mouth, the spark shot out with a crackle and flew directly into the vapor column. Apparently, Nezraut's exhalation was combustible, for the small spark ignited the entire column into an arching ribbon of fire. The flame followed the vapor trail like a fuse to a stick of dynamite. The sap sphere burst into flame, showering new sparks in all directions, some of them feeding fire to the other spheres. Within seconds, every ball of sap was brightly burning, tongues of orange and yellow fire blending and separating in swirls of rotating heat.

A jagged, snarling scream rent the air. It was Nezraut's three word command. "Burn them all!" The dark Flurn complied, lifting their thorny branch arms above their heads. The flaming sap spheres were momentarily stationary, like the raised torches of an angry mob, before being hurled at the Flurn Elders.

"Within seconds, a raging inferno . . ." Gnarl's voice faltered and then stopped. He took a deep breath while regaining his composure before returning to his narrative. "They were all set afire," Gnarl said as he looked down at the deck. "Bellock, Merum, and the other Flurn Elders were all burning. I tried to help, tried to break through the circle of dark Flurn, but it was in vain. They were so much stronger and larger. I was tossed backward like a twig."

"Are you saying," cried Harvey, "that they're all dead?"

"I am so sorry, Harvey," continued Gnarl in a soft and sorrowful voice. "They continued to burn until there was very little left of the living Flurns they once were. When it was all over, nothing but charred stumps and ashes remained. Nezraut and the dark Flurn left me behind and traveled to where I know not. Once they were gone, I immediately left for the Shellow Plain and warped myself to Earth and your home."

Tears were freely streaking the green bark of Gnarl's face. Harvey, white and expressionless, appeared as if he had turned to stone. He stood staring absently at Gnarl, recoiling from the shock of his words.

Harvey felt as if he had fallen backwards into a deep well and was rapidly plummeting downward. He could still hear voices speaking on the deck, but they were quickly growing distant and faint.

Trail-tears had formed on Sheef's cheeks as well. Hanging his head, he stroked his eyelids with his index finger and thumb in the direction of his nose. There they met in a pinch, his nose being held tightly in between.

Without looking up, he said dejectedly, "I suppose that's it then. Ecclon has fallen and soon shall we."

Gnarl turned in his direction, and while wiping tears from his face with his rootlet hands, he said, "No, Sheef, the battle for Ecclon is far from over. There is still a chance to keep it free from the clutches of the enemy. It is even possible to save Bellock and the Flurn Elders."

Dubious and upset at the words Gnarl had spoken, Sheef asked in a hurt and angry tone, "What are you going on about? You just informed us of how they were burned to death, so how in the world can you now stand there and say that there's still a chance of saving them?"

"I do not understand how my posture is of any relevance, Sheef. Whether I stand or sit has little bearing on the veracity of my words. Now I understand how upset you and Harvey must be, but I would never dare to say that there was a possibility of saving them if it were not so."

The notion that Harvey's Flurn friends might still have a chance halted his descent down the well and began to lift him slowly upward. The voices of the others on the deck soon grew louder and more distinct.

"But how?" asked Harvey. "They're gone."

"Gone in this present reality, that is true. However, if you were to change the roots of this present reality."

"You mean warping into the past, don't you?" asked Sheef.

"Yes, Sheef. Only by warping to the past will you be able to prevent millions of humans from turning away from the thought energy of the Unseen. You must find and destroy the Narciss Glass. This, as you already know, will save Ecclon, and also the life of Harvey's mother. What you are just now realizing, however, is that in saving Ecclon, you will also alter, or keep from ever happening, the latest series of unfortunate events."

"Stopping Bellock and the others from being burned by Nezraut!"

"Nothing, my friend, is a certainty, but I feel the probability of preventing their deaths is very much in our favor."

"That's good enough for me," said Harvey, a steely resolve beginning to harden his eyes.

"Well," said Sheef, "Looks like it's time to chat with your mother again."

13

"Mary Anne, I'm sorry, I mean your highness, Princess Dwen, do you have any idea of where or when to look for the Narciss Glass?" Sheef asked, stumbling over his own words.

"Please, call me Mary Anne. I never felt comfortable with that royal title anyway. It always seemed a little too impersonal. In answer to your question, Sheef, I do know the where and when, but in order to explain, I need to show everyone a scene from a movie."

"Mom, are you serious?" asked Harvey. "This hardly seems the right time."

"I know it sounds strange, son, but if you ever hope to locate the Narciss Glass and destroy it, then you need to see what I've discovered hidden in a film."

"Okay then," said Sheef, clearly befuddled.

As the group began shuffling across the deck to the back door, a high-pitched squeak from the backyard pierced the air and irritated everyone's hearing. Heads turned and looked in the direction of the sound.

Fifteen feet from the deck was a line of squirrels, two dozen or more, all sitting upright and at attention. They were shoulder to shoulder with tails aggressively flicking – a hindquarter's gesticulation mirroring the vicious hissing of their fang-bared faces. Their eyes were all unblinkingly locked on one person. Harvey.

The squirrels looked desperately famished, but a wicked delight flickered in their eyes. They had scented a most appetizing meal to satisfy their hunger.

Harvey could feel their cold, appraising eyes. A shiver chased down his spine. He knew that he had seen that same desperate hunger somewhere before, but at that moment, he couldn't quite remember where.

Everyone stopped walking towards the back door as if paralyzed by the squirrels' unsettling stares. Harvey's mother broke the tension and got everyone moving again with an unconvincing explanation. "The squirrels, why they tend to get bent out of shape this time of year, gathering and protecting their acorns and what not. Why don't we get inside and let them be. They'll settle down once we're gone."

But it wasn't the time of year for acorns to be on the ground; Harvey knew this, but decided not to say anything. He followed the others inside, but not before glancing back at the numerous eyes which were following his every movement across the deck.

Soon everyone but Gnarl had gathered in Harvey's mother's bedroom where the only functioning television was located. Fromp didn't see the squirrels in the backyard. After Harvey, Sheef, and Thurngood climbed down from the attic, the warphound decided that additional investigation of a very cushy surface was needed. When Harvey entered his mother's bedroom, he found Fromp plopped down in the middle of his mother's bed.

Gnarl had elected to wait on the deck. At eight feet tall, though still short for a Flurn, it was too cumbersome for him to navigate back through the human home. He had already cut a nasty gash in the smooth, verdant green bark-skin of his right branch arm. Waiting on the deck also afforded him the opportunity to think, to mull over the peculiarity which everyone had just observed.

The creatures in the backyard, what Harvey's mother had referred to as squirrels, appeared to have scented something in the air around Harvey. And by the aggressive glint set in their eyes, Gnarl assumed that it wasn't anything good. He suspected that Harvey was harboring dark thoughts, and whatever they were, their stench was already attracting uninvited guests.

Gathering in the bedroom, Harvey's mother sat on the edge of her bed in front of her television. Harvey and Sheef were utterly confused as to how a film clip could possibly have any relevance to Ecclon and the Narciss Glass.

"As I was telling you before Gnarl's unscheduled meeting with my roof and attic, Harvey's father and I had reached the conclusion that Millud had stolen the Narciss Glass from the Ecclonian Hall of Artifacts and fled with it to Earth during the planet's early 1930's. When we warped here in search of the Narciss Glass, we determined that the best way of finding it was to establish what happened to Millud after his arrival. For months, we searched for the slightest clue concerning his whereabouts and uncovered nothing. And then, when we had all but given up, Millud literally appeared before our very eyes.

"It was the weekend, and I suggested to Arrick, Harvey's father, that it might do him some good if he tried to forget about Millud and the Narciss Glass for a few hours. I proposed that we explore some television programming.

"It took your father an hour to figure out how to control the remote. Once he got the hang of it, though, he was cycling through the two-hundred-plus channels like a channel surfing pro. In the middle of his fifth rotation, a screen image suddenly arrested his flipping. There, on the Hollywood Classics movie channel, was Millud himself. He was being interviewed about a film he had directed.

"We were able to recognize Millud from a photograph of him we obtained from the Hall of Artifacts. And though his hair was thinner and grayer, there was no mistaking who it was. The face on the screen had exactly the same beady eyes and beak-sharp nose.

"This was the first clue to the Narciss Glass's whereabouts. Millud had apparently traveled to Hollywood and somehow managed to squirm his way into becoming a director in the film industry."

"You're not talking about H.B. Millud are you?" asked Sheef.

"Houston Bernard Millud, the one and the same," replied Harvey's mother. "His first name became his last. He obviously made up the first and middle."

"Didn't he direct *The Tempest's Fury*?" asked Sheef.

"Yes he did. Very good, Sheef, you know your film history. It's still considered a cinematic masterpiece."

"I don't get it, though," said Sheef. "How did an Ecclonian artifacts clerk, who had never heard of Hollywood, make it as a major director in Tinsel Town?"

"It wasn't because of talent," replied Harvey's mother. "He likely used the Narciss Glass to open doors. That's what Arrick believed anyway. Once he saw the interview, he spent day and night trying to track down any information he could about Millud's time in Hollywood."

"Millud's not still alive, is he?" asked Harvey.

"No," replied his mother, "he died nearly twenty years before your father and I warped to Earth, but after seeing that interview, your father read everything he could on Milllud's Hollywood career. While he was reading, I watched every movie that he was ever involved with, no matter how insignificant the role was. And let me tell you, there were a lot of movies to watch. This was, after all, Hollywood's most prolific period. Major film companies were cranking out a new film every week.

"Millud, we found out, began his film career as an assistant gaffer, which is the term for a lighting technician. From there, he landed minor roles in some B movies, and then transitioned into directing, primarily B movies as well."

"B movies?" asked Harvey.

"Lesser known and typically lower budget films," explained his mother. "He only acted in three, but directed more than twenty. I watched them all: corny monster horrors, predictable murder mysteries, ridiculous adventure tales, and sappy romances. And I have to tell you, every single one of them, especially those that he acted in, were hard to get through. Some of the early films, however, when he was just an assistant gaffer, were quite good, so good, in fact, that it didn't take long for me to get hooked on classic movies.

"Harvey's father and I watched every film that Millud had anything to do with, intently searching for any clues that might help us determine what happened to the Narciss Glass. It was a longshot that a movie would reveal anything, but we had nothing else to go on."

"Did you ever find anything?" asked Harvey.

"Your father did. He uncovered a clue in one of the films."

"What was it?" asked Harvey, who had become so enmeshed in the narrative that he felt as if he had been present with his father when the clue was spotted.

"I didn't know at the time," replied Harvey's mother pensively. "He said that it was probably nothing, just a crazy hunch, not even worth the effort to pursue it."

"I don't get it. Why didn't Dad simply tell you what he had seen?"

"Harvey, you were still a baby, and a sickly one at that. As I look back on it now, your poor health was likely a consequence of your young Ecclonian body attempting to adjust to earth's environment. I suspect that your father didn't want me to worry about him. I suppose he figured that I had enough to fret over without the added burden of being anxious about his safety. And he was right in keeping it from me. If I'd any notion of what he was up to, I wouldn't have let him go."

Harvey's mother continued speaking as she walked over to her bedside table in order to retrieve a remote control. "I have the scene already cued up. As soon as you arrived, I knew you would need to see this." And with that, she pressed "play".

On the screen before Harvey and Sheef, a worn black and white film began to play. If it had been a book, the pages would have mellowed into an aged yellow.

The setting looked to be a parlor in an opulent chateaux or manor house. Seated in two hand-carved, luxuriously upholstered chairs, which were arranged around a small wooden table with a thick marble top, were a brother and sister. Both were somewhere between the top step of adolescence and the bottom rung of adulthood. They were invitingly attractive, dressed formally to receive the rich and airy meringue of society's upper crust.

They smiled pleasantly, but their expressions were far from genuine. Pasted, plastic smiles were clearly a requirement for the evening's celebration.

"I've seen this before," said Sheef. "Isn't this from *The Tempest's Fury* ?"

"It is," said Harvey's mother as she paused the movie.

"Well, it's completely lost to me why the critics rave so much about the film. I just don't see the appeal. I tried to watch the entire movie years ago, but I didn't make it more than twenty minutes before I turned it off. It was awful."

"And that," said Harvey's mother, "is why you aren't a fan of the film. If you had let the film play for another twenty minutes, though, you would likely agree with the critics. The interesting thing, however, is that if someone were to ask you why you enjoyed the film so much, you wouldn't be able to provide much of an answer."

Sheef cast her a quizzical look.

"Mom," asked Harvey, "what's the big deal about the movie, and why have I never seen it? I thought you showed me all the classics."

"Trust me, Harvey, it was intentional, the reason why, you will soon learn. Before I restart the movie, though, let me give you a summary of the film. *The Tempest's Fury* tells the story of a paranoid, elderly uncle who never married or had any children of his own. Instead, he set his nose to the proverbial grindstone, amassing an enormous fortune in maritime shipping. He was a miser his entire life, never sharing a dime with his seven siblings. Apparently, his avaricious ways acted as a preservative, giving him a longevity that outdistanced that of his brothers and sisters.

"The movie opens just before the uncle's one hundredth birthday. One of his nieces has planned an elaborate party to mark the centennial achievement, and she has invited the other dozen or so nieces and nephews. In his paranoid and delusional mind, though, the uncle believes that they're all conspiring to murder him, but not before deceiving him into altering his will.

"They have no such designs whatsoever, but there is no reasoning with the deranged uncle. In order to keep them from taking his life and fortune, he decides to beat them to the punch."

"What do you mean?" asked Harvey.

"She means," offered Sheef, "that he starts killing off his relatives."

"That's terrible."

"It is, son, but it shouldn't come as a surprise that someone like Millud, who always felt like people were out to get him, would choose to make such a movie."

"All right," Harvey's mother continued, "let me play the rest of the scene. I want you to watch very carefully and tell me if you observe anything unusual."

When the film resumed, the brother and sister were being served tea when the outraged uncle burst into the parlor, screaming at the top of his lungs about their double-crossing scheme to bilk him out of his fortune.

In the middle of his tirade, he grabbed a teapot and hurled it into an enormous mirror attached to the parlor wall. The volatile behavior of the uncle caused the brother and sister to spring out of their chairs. They stood with the small table between them and their uncle.

The uncle, meanwhile, picked up one of the large glass shards from the broken mirror and held it menacingly like a weapon at his niece and nephew. They ran from the parlor, screaming hysterically.

Harvey's mother stopped the movie and said, "Well, did you observe anything out of the ordinary? Harvey, Sheef, did you hear what I said?"

"I'm sorry, Mary Anne," said Sheef. "I don't know what came over me. I lost my train of thought or something. I don't quite know where I was. What did you say?"

Harvey's mother gave Sheef a knowing look and said, "Your reaction to the scene is typical. I'll explain in a minute, but tell me, did you observe anything out of the ordinary?"

"Nothing other than the entire scene being bizarre; that uncle is completely unhinged," said Sheef.

"I quite agree, Sheef," replied Harvey's mother, "but did you notice anything peculiar about the uncle's appearance or the object in his hand?"

After a half minute of silence, Harvey, while staring intently at the television, said, "They're not the same."

"What do you mean?" asked Sheef.

"The actor playing the uncle is not the same person. Very similar looking, but definitely different. They must have had a great makeup department. The man who throws the teapot and the one who picks up the glass shard are two different actors. It's hard to see, but the man who picks up the glass is shorter, skinnier, and has thinner hair. I would've missed it if I wasn't searching for something wrong."

"Well I sure missed it," said Sheef shaking his head. "Mary Anne, would you play the scene again?"

"I will, but I'll stop it before the uncle picks up the piece of broken mirror. It's too dangerous for you to it see a second time so quickly."

Sheef tilted his head in curiosity at her words as Fromp was prone to do. Harvey's mother reversed the movie and replayed the scene, pausing it when the uncle bent down to pick up the glass shard.

"You're right, Harvey," said Sheef grinning. "I can't believe I didn't notice it, but you're spot on. They're clearly not the same actor. I assume you know the reason for this, Mary Anne?"

"I do. According to my research, the actor who played the uncle in the first part of the movie, a gentleman by the name of George Cloy, apparently suffered a heart attack immediately after throwing the teapot. I was never able to find a record, however, of an autopsy being performed to determine if this was the official cause of death. With what I learned about Millud's character, though, I wouldn't be at all surprised if George Cloy was the victim of foul play."

"So Millud stepped in and took over the role?" asked Harvey.

"He did, but not just so that the show would go on. He had much larger plans. Anyone care to venture a guess as to the origin of the glass shard he held in front of the camera for seven seconds?"

14

"It's the Narciss Glass, isn't it?" asked Sheef.

"It is," answered Harvey's mother. Apparently, Millud removed the rectangular piece of mirrored glass from its handled case and placed it on the floor before they finished shooting the scene. But instead of picking up an actual fragment of glass from the shattered mirror, he grabbed the Narciss Glass and held it directly in front of the camera for the entire world to see."

"Well, no wonder it became his first big hit."

"You're exactly right, Sheef," said Harvey's mother. "If viewers made it half way through the movie to the particular scene which you just watched, they would be hooked. Looking at the Narciss Glass for longer than a few seconds is more than enough time to captivate one's attention. This is why, Sheef, you were momentarily dazed the first time you watched the clip, and why I didn't let you view it a second time."

"But, mom, it's just a movie," said Harvey.

"It doesn't make a difference, honey. It still has exactly the same effect as if someone were physically holding it in his hands.

And do you remember what that effect is? The Narciss Glass enthralls and infatuates a viewer with his own reflection, and it takes only one look at it to become enamored with one's own beauty and magnificence.

"For humans, especially, indulging one's selfishness is highly addictive, though not at all satisfying. Being consumed with one's self always leaves a person empty inside, and unfortunately, humans, more often than not, attempt to fill this emptiness by focusing even more intensely on themselves. It's a downward cycle from which it's extremely difficult to escape, and when you add the Narciss Glass into the equation, the process happens with much greater velocity."

"So that's why the movie is so loved, especially by the critics. It entices the viewers, feeding their pride and selfish natures," remarked Sheef.

"Makes sense doesn't it?" asked Harvey's mother. "Many film critics are full of themselves, so it's no wonder that they would fall all over themselves in praising the film. And by the way, *The Tempest's Fury* is one of the most viewed movies in Hollywood's history. In fact, I've heard that some fans have watched it hundreds of times, while others have purchased dozens and dozens of copies of the movie. And what's so interesting is that when these fans of the film are asked what makes it so unique and special, they're typically at a loss for words. Anyway, now you know how Millud made a name for himself in the industry"

"A horrendous film turned into one of the most lauded classics, all because of the Narciss Glass," said Sheef. "Unbelievable. Absolutely unbelievable. I don't suppose Millud ever considered the consequences of placing the object in the film?"

"I doubt that he could see beyond his own selfish ambitions. Unfortunately for Earth and Ecclon, the use of the Narciss Glass didn't end with *The Tempest's Fury.*"

"You mean he used it in other movies?" asked Harvey.

"By my count, at least a dozen more. After *The Tempest's Fury* was released, critics and moviegoers were fanatical about every new film he directed. And to be honest, they're no better than all the "B level" movies he directed in his early Hollywood days. I've watched them all, and in each, somewhere in the film, the Narciss Glass makes an appearance. It's been used as a hand-held mirror in a romantic comedy, a small decorative mirror in a murder mystery, and even as one of the panes of glass in a paneled bar window in a hokey western."

"And you were able to spot it in all those movies?" asked Sheef.

"I didn't see it, not initially, if that's what you mean. Rather, I felt it. I learned to recognize the dark, sucking pull of the object whenever it was used in a scene, and it was only after this unnerving awareness did I scrutinize the scene to locate where it was. Once I spotted it, I immediately cut the movie off. Like I mentioned before, you stare at it for more than a few seconds, and you risk losing yourself to it."

The circumference of Harvey's eyes suddenly increased. "That's why you spent all that time watching those old movies. It makes total sense now."

"I was doing research, sweetie, but to be completely honest, there were many occasions when I viewed movies from this era for nothing but sheer entertainment. But don't forget about the television detective shows."

"What?"

"The detective shows. How else was I going to learn the skills of deduction and to properly arrange clues to solve a mystery?"

"Are you serious?" asked Sheef in a tone of disbelief. "You're telling me that you learned how to sleuth from watching television?"

"On most days I was simply too tired to read, and I had to learn those skills from somewhere."

Sheef glanced down at the rug while lightly pinching the bridge of his nose. When he looked back up, the crow's feet on the outer edges of his eyes were merrily wrinkling, their bottom tips almost touching the rising folds of his grinning cheeks.

"Sheef, why are you smiling?" asked Harvey.

"It's just that . . ." Sheef began to laugh, finding it difficult to form a coherent sentence without his own laughter butting in and interrupting.

"It's just that," he finally managed to get out, "saving Earth, Ecclon, every other world, and possibly reversing the deaths of Bellock and the other Flurn elders, all comes down to following the discoveries made by a person who learned her problem solving techniques from watching fictitious TV detectives."

"I must admit," remarked Harvey's mother, "when you put it like that, I guess it's pretty funny."

"But, mom, those are old movies. There can't be that many people watching them today."

"Actually, with easy access to almost any movie Hollywood ever produced, there are likely more viewers of Millud's films today than there were decades ago, but even if this isn't the case, people are still being affected by the films, even if they've never seen any of them."

"How?"

"The movies with the Narciss Glass are like a contagion, a virus of pandemic proportions. Anyone who watches them is soon engulfed in self-adoration. This worship of self, this insidious infection, however, doesn't restrict itself to the initial viewer. It quickly spreads to others, destroying relationships, including those with the Unseen."

"And that's why," remarked Sheef, "during the last sixty or so years millions of humans have turned away from the thoughts of the Unseen."

"And darkened the clouds of Ecclon," concluded Harvey.

"It's obvious that we need to go back in time and destroy the Narciss Glass before Millud can use it in his first movie. So how do we do that?" asked Sheef.

"I'm not exactly sure," replied Harvey's mother, "but, Harvey, before your father disappeared, he jotted down two names multiple times in some of the notes he left behind. 'Sadiki' and 'Madora'. I have no idea what they mean, but I believe there is someone who does."

"Gnarl," replied Harvey.

Harvey's mother responded with a nod.

15

When Harvey, his mother, and Sheef walked out the back door and onto the deck, they interrupted Thurngood and Gnarl who were engaged in what appeared to be a very serious conversation. They were standing next to each other while staring intently into the backyard. The line of squirrels was still there, each animal standing on its hind legs and chattering. On the deck by Thurngood's feet lay two backpacks.

When Thurngood turned to Harvey and Sheef, Harvey observed a quick transformation of expression, from grim and pale, to carefree and flush.

"I have no idea," said Thurngood, "what exactly is in store for you two, but hopefully the items in the backpacks will help bring you back in one piece. Each of you has two bottles of Kreen nectar, which I just hand-squeezed myself, thank you very much. And I suggest that once you get to wherever it is you're going, you put these on."

Thurngood pulled out a light brown shirt from each of the backpacks. "It's an Ecclonian Lignum shirt. Craftsmanship doesn't come any finer. The material is a tight weave of thread-thin wooden fibers from a living Flurn. Don't worry though," said Thurngood chuckling, "the fibers were voluntarily donated. No Flurn was hurt in the process of making this product."

Thurngood threw one of the shirts to Harvey. "Look it over. It's amazingly light." Harvey studied the shirt with his hands and fingers, rolling it, stretching it, and then lifting it up and down in quick jerks to gauge its weight. It was light, incredibly light. The material was paper thin and supple. To Harvey, it felt more like silk than wood. Thurngood tossed the other shirt to Sheef.

"Lignum is practically impenetrable," Thurngood continued. "Because the weave is so tight and the wooden fibers are so tough, it can stop even the sharpest of blades. Harvey, try it on. I'll show you what I mean."

Harvey pulled off his shirt and warily placed his arms into the sleeves of the Lignum shirt as if he were inserting them into the wide, open mouth of a python. He wasn't necessarily afraid of the shirt, but rather what Thurngood planned on doing to him once it was on.

The fabric was so light that its weight was almost undetectable. The soft and silky contact with his skin had a soothing effect on Harvey, and he soon began to relax. It was short lived, however, for the Lignum fabric started to tightly contract around his torso and arms. Panic stricken, Harvey cast a facial plea of help and explanation to Thurngood.

"There's no reason to be frightened, Harvey, the shirt is just fitting itself to your body. It's perfectly normal."

"Normal for you maybe," Harvey said as his breath went shallow in weak, hyperventilating puffs.

"Don't worry. I promise the tightening will pass in few seconds."

"Hopefully before I suffocate."

Fortunately for Harvey, Thurngood's promise quickly proved true. Seconds later, the constrictions ceased. In fact, to Harvey, it felt as though the shirt had suddenly dematerialized.

"What happened?" asked Harvey somewhat befuddled. "Where did the shirt go?"

"You're still wearing it," said Thurngood. Take a look at your arms again."

Harvey looked down at his right arm, and sure enough, the shirt sleeve was clear for anyone to see, but in the blink of an eye, it appeared to vanish into thin air, and yet, as he continued to look, it was suddenly there again.

"Thurngood," asked Harvey, "what's it doing? It keeps disappearing and reappearing, and I can't feel it touching my skin anymore."

"It's not disappearing; it's pulsating with your heartbeats. The Lignum fibers have intermingled with your skin. That's why you can no longer feel its presence. With each beat of your heart, the pulse excites the Lignum, causing its pigmentation to match that of your own skin. It practically becomes indistinguishable. However, when the pulse passes, it returns to its original color, creating the illusion of the material disappearing and reappearing."

"Then, is it alive?" asked Harvey, clearly astonished.

"It is. The wood fibers from the Flurn are sealed in barrels of Kreen nectar for at least one Ecclonian year. When the nectar ferments, it's absorbed by the spongy wood fiber. The enhanced nectar brings the wood cells back to life, and before long, respiration, photosynthesis, and mitosis are once again occurring."

"So my shirt will grow by itself?"

"It wouldn't grow any larger, but new cells are continually created to replace the dying ones."

"But how do I get it off?"

"Seeing as it's a living organism, why don't you just tell it to."

"Dad, I mean Thurngood, it's a plant," Harvey snapped sarcastically. "It can't understand what I say!" His frustration and annoyance was in reaction to much more than the shirt. The underlying hurt of being lied to was beginning to surface.

"I know a number of Flurn who would disagree with you on that point," Thurngood replied with a wry grin, attempting to diffuse the situation with humor.

"So what exactly do I do?" asked Harvey, still clearly annoyed.

"The impact of human thought is not restricted to the illumination of Ecclon's orb clouds."

"You mean I can think the Lignum shirt off?"

"You saved my life and won your first battle with Nezraut with nothing but your thoughts," offered Sheef.

"Okay then," said Harvey, his annoyance reduced to a simmer. He closed his eyes and created an image in his mind of the shirt loosening and extricating itself from his skin. A moment later there appeared the folds and wrinkles of a loose-fitting shirt.

"That's so bizarre," said Harvey while laughing to himself.

"To form-fit it again," said Thurngood, "either take it off and put it back on, or simply think it tight."

A millisecond after Harvey sketched out the opposite image on his mind's eye, the Lignum shirt once again contracted and merged with his skin.

"Sheef," Harvey called out as he turned his head to face him, "try yours on. It feels amazing."

In the next second, while Harvey was still facing Sheef, Thurngood shouted out Harvey's name as he swung his sword in an enormous arc, landing its razor-sharp edge on Harvey's chest. Harvey briefly glimpsed a blue flash in his peripheral side mirror, but it made no difference. The blade struck with such lightning fast quickness, that the possibility of doing anything but absorbing the blow was out of the question.

The inertia of the moving sword colliding so forcefully with his chest altered Harvey's orientation with the deck from perpendicular to parallel. For a sliver of a moment, his body hovered in the air as if it were being levitated by unseen spirits.

The back-pound on the deck knocked the air in Harvey's lungs free. When his breath decided to rejoin his body, he said gaspingly, "Was that really necessary? You didn't have to hit me so hard to make your point, and don't you think you could've warned me?"

"I did. I called out your name, and trust me, the enemy is full of surprises and swings much harder than that. You'll always have to be on the guard for what you're about to warp into. The point of hitting you, though, was to test the shirt. How's your chest?"

Harvey examined himself externally and internally. Thurngood's blade hadn't made the slightest incision in the Lignum shirt, and though the blow had flipped Harvey on his back, to his surprise, the bones and muscles of his chest weren't sore in the least.

"I guess I'm okay," said Harvey sourly as he slowly regained his perpendicular orientation, Thurngood's physical blow only feeding Harvey's grudge.

"Lignum is like armor, only vastly lighter and exponentially stronger," said Thurngood, not knowing how to properly respond to the bitterness in Harvey's voice. "If you wanted to achieve the same results with steel, the armor would have to be multiple inches thick. I also have pants and gloves to complete the ensemble for both of you. Once everything is on and fused with your own skin, you'll forget you have it on. Go ahead and wear your regular clothes on top."

"So, in essence," remarked Sheef smirking, "You've given us the world's toughest underwear."

"I've never thought about Lignum clothing in those exact terms, but yes. However, it's more likely the universe's toughest underwear, not just this world's."

"But, Thurngood," asked Harvey as he thought off the shirt and placed in his backpack, "why didn't Bellock share this with Sheef and me when he first recruited us. Seems to me that Lignum wear should be standard issue for anyone setting out to do battle with the Vapid."

"I can only guess at Bellock's reason for withholding it from you, and my best guess is that he wanted you to first learn how to battle with your most formidable offensive weapon."

"My thoughts?" asked Harvey.

"Still the greatest weapon ever forged by the Unseen," replied Thurngood.

Suddenly, shooting off from the grass in rapid succession, the entire line of chattering squirrels leapt airborne towards a particular target standing on the deck. They flew at Harvey like lemurs soaring for a tree trunk. Unfortunately for them, none made it past the end of Harvey's sword blade in one piece.

When the first squirrel initiated the leaping attack, Thurngood shouted Harvey's name as he tossed him a sword. Harvey's arm was already swinging forward when the grip landed gracefully in the cradle of his hand.

The rapidity of Harvey's sword play reminded Sheef of a Japanese chef's blurry knife acrobatics. The results were similar as well, but instead of onions, mushrooms, and shrimp sliced and diced into smaller pieces, the sectioned particulars of squirrels were soon flying in every direction.

Chunks of squirrel plopped down, marring a good portion of the deck, while Sheef and Thurngood shook their heads in disbelief. Though they had witnessed Harvey's natural ability with a blade earlier in the day, this was something entirely different.

"Harvey," said Thurngood dazed and practically speechless, "I don't know how you ended up with fighting skills like those. I've never seen anyone handle a Querreck blade like that."

Harvey was breathing heavily, his mind catching up to his reflexive actions with the sword. Gnarl, who had been quietly studying both the squirrels and Harvey ever since the group reconvened on the deck, now spoke up.

"Those were no ordinary animals. They had been taken possession of by the enemy. I am certain of it."

"Insips?" asked Sheef.

"There is no other logical explanation," said Gnarl. "It appears that something drew them here, and considering the fact they attacked young Harvey, I believe that something to be him."

"Well of course it's him," said Thurngood. "He is, after all, the one chosen by Bellock, as well as the one who defeated Nezraut. I imagine that the Vapid sent scouts here."

"Perhaps, Thurngood, but the appetites of the Insips which took possession of the squirrels were aroused by some manner of foulness. They were all but salivating, desperate to feast upon what young Harvey had prepared for them."

"Gnarl, that's insane!" Harvey blurted out. "I haven't done anything to attract them. And what do you mean by preparing something?"

"Harvey," said Gnarl gently but directly, "there is a festering in your heart. You are harboring something toxic, perhaps a feeling or a thought. Whatever is the case, its fumes are now attracting outside attention, and if you fail to release it, your lack of action will prove detrimental to you and everyone involved in this mission to save Ecclon, Earth, and our Flurn friends. Every move you make will leave a pungent trail for the enemy to follow. And your skill at wielding that most formidable weapon which you just mentioned, will be significantly dulled."

"Gnarl," said Harvey defensively, "I'm telling you, I don't know what you're talking about!"

"Search your heart, Harvey, and you will find that my words ring true, though I am confident that you already know this."

Harvey looked away from Gnarl to the squirrel carnage covering the deck. The ancient sage's words revealed to everyone that he was holding hostage a cognitive or emotional malignancy deep within his being. He knew exactly what it was, but he couldn't admit it. Not yet anyway. The wound was too fresh, the emotional cut too raw. Gnarl was right; the wound had already begun to fester, but for some inexplicable reason, Harvey found himself enjoying its putrid odor.

A flush of conviction spread its hands around his head, its finger tips digging into his forehead, crafting the beginnings of a splitting headache. A patting on his shoulder distracted him from his mulling. He turned in the direction of the pat. Fromp was sitting next to him, his boxy head equal with his. The warp-hound whined and pawed at him a second time. A pleading look, as if he was asking Harvey to throw a ball again, was weighing heavily in his large brown eyes.

16

Thurngood picked up the pieces of squirrel, placed them in a pile in the corner, and then washed the deck clean with a hose attached to the back of the house. Meanwhile, Sheef and Harvey's mother sidled up next to Harvey.

"What's going on, kid?" asked Sheef. "A Flurn as wise and discerning as Gnarl doesn't waste words. He wouldn't have said what he did if there wasn't something to it."

"Sheef," said Harvey, his words a hair above a whisper but sharp with annoyance, "I don't know what he means. I just . . . can we please change the subject. We have two words that apparently my dad thought were important enough to write down more than once in his notes. I don't want to waste any more time thinking about something I'm supposedly harboring. I know it's Gnarl and all, but everyone, even a famous Flurn, is capable of making a mistake."

"Okay, okay, settle down. I'm not the enemy here; I'm just trying to help. If you say there's nothing, then that's the end of it. I didn't mean to upset you, but I felt like I had to ask."

"Honey," said Harvey's mother tenderly, "if there's anything you need to talk about, I'm here to listen."

"There's not!" Harvey snapped. He immediately turned red and sighed. "I'm sorry, Mom. Sorry, Sheef, I didn't mean to snap at you two. I'm just so worried about you, Mom, and Bellock, and Ecclon, and everything else. We're supposed to save planets and people, but we don't even know where or how to begin."

"It's quite all right," said Sheef. "Apology accepted. Let's begin by asking Gnarl about those words, and by the way, it's not up to us to save anyone or anything. The Unseen is the designer of the rollercoaster we're about to step into. You and I are only along for the ride."

"Gnarl," Sheef said as he, Harvey, and his mother walked closer to where the Flurn was standing on the deck, "Harvey's mother gave us two words that her husband had written down in his notes. None of us have ever heard of them before. She thinks you might be able to help."

"Certainly," said Gnarl. A pleasanter, less scrutinizing demeanor washing over his countenance. "Please, show me the two enigmas."

Harvey's mother handed Gnarl a piece of stationery she had scribbled the words upon. Gnarl read the words and then audibly rolled them about on his tongue with "hmm's", "um's", and the occasional "ah, yes". He marinated on the words for no less than thirty seconds before speaking.

"I only recognize the word 'Sadiki'. However, it has been many earth years, centuries in fact, since I last heard it used. Very ancient indeed. Not originally from this planet either. The word is early Ecclon if my memory serves me correctly. Princess Dwen, do you have any conception as to why it was important to your husband?"

"Arrick never told me what or who it referred to, but he did say that he needed one in order to retrieve the object."

"Why yes, it makes sense then," Gnarl mumbled to himself, but loud enough for everyone to hear, "if he traveled there, and where else would he travel if his intention was to go backward in time? Not a direct route to the past, mind you. Very circuitous, but it could be exploited in order to send a person back. Likely the only way, too. It could not be done, though, without the use of a Sadiki – most essential to have one, but I would be astonished to learn that one still exists."

"Excuse me, Gnarl," said Harvey's mother politely, "I don't mean to be rude, but would you mind explaining your thoughts to us?"

"I apologize, Princess Dwen. I did not realize that I was thinking audibly. It is a consequence, no doubt, of centuries of thinking and meditating alone. Yes, by all means I will share with you my thoughts. I suggest, however, that everyone take a seat."

Harvey took a seat as did everyone else, but soon after sitting down he was already squirming restlessly in his seat. The squirrel attack had released a surge of energy from his adrenal glands. He was ready for action. For him to be confined to his seat in this amplified state made him feel like he might explode at any moment.

Once everyone was settled, Gnarl began to explain his thoughts. "If your husband, Princess Dwen, located and used a Sadiki, it can only mean one thing. He warped to the Phantasian as a way back in time.

"The Phanta . . . ? I'm sorry, Gnarl," said Harvey's mother, "he warped where?"

"The Phantasian. Well, yes, it is quite understandable that you would have no knowledge of it," Gnarl said and then paused for a moment. "Let me see . . . where shall I begin? Ah yes, as fitting a starting place as any. The Phantasian is a vast collection of worlds located in a dimension which is not easily accessed, and let me assure you, the universe is a much better and safer place because of this fact. Now, these particular worlds are unlike any other world in any of the myriad dimensions, for these worlds were not created by the Unseen."

This unexpected statement from Gnarl triggered simultaneous jaw drops of disbelief and dumbfoundedness.

"But that's impossible," commented Sheef. "Anything and everything that exists owes its existence to the creative workings of the Unseen."

"That would seem to be the case, would it not? Anyone hearing my statement would likely respond, as you did Sheef, that what I said violated an inviolable law of the universes, namely, that if any object, law, or process does exist, then it can be logically inferred that its existence was the result of the creative action of the Unseen."

Everyone nodded, though, not completely confident that they had grasped all that Gnarl had just said.

"But you must remember, especially you humans and Lacit, that you were created in the image of the Unseen, and as His image bearers, you yourselves have incredible creative abilities. Harvey, I am certain that Bellock explained this to you when he taught you about the effect of human thought on the orb clouds of Ecclon."

Harvey nodded, as small bubbles of remembrance from Bellock's extensive explanation on the topic rose to the surface of his memory.

"You're not telling us, are you, that humans or Lacit created these Phantasian worlds?" asked Thrungood.

"I am. As unbelievable as it sounds, this is the truth of the matter, though it is primarily humans who are responsible for the majority of the creating. In order to comprehend how this is possible, think again of the way in which the Unseen created our worlds and then how a similar process might be applied to humans.

"The Unseen first conceives of something, such as a world that He desires to create, in His imagination. Once conceived, He speaks, and that which he imagined takes on physical form in another dimension. For example, at one point He imagined the Flurn – their appearance, intellect, demeanor, purpose, and so on – and then He spoke the Flurn into existence."

Everyone nodded, acknowledging that they were tracking with Gnarl's explanation.

"Suppose a human author spends hundreds upon hundreds of hours imagining and creating the characters and plot of a novel. The author writes and publishes this work. The novel is read, and the imagined story world, which the author created, now exists in the reader's imagination. But did the imagined world ever take on physical form outside the mind of the author or the reader?"

"No," said Harvey, "other than there being a physical book that you can hold, the world which the author created is still just in the mind."

"One would think this to be the case, but recall what occurs with the Unseen."

Gnarl stopped speaking in order to let his words settle. A long minute passed in awkward silence. The epiphany struck Harvey first. "The Phantasian! I was wrong. Wasn't I? The story that the author created really would exist. I mean physically, beyond there just being a book that could be held. I'm betting that the world in his imagination would take on form and matter in the Phantasian."

"Very, very good, Harvey, though the human author would have no idea whatsoever that his fictitious world had become a real one in another dimension."

"Whoa, whoa, whoa!" said Sheef, combing through his hair with his hands and then wrapping them together on the back of his neck. He stood up and began pacing the deck. "Do you mean to tell me that everything that humans have ever imagined throughout all of history has become a real world in this Phantasian place?"

"Not quite," said Gnarl. "Birthing a new world in the Phantasian does not occur unless it is preceded by long periods of very concentrated thought. If you, for example, were to spend five minutes imagining a world in which you were able to fly, the thought energy behind it would not be sufficient to manifest such a world in the Phantasian. However, if you were to spend months thinking about it, and if this cognition was followed by your actually writing it down, and then vast numbers of people read what you had written, then there would likely be enough concentrated thought energy to launch a world in which you were flying."

"Does that mean that every novel has become an actual world in the Phantasian?" asked Harvey.

"Not necessarily. If it was a very obscure book, read by few, it is likely that there would not be adequate thought energy to engender a world, but the more popular novels, yes, most definitely. And do not forget plays and movies."

"So, let me get this straight. "You're saying that there is a *Wizard of Oz* world in the Phantasian that is actually inhabited by witches, singing munchkins, and flying blue monkeys?" asked Sheef.

"I'm not familiar with this work."

"Oh sorry. *The Wizard of Oz* is a very famous book, and an even more popular movie."

"Well then, certainly. If the characters you mentioned – witches and flying monkeys – exist in the book and movie, then they would exist in the Phantasian world. In fact, if you went to this particular *Wizard of Oz* world, you would be able to interact with the different characters just as you are doing with me now."

"So who knows about this place?" asked Harvey's mother.

"Fortunately, very few are aware of its existence. Though in times past, more than one ancient people were acquainted with the Phantasian, most notably the Egyptians and Greeks. It was from the worlds of the Phantasian, incidentally, that the Egyptians learned the engineering requisite to construct the pyramids."

"But that doesn't make sense," said Thurngood. "Such engineering knowledge wouldn't appear in books and movies for centuries. The ancient Egyptians would've been long gone before there was any useful information that they could glean from these future worlds."

"That would be true, Thurngood, if the Phantasian worlds were subjected to the flow of time, but this dimension does not ride on any such current. There is no past or future...only the present. A Phantasian world, for example, formed by a novel written one thousand years from now, would have always existed in this dimension; hence, it would have been available to any ancient people, including the Egyptians."

"So any technology that appeared in a story, say from 2050 AD, would've been available to people living in Egypt in the year 2500 BC?" asked Sheef in disbelief.

"If they had the knowledge and means to access the Phantasian, then it would have most definitely been available to them. And when you consider the number of incredible architectural and engineering breakthroughs and accomplishments that occurred during this period, I believe that these ancient people accessed these worlds frequently. The Phantasian worlds, apparently, also had a tremendous influence on many of the oral tales, myths, and epic poems of the later Greeks."

"I'll tell you one thing," said Sheef chuckling, "this completely flips on its head my understanding of history. Imagine it! There are worlds out there in which a vampire, Medusa, and even a talking dog actually exist. Absolutely incredible."

"Incredible," replied Gnarl, "but also extremely perilous. Anachronistic knowledge can be highly destructive."

"Anachronistic?" asked Harvey.

"Something belonging to another time period," replied Gnarl.

"A horse and buggy traveling down a modern highway or a supersonic fighter breaking the sound barrier over the head of cowboy living in the year 1885," offered Sheef.

"Oh, I get it," replied Harvey. "So how can anachronistic knowledge be destructive?"

"Where do you think the idea for an atomic weapon originated?" asked Gnarl.

"I see what you mean."

"And you believe," interjected Harvey's mother, "that Arrick learned of these worlds, somehow figured how to warp to one of them, and then used it to travel back to Hollywood, planet Earth, in the late 1930's, in order to retrieve the Narciss Glass? But how?"

"From what I have learned of your husband, he was a very brilliant man, quite adept and clever in solving enigmas. As the head administrator of the Hall of Artifacts, he would have had access to a voluminous amount of ancient writings. One of these, no doubt, was inscribed with revelatory information about the existence of the Phantasian, as well as the means of traveling to it: a Sadiki."

"Is a Sadiki some sort of talisman that transports people?"

"No, a Sadiki is not a magical object. Sadikis are alive."

"Alive?"

"They are planet Earth's oldest and most cherished canines."

"A Sadiki is a dog?" asked Harvey in disbelief.

"Your planet's very own warp-hound."

The eyelids covering Fromp's eyes, which were heavily shut as he peacefully snoozed on the deck, were suddenly flung open. His ears stood tall atop his watermelon of a head.

"We have a dog that can do what Fromp does?" asked Sheef.

"Only to and through the Phantasian," replied Gnarl.

"Which is exactly what we need," said Harvey. "So where do we find one?"

"In a place where they were once revered. Egypt, of course."

17

The group spent the rest of the afternoon planning their next move. They gathered on the back deck for an early dinner of sandwiches that Sheef and Thurngood had hastily assembled to discuss whether or not anyone else would accompany Harvey and Sheef to Egypt, when their meal was abruptly interrupted.

"Thoughts and swords on guard!" Thurngood's shouting command rent the tranquil twilight. Male fireflies, casually wafting atop folds of humid air, had already begun their signaled serenades when Thurngood's voice shook the atmosphere.

And then, seemingly from nothing, a glowing warp hole appeared in the sky ten feet off the ground. Thurngood hastily led Sheef and Harvey down the deck stairs. Their three blue Querreck swords stood up and out like the raised horns of a triceratop bracing for battle.

Thurngood instructed Harvey and Sheef to spread out. They each took a number of steps away from one another, forming a triangle around the hovering warp hole. A growling Fromp stood in between Sheef and Harvey, a dorsal fin of hair rising along the ridge of his back.

Harvey tightened his grip on the sword handle as a bead of nervous sweat followed the contours of his forehead. It rolled effortlessly over his eyebrow before making stinging contact with his eye.

"We'll have a few seconds' jump on whatever's about to drop down on us," said Thurngood. "Vanquish lies with truth and flesh with sword!"

A quaking boom shook the branches and hanging moss of the oak trees. This was followed by a sharp pop and the blinding explosion of light that heralded the warping arrival of an unknown visitor. Two large silver-gray objects landed at their feet.

"It's the girls: Jules and Joust!" shouted Sheef as Jules stumbled and collapsed on the ground. "Jules is badly hurt!"

Sheef dropped his sword and knelt down next to the whimpering warp-hound. A deep laceration ran diagonally from the scruff of her neck to the middle of her chest. Smaller and shallower cuts crisscrossed her back and flanks. Joust, who had similar surface wounds, was rendering aid the only way she knew how. Within seconds, Fromp had joined her.

Their tongued nursing of the injury was so intense that Sheef had difficulty clearly seeing the wound. He lightly pushed aside the boxy snouts.

"The wound's pretty deep. Likely a gift from one of those dark Flurn. Thurngood, you and Harvey help me get her up on the deck."

The three of them gently lifted the large warp-hound and carried her to the middle of the deck. By the time they had set her down, Harvey's mother emerged from the house with her hands full of gauze, strips of cloth, and antiseptic.

Just before dinner, Sheef, who had observed how fatigued Harvey's mother appeared and who knew how important it was for her to be alert during the discussion, offered her a piece of Kreen. The fruit of Ecclon provided her with a surge of energy and gave her the strength to nurse the animal's injuries.

"Thurngood, would you keep Joust and Fromp away so that I can dress the poor girl's wound?"

"They must have followed my scent to the Shellow Plain," said Gnarl.

"Based on their condition," remarked Sheef, "only after they fought with the enemy. They were probably trying to protect the Flurn Elders."

"How do you think they survived then?" asked Harvey.

"No way to tell," replied Sheef. "Maybe they were knocked unconscious during the fight, and when they regained consciousness, the battle was over and the enemy was gone. Joust must have scented Fromp's warp trail and followed us here."

"Harvey," said his mother who was kneeling beside Jules, lightly dabbing her wound with an antiseptic-soaked cloth, "you're not safe here. You and Sheef must leave immediately."

"She's right," said Thurngood. "Two warp holes from Ecclon opening up in the same place on the same day is highly unusual and very noticeable. If Nezraut wasn't aware of something going on here before, I can guarantee you that he knows now."

"But, mom, I can't let you fight them alone!"

"Harvey, listen to me. You, son, have a fight before you, but this is not it. You know what you need to do. It's why He chose you. I'll be all right. Besides, I have Joust and the captain of the Lacit Royal Guard to protect me."

"Harvey," said Thurngood as he swung his sword menacingly. "You should actually feel sorry for anything that comes against your mother. It would first have to go through me, and let me assure you, I won't be selling it toilet paper!"

"Your mother is correct, Harvey. There is too much at stake for you to linger here any longer," said Gnarl.

"But where exactly do we warp? And how do we even begin finding one of those Sadikis?"

"Simply warp to the pyramids of Egypt. They are still active, and thus, closely watched."

"Active? Watched? What do you mean, Gnarl?"

"Harvey," said Gnarl beginning to lose his patience, "there is no time to delve into those waters now.

"VAPID LORDS!" yelled Sheef. "THEY'RE CLOSE; I CAN FEEL THEM ARRIVING! HARVEY, LET'S MOVE IT!"

Gnarl had already sent a thought to Fromp for him to open a warp hole, and he was well into rotating an exit when over thirty shimmering distortions refracted the last light of day.

Fromp's warp hole was swirling, available and waiting, when Sheef yelled again. "Harvey, it's now or never!"

"But how will we find the Sadiki?" shouted Harvey to Gnarl, his voice striving to overcome the sucking sounds of the distortions which were now open for the enemy's arrival.

"You will not! She will find you!"

"She?"

"No time. Go!"

A fire ball shot out of one of the warp holes and streaked across the backyard. Harvey followed its projected trajectory.

"Mom, watch out!"

The alacritous agility and Kreen-induced strength of Harvey's mother's movements were a glimpse of her true nature – a memory of what she and Ecclon had been when both had vibrantly pulsed. Milliseconds before the flaming sphere burst into fiery fragments on the back of the house, Harvey's mother scooped Jules into her arms, stood, and then vaulted into a backwards flip. The chain of fluid motion events occurred so quickly and seamlessly that Harvey wasn't even sure that what he had observed had actually happened.

She was in mid-flip, with her body parallel to the deck, when the fireball passed mere inches beneath her. She landed squarely on her feet, tightly holding the still whimpering warp-hound.

Harvey's mother stood resolutely. She shouted a command to her son, sounding more like a warrior than a mother.

"Go now!" she screamed.

A violent tugging on Harvey's shirt sent him stumbling backwards. Sheef had grabbed him from behind. As their feet tangled together, they both fell in and through the waiting warp hole.

Fromp quickly followed as additional fireballs launched like torpedoes from the enemy's opening portals. Patches of fire burned brightly on the deck and wall of the house. Thurngood immediately responded with water from the garden house.

The door of Fromp's warp hole snapped shut and disappeared. Sheef, Harvey, and the warp-hound were gone, but into their wake the enemy appeared. Swarms of shrieking Insips scattered from the warp holes like shotgun BB's, their spread covering every inch of backyard. Closely on their wings were packs of snarling Volkin Wolves. The Vapid Lords emerged next. And finally, Nezraut stepped through, the lords and wolves parting and arranging themselves as if welcoming royalty.

Nezraut began speaking in words well-seasoned with faux refinement. The snarl evident on his double mouths, however, betrayed his language.

"How unfortunate! It appears that I missed the backyard family reunion by only seconds. What a disappointment and shame, for I do so enjoy family gatherings."

Nezraut glanced to the corner of the deck where pieces of sliced and diced squirrel segments were piled.

"I see that you parted – please pardon the pun – with many of my Insips, but fortunately for me, you did not decimate them all. A few scouts made it back and shared with me the most intriguing tidbits of information. You cannot imagine my surprise when I learned that an Ecclonian princess is living here on Earth, and that she, believe it or not, is the mother of a beloved teenager."

Nezraut turned in the direction of Harvey's mother before continuing. "Princess Dwen, thank you for welcoming me to your little backyard soiree, and let me take this opportunity to formally introduce myself."

Nezraut stopped speaking and walked with an imperial air across the yard. His highest ranking Vapid Lords fell in and followed at a deferred distance. By his side was Sköll, the leader of the Volkin wolves. When he reached the deck, his advance up the stairs was halted and blocked by Thurngood's body and blade.

"It's okay, Thurngood," said Harvey's mother. Let him through."

"But, Princess Dwen."

"It matters not what this Vapid Lord and his toadies to do us. Harvey is gone and on his way. Our lives are of little importance now."

She said this as she set Jules back down on the deck and gently stroked the warp hound's head. Harvey's mother was struggling to maintain consciousness. Even with the energy surge from the piece of Kreen she had eaten, her acrobatic feat while holding Jules had left her exhausted.

Thurngood stepped aside, allowing Nezraut and Sköll to pass. Joust stood up, baring her teeth and growling at the approaching Volkin wolf. When the Vapid Lord was mere feet from Harvey's mother, he stopped walking and tipped her a slight condescending bow. Sköll sat down at his master's side, staring at Joust with a venomous scorn.

"Princess Dwen, mother of my mild irritant, do you realize that your son's antics have begun to fray the ends of my patience? He is, if truth be told, a most unruly boy."

Fighting to suppress both fear and utter revulsion, Harvey's mother defiantly replied, "I think that my 'unruly boy' has done far more than merely fray your patience. From what I understand, he not only derailed your plans, but defeated you in battle as well."

"His victory, Princess, if you choose to call it that, was, I can assure you, an anomaly. You see, I made the mistake of endeavoring to make him a prisoner of thought. Next time, I shall not bother with deception and mind tricks. I shall simply kill him.

And as for derailing my plans . . . Ecclon is already mine. The Flurn Elders are no more, and the clouds are even now gasping their last flicker of light. Whatever your boy and that fool of a friend of his are up to, it is inconsequential. Nothing and no one can stop me."

"Is that so?" asked Harvey's mother with a growing smirk. "If everything you said is true, then why are you here in my backyard with such an impressive show of force?"

Nezraut was momentarily stunned, briefly unsure of how to respond. He soon recovered his smarmy composure, narrowing his eyes to glowering slits.

"You, my infirmed princes," said Nezraut viciously, taking two steps closer to her, "should be more careful in the manner with which you address me. I am not one to be trifled with."

Nezraut's pleasantries, though, quickly returned as he continued. "Now, why not be sensible? Lessen and lighten the impending torturous suffering for you and Thurngood by telling me what I want to know. If you do so, I promise to be merciful and kill you expediently. If you refuse, my Volkin Wolves will make a slow and savory meal of you both. The choice is yours. Let us begin by your telling me everything about the object."

"I don't know what you're talking about," stammered Harvey's mother unconvincingly.

"Oh please, Princess, do not take me for a fool. The surviving Insip scouts returned very agitated, which is understandable considering what they had witnessed. They were babbling on incessantly. Most of what they said was a muddled mess, but there was one word, and a very unique one at that, which they said multiple times: Narciss Glass.

Now I suspect that your son and Sheef are on a quest to find this object, but I am embarrassed to admit that I do not know why. Would you, therefore, be so kind as to explain what it is and why they are after it?"

"Not on my life," responded Harvey's mother without the least quibble of irresolution in her voice.

"Then on your death. So be it, if that is your choice."

Nezraut was on the verge of saying something else when a familiar and pleasing odor caught hold of his nasal attentions. He titled his head back and forth three or four times in order to snatch a larger sampling. He wickedly grinned.

"Not a typical backyard aroma by any means. Far from the odiferous offerings of the barbeque or grill that humans find so enjoyable, but an exceedingly lovely one nonetheless. Very powerful, too.

Harvey's mother and Thurgood exchanged baffled looks before Nezraut continued.

"Insips, you know, are not the only creatures that are able to detect thought odors. Vapid, you might be surprised to learn, are equipped with a unique olfactory, capable of scenting the slightest of aromas arising from unpleasant human thought. And based on the unique bouquet of fragrances in the air today, I would say that someone, a young man perhaps, is harboring a hurt in his little heart, and it has spread to his mind, making some of his thoughts quite rancid and easily identifiable. I do believe a trail has been left for us to follow. How very thoughtful of young Harvey."

Perplexed, Harvey's mother replied, "You don't know what you're talking about. He's left nothing for you to follow. Why would he do that? You're bluffing."

"I can assure you, Princess, I know precisely what I am talking about, and you should also know, I never bluff."

Nezraut looked down at Sköll and whispered loudly enough for the wolf and anyone close by to hear, "I can see, my pet, that you have detected it as well. Open a warp hole and track that scent to wherever it leads that snout of yours. Take a swarm of Insips with you, but when you locate Harvey and that fool mentor of his, do not attack. Listen to everything they say about this Narciss Glass. Then report back to me immediately with their location.

In less than three minutes, Sköll had opened a new warp hole and bolted through. He was accompanied by a screeching swarm of Insips. His flaring, hungry nostrils led the way.

Once the Volkin wolf was gone, Nezraut turned back to Harvey's mother.

"It appears," said Nezraut while clapping his hands together, "that I will soon know the whereabouts of your son and discover the secrets of this Narciss Glass which seems to have captivated everyone's attention."

"Even if you do find them, what makes you think that Harvey won't defeat you in battle for a second time?"

"Defeat me in battle?" Nezraut chuckled. "How you amuse me. I told you, only minutes ago, that the next time I met young Harvey I would simply kill him and forgo all those tiresome attempts at deceiving him into my service. This scent changes everything, however."

Harvey's mother's confused look asked for elaboration.

"I know the particular thought odor emanating from your son's mind quite well. As you already know, whether you are ready to admit it or not, it leaves a definitive trail, but what you do not know is that it also creates a very nice chink in his thought armor. I will admit that Harvey's thoughts were well fortified by the Unseen's truth during our initial engagement, but when we meet again, his defenses, as he will find out too late, will have been undermined by his own putrid thinking."

Here Nezraut clapped his hands together for a second time.

"And this should be good news to the ears of his mother, for I may not have to kill him after all. With vulnerable thoughts, it is highly probable that this time he WILL succumb to the power of my deceptions and willingly become my own personal pawn. And what a prize young Harvey would make!

"That robust and efficacious mind of his, once bent to do my bidding, will be used to manipulate millions upon millions of creatures throughout the universes. The thought of a young protégé, twisted to carry out my designs . . . well . . . to be honest, it threatens to play upon my emotions," said Nezraut smiling.

Thurngood continued to stand silently on the deck. The captain of the Lacit Royal Guard strove with every fiber of his being against lashing out with his blade at Nezraut. His close proximity would enable him to inflict a serious wound, but there were too many other Vapid and Volkin Wolves to contend with.

He was a skilled fighter to be sure, but no single fighter, regardless of skill, could hope to vanquish such a horde. Discretion may be the better part of valor, but it certainly is a bitter pill to swallow, especially for the passionate warrior.

Instead of attacking, Thurngood continued to watch Gnarl who had positioned himself amongst the oak trees in the yard. He blended in so well that he would've only been noticed if someone was intently looking for him.

Thurngood hadn't the slightest idea as to what Gnarl was up to, but the nonverbal communique was clear. The illustrious Flurn had held up his branch hand more than once, telling Thurngood to stop whatever he was planning on doing and to wait for his lead.

Nine oak trees were situated in the backyard. Three of the largest sunk their roots into the moist and velvety soil close to the deck, their stout branches reaching out far enough for their fingers to scratch the roof.

Above ground, the trunks of the trees were separated by spacious patches of green, but underneath, their root systems were intertwined with one another, as if the trees were all part of a single subterranean organism.

Gnarl's roots easily penetrated the loose soil. Small exploratory rootlets tunneled in every direction, mingling and wrapping themselves around every oak tree root they met. He was soon connected to every one of the trees, and more importantly, in control of them.

A thought rifled down Gnarl's trunk and into the communicative root wiring underground. The oak branches over the deck briefly shook. Nezraut, however, was too busy basking in the light of his own cleverness and false assurance of victory to notice the movement.

"It seems, Princess, that the lives of you and Thurngood have become more of a liability than an asset. You will not divulge anything about the Narciss Glass. This is unfortunate enough, but now you also know that I am able to easily track your son. I am sorry, but I cannot chance your warning him, not that it would do much good. Do take heart, though. Knowing that I can follow your son's trail wherever he may warp, makes me feel much more amiable, which is good news, for it means that your deaths shall be relatively quick. Painless? Well, I must maintain standards. Reputation and what not. I am sure you understand."

"Now let us see," continued Nezraut, "how shall we do away with you two? Oh, I know. Given that we are in a backyard, I believe it would be more than appropriate to provide you with a death complimentary to this setting. What is it that you humans say? Ah yes, light the grill!"

With these words, a sphere of undulating molten flame emerged from Nezraut's hands. The other Vapid Lords followed suit. Within seconds, balls of fiery light shone out in the early evening shadows like the beacons of many lighthouses. The hollow, expressionless faces of the Vapid were eerily illuminated.

"Do you have any last words," asked Nezraut smugly, "that you would like me to pass along to young Harvey?"

Yes, I do. "From the height of pride, comes a painful fall," responded Harvey's mother with steely resolve.

"Interesting choice, but I fail to understand why you would select these to be your parting words?"

"It's a proverb from the writings of Gnarl the Deep that I memorized when I was a young girl."

"How quaint. And yet, I still am unable to see why you would want these to be the last words that cross your royal lips and what relevance they would have for Harvey."

"That's because they're not meant for him. They're meant for you." The fire in Harvey's mother's eyes was burning more intensely than the one in Nezraut's hands.

All at once, hundreds of dirt eruptions occurred throughout the yard. It was a veritable minefield of soil explosions. Roots blasted through the ground. The branches overhanging the deck, within striking distance of Nezraut, swung low and hard. A solid connection between wood and skull sent Nezraut twirling unconscious over the deck railing.

With the crushing squeeze of a constrictor, the oak tree roots grabbed hold of each Vapid Lord, binding their arms to their bodies. Flaming spheres fell to the ground where they smoldered into ashes.

Gnarl tightly held each of the Vapid until deprivation turned to fainting, then released them to collapse onto the lawn.

"Okay," said Thurngood, flabbergasted and amazed, "I didn't see that one coming! Gnarl, I must admit. I am impressed."

"There is really nothing much to it," responded Gnarl, "Earthly trees are easily controlled with only a modicum of focused thought."

"Well, really not what I meant. Anyway, we should probably warp out of here and warn Harvey and Sheef before our friends regain consciousness."

"Agreed," said Harvey's mother, staggering backwards for the support of a chair.

"Dwen," said Thurngood, "it might be best if . . ."

"Don't even suggest it, Thurngood. I'm going after my son."

"All right then. I'm wise enough to know not to pick a fight with a protective mother. Why don't you rest until Joust opens a warp hole."

"What about Jules?" asked Harvey's mother.

"I will take her with me," said Gnarl.

"What do you mean? You're not going with us?" asked Thurngood.

"I am a Flurn, a protector of Ecclon. My place is with my planet and its people."

"But what can be done at this point? The orb clouds are all but extinguished."

"All the more reason for my return. What manner of Flurn would I be if I abandoned Ecclon in her most dire hour? And besides, though the light of the clouds has dimmed, that of the Unseen has not. He has not been caught by surprise. No breath is drawn, no droplet falls, no seed is sown without His knowledge."

"I remember reading that proverb," said Thurngood. "I just wish that I believed it right now."

"Then, now, or tomorrow never alters the truth. Do not strive to make yourself believe. The truth will believe for you, if you will only let it."

MADORA

18

With a loud crack, Harvey, Sheef, and Fromp flashed into the desert night sky, mere feet above the pinnacle of a large pyramid. The top of the structure had eroded away, creating a small level surface. Fortunately, Fromp opened the warp hole directly above this area, though it did nothing to soften the landing on solid rock.

"If our goal was to get noticed by a Sadiki," said Sheef as he stood up and began dusting himself off, "that certainly did the trick."

"You got that right," replied Harvey, who was rubbing the small of his back. "But what do we do now?"

"If it wasn't dark, I would suggest climbing down, but it would be foolhardy at best to attempt a descent now. We'll have to wait until morning."

"So I guess that means we're camping out on top of a pyramid."

"Minus a tent, sleeping bags, or pillows," said Sheef good naturedly, "but I believe we can make do for a few hours."

Sheef bent down and picked up two bread-loaf-sized limestone chunks and handed one of them to Harvey.

"Here you go, an ancient Egyptian pillow."

"As tempting as it is to lay my head on a chunk of limestone, I think I'll stick with Fromp," said Harvey while pointing to the warp-hound who was already lying on his side, offering his soft and substantial belly as a headrest.

"It even vibrates," said Harvey as he lay his head on Fromp's belly, allowing his fur to gently envelope his head.

"Hope he's flea free," remarked Sheef as he positioned himself next to Harvey and Fromp.

Fromp responded by turning his head around and laying a large wet one across Sheef's cheek and lips.

"You rotten slug mouth," said Sheef in disgust as he wiped a glistening layer of hound saliva from his face.

It was a moonless night. With no lunar light to bully and diminish the stars' brilliance, they were free to dance about the heavens. It was breathtaking to behold, and the sight reminded Harvey of a conversation he had with Sheef about being in an environment free from distractions, so that the power of the Unseen might be experienced.

A heavy fullness soon enveloped Harvey. In fact, it was so dense and near, that he felt if were to just reach out, he would touch the presence.

"Harvey," said Sheef, breaking the moment and the silence, "that thing Gnarl said you were holding on to. Do you want to talk about now?"

After more than a minute of silence, Harvey responded. "Sheef, as I said before, I honestly don't know what he was talking about, and I'd really rather not discuss it anymore. Besides, I'm wiped out, and I have a feeling that we'll need to be rested for tomorrow."

"All right, but you know I'm here for you if you need to get something off your chest."

"I know, Sheef . . . and thanks."

"Don't mention it."

Harvey lay on his back, wallowing in the guilt of his own making. He honestly did know what Gnarl was talking about, and lying to Sheef was the last thing in the world he wanted to do, but opening up was even less desirable. If he voiced what was going on inside his heart, he knew that he would be forced to do something about it.

Harvey turned on his side away from Sheef, which allowed him to look out into the darkness. In the distance, he thought he saw two glowing green lights. The sight triggered a wispy and indefinite memory. Initially it was difficult to grasp; however, when he was finally able to lay hold of it, a jolting fear raced through his body. They were eyes. Volkin Wolf eyes.

As soon as sight and memory converged, the glowing lights vanished. Though they were gone, Harvey sensed something was still watching him.

19

Harvey and Sheef awoke to the frantic barking of Fromp. He was scurrying away five desert vultures that were attempting to land in order to investigate a possible scrumptious, meaty breakfast.

When Harvey opened his eyes, the blinding early desert sun was blinking on and off every few seconds by shadows cast from the circling vultures.

"We better start moving and let them know that we're still alive and kicking," said Sheef while stretching. "We need to get going anyway. I doubt that we're allowed on these pyramids without permission. The last thing we need right now is to get entangled with the Egyptian authorities."

"Agreed," yawned Harvey, "but before we begin, shouldn't we eat or drink something?"

"I was just about to suggest that."

Sheef unzipped the backpack Thurngood had given him. Before they had warped, Sheef had put in five Kreen. He pulled out a pocketknife and cut out two pieces. After only one bite, they were both reinvigorated and energized.

"You know," said Harvey, "we could just have Fromp warp us down."

"We could, but then he wouldn't be able to open another warp hole until he recovered enough strength, and there very well might be a more urgent reason to warp somewhere quickly once we get into whatever it is we're getting into."

"On second thought, I say we climb down."

"I thought you'd see it my way. Now we just have to find a route off this thing."

"Why not let Fromp lead. I mean, he's the one that got us up here, shouldn't he be the one who gets us down? With his senses and agility, I'm sure he can find a route much faster and easier they we can. Besides, I just ate some Kreen, sending him a thought will be a piece of cake."

"Then let the hound lead the way," said Sheef with a dramatic sweep of his arm.

Harvey created an image in his mind's eye of Fromp taking the lead and guiding them down the pyramid. Immediately after sending the thought, the warp-hound barked and reared up on his hind legs, indicating his affirmation and excitement.

Fromp walked methodically and slowly around the summit with his snout scenting the wind. He looked down numerous times. Each of these looks was accompanied by a whine. When he had nearly completed walking the perimeter, though, he began barking enthusiastically while running in circles.

"That must be our trail," said Sheef as he hefted his backpack on his shoulders. Harvey followed suit, and soon they were off.

Fromp alighted with the grace of a gazelle from one stone to another, making his speedy descent difficult for the humans to keep pace with. Multiple times the hound leapfrogged from one block to another, leaving Sheef and Harvey behind to lower, hang, and drop a distance which was too high for them to jump. Fromp ended up reaching the desert floor a good ten minutes before they did.

"Now what?" asked Harvey once they finally reached the bottom.

"I suppose," said Sheef as he wiped the sweat off of his brow with his shirt sleeve, "we wait for something atypical, like that, to appear."

Sheef was pointing to a rapidly moving column of dust streaking across the desert.

"Sheef, is that a car?"

"Can't be. Moving way too fast to be a car driving through sand."

"Then what?"

"Don't know, but it looks like we're about to find out."

The streaking dust column made a 90 degree turn, putting it on a trajectory directly towards them.

"What do we do now?" asked Harvey stepping backwards.

Fromp crouched down. The fur along the ridge of his back stood straight as porcupine quills. A low growl rumbled in his throat.

"Nothing to do," replied Sheef nervously. "But it might not be a bad idea to remove those swords from our bags."

Harvey reached down for his backpack, but before he was even able to touch the fabric, the sand cloud was upon them. It abruptly stopped just in front of where they were standing.

The sand of the billowing cloud was slow to settle back to earth, delaying the unveiling of whatever was hiding within, but when the air finally did clear, the outline of a dog's head and body began to take shape. Fromp excitedly barked.

Soon, enough sand had sifted out of the air to reveal the most beautiful and stunning animal Harvey and Sheef had ever seen. A Sadiki had appeared.

The dog was medium-sized. She had the triangular ears and snout of a shepherd. Her fur, a soft blend of gold and rust orange, fluttered lightly in the breeze. Curling back over itself, a majestic tail stood proudly like a royal banner.

It was impossible to look upon the Sadiki and not be awed. Her bearing was not only regal but otherworldly, as if the hero of an ancient myth had stepped forth from the pages of an epic poem.

Fromp wasn't merely awed, he was already well on his way to being seriously smitten. A goofy grin bent his black gums, and from his mouth, his prodigious pink tongue dangled waywardly.

He pawed at the ground, desiring to approach the Sadiki for a more intimate sniff. A fear paralyzed his forward mobility. It wasn't, however, a fear of being harmed or injured. The feeling was utterly foreign to the warp-hound. For the first time in his life, Fromp's paws felt heavy, clunky to be precise. He was unsure of himself. His head swam with dizziness, similar to the way he felt when he had gone more than a day without sleep. He looked over to Harvey and Sheef with pleading and questioning eyes. Unfortunately for Fromp, the two humans were also transfixed by the stunning creature before them.

"Does that dog appear to be shining?" asked Harvey.

"Shining or shimmering, take your pick. I've never seen any-thing to compare. I suppose we've been found by whatever Gnarl said we needed to find.

"A Sadiki."

"Exactly."

Harvey smiled.

"What is it?"

"Nothing, just that it wasn't long ago that another dog appeared out of nowhere and whisked me off to the unbelievable-made-believable.

"And now?"

"I've exactly the same feeling."

While they were conversing, Fromp inched with turtle steps closer and closer to the Sadiki.

"Looks like we're not the only ones impressed with our shim-mering new arrival," remarked Sheef while tapping Harvey on the shoulder and motioning with his chin towards Fromp.

The Sadiki was still standing in precisely the same posi-tion. Her statuesque pose was that of a loving obedience, wait-ing patiently for the object of her affection to appear. The Sadiki didn't have long to wait.

The roar of an off-road motorcycle reverberated off of the pyramid's limestone blocks, and though the sound continued to grow until it was deafening with its annoying proximity, Harvey and Sheef still couldn't see its source.

Suddenly, the dirt bike emerged from the side of the pyramid, which had until then screened its movements. From the fifth row of stones, the rider launched the bike airborne, thirty feet above the sand.

Harvey was certain that the front tire would hit first, cart-wheeling the rider over the handlebars. And this is precisely what didn't occur.

Rather, the bike and its rider soared gracefully through the dry desert air, directly over the head of a wildly barking Sadiki. The landing turned out to be just as smooth as the soaring. The back tire lightly kissed the sand, allowing the rest of the bike to fall forward and safely find its footing.

A second after, the rider gunned the engine while turning the bike 180 degrees, sending a fishtail of sand spray high into the air. The bike came to a sliding stop only a few feet from Harvey and Sheef.

Legs clad in dark brown leather extended from either side of the motorcycle. Boots of the same color and material sunk assertively into the sand. With the bike now stabilized, the rider reached up and removed the helmet.

Long, flowing black locks of hair unfurled themselves, their ends dropping just below the waistline. Now it was Sheef and Harvey's turn to stare stupidly with goofy grins bending their own gums.

The woman shouted at them in a foreign language. Harvey, dumbfounded, looked to Sheef and said with faltering words, "Sheef, why is she shouting at us?"

"I have no idea. I didn't understand a word she said. Sounds like Arabic."

The woman gave a slight nod, and then spoke in words easily understood by Harvey and Sheef. "You speak English," she said in words seasoned with a foreign accent. "No matter, I speak all tongues. I see that you've already met Akeila." She thrust her helmet at Sheef's chest. He caught it, but its force knocked him back a step or two.

She gave Harvey and Sheef a scrutinizing once over before continuing to speak in a most unpleasant tone. "You have exactly twenty seconds to explain warping into my realm before I kill you!"

20

"Well? One good reason for your lives?" asked the women as she placed her right hand upon the hilt of a sword resting in a scabbard attached to the side of the motorcycle.

With the seconds quickly slipping away, and the woman now beginning to unsheathe her blade, Harvey blurted out the one word that he thought might possible save them.

"Ecclon!" he blurted.

A flash of recognition and piqued interest. The muscles in the woman's face relaxed a bit.

"You've bought yourself a minute to explain why and how you know that word."

Harvey shifted uncomfortably as he stole a look at Sheef.

"Tell me now!" she said, her muscles once again tightening. "I'm waiting on pins and needles, and your time's slipping away."

"I'm Ecclonian," said Harvey, his nervousness inflating his voice an octave, "but I've spent most of my life here on Earth. I only found out about Ecclon and warp-hounds a little over a month ago."

"Anyway," he continued, his words spilling out in a hurried, tangled mess, "I was warped to Ecclon by Fromp, the warp-hound over there, and was told by a Flurn by the name of Bellock that the planet was dying because too many humans were turning away from the thoughts of the Unseen and that Nezraut had . . ."

"SILENCE!" The woman said abruptly. She stepped off her motorcycle, recklessly letting it drop to the sand. She unsheathed her sword and then speedily walked over to where Harvey was standing. Before he realized what was occurring, the tip of her blade was pricking the skin of his throat. The swiftness of her movements gave no allowance for Harvey or Sheef to react.

Sheef did take a step in Harvey's direction, but his movement was immediately curtailed by the woman's threat. "Take another step, old man, and I stick the boy." Sheef stepped back.

"What foul name did you spew in my presence?" seethed the woman. She lifted the sword ever so slightly, breaking Harvey's skin with the blade's point. A drop of blood trickled down his throat and onto his shirt.

Harvey, now hyperventilating, managed to snatch just enough breath to squeak, "Nezraut."

"That is what I thought you said," she replied while pushing him backwards with the flat of her blade against his chest. Harvey reached up and grabbed his neck, inspecting the small wound and attempting to regain his composure.

The woman thrust her sword into the sand. "I've decided to let you live for the time being, provided that you tell me everything I want to know." Her voice was still far from pleasant, but the threatening tone had been dialed back significantly.

She looked over at Harvey massaging his throat and said, "It's just a scratch. No permanent damage. You, boy, are going to tell me every detail about what's occurring on Ecclon and how that bag of maggot puss, Nezraut, is involved. But out here in the open is not the place." She stopped speaking and quickly panned the desert. "It wouldn't surprise me if Nezraut's sniveling bats are already watching us. There is a place not far from here where you can safely speak."

She walked back over to her motorcycle and stood it up. "Your warp-hound can run alongside Akeila. You, Ecclon boy, straddle the gas tank. Hold on tightly to the middle of the handlebars. Your father, or whoever he is, can ride on the seat behind me.

Harvey and Sheef made eye contact and shrugged. Since there was no option "B", they followed the woman's directions and were soon uncomfortably seated in their assigned positions.

"Hold on tightly. Biking the desert isn't for the faint of heart. And be careful where you place those hands of yours," she warned, looking back at Sheef. She then popped the clutch and sped off across the desert, away from the pyramids.

For Harvey, the ride atop the gas tank was even worse than the one he experienced on Fromp's tail during the warp-hound's high-speed chase of a fleeing Zuit back on Ecclon.

Even with the additional load of two passengers, the woman was still able to expertly handle the motorcycle. The problem was, however, that she rode it a little too expertly, too much like a motocross professional. For example, rather than decelerating when approaching a small sand dune, she gunned the engine, ensuring that she and her distraught passengers experienced the stomach-dropping thrill and trepidation of a rapid ascent and descent.

Harvey clutched the handlebars so fiercely that he feared that if he ever stepped upon solid ground again, his fingers would be frozen in a death grip. Sheef, meanwhile, clung to the woman like a barnacle on the hull of a ship.

For over thirty minutes, adrenaline surged through Harvey and Sheef's wobbly and weary bodies. Harvey was beginning to suspect that the woman had lied about taking them to a safe place, and was instead riding them far into the wilderness where she would abandon them to suffer death by exposure. He was also concerned about how much longer Fromp could keep up with Akeila, when the woman finally down-shifted gears. They rolled to a stop before an outcropping of rock, sticking out of the sand like a small, uninhabited island.

Shards and boulders of dark granite were piled atop one another in what appeared to be a disorganized mess. Closest to the group were two large pieces, each about fifteen feet in length. They were propped up against each other, creating a small "A"-shaped opening.

"We're here," said the woman as she stabilized the motorcycle with her feet so that Harvey and Sheef could get off. "Let's get in and out of the open as quickly as possible. Warping to the top of a pyramid likely caught the attention of more than one unsavory creature. By the way, you two could've been less flashly in the manner of your arrival."

The woman guided the motorcycle through the opening and rested it against a granite boulder. She then descended a flight of carved stairs into a subterranean tunnel. Akeila, and a heavily panting Fromp, were close on her heels. Harvey and Sheef tentatively followed.

There was soon scant amount of natural light. The woman pulled a flashlight from a knapsack that was slung over her shoulders. The light was only able to illuminate ten feet into the tunnel before being consumed by the stale, dark air. The temperature rapidly plummeted, a refreshing reprieve from the desert furnace. They climbed down the equivalent of twelve flights of stairs before the tunnel leveled out.

The woman shone her light on a large gray electrical box affixed to the tunnel's wall. Using both of her hands, she heaved a metallic lever upward. The hum of an electrical current sounded above them as a series of overhead lights flickered on, lighting the remainder of the tunnel which continued on for another sixty feet.

"Solar power. Panels hidden amongst the granite rocks on the surface. A never ending energy source in the desert," she said nodding upward. "Also have satellite uplink for the computers. My job requires that I know what's going on in the world." Sheef shook his head in disbelief.

Two doorways on both sides of the tunnel, each equally spaced from one another, were carved into the walls. They opened up to rooms that had the exact same dimensions.

Stopping in front of the first set of doors, the woman turned around and directed Harvey and Sheef to enter the room on their right, and for the first time she spoke in a pleasant tone. "Welcome to my home. I am Madora, keeper of the Sadiki."

21

Harvey and Sheef entered into an opulently decorated room. Rich tapestries, accented by exquisite rugs atop polished granite floors, hung on every wall. Plush couches and chairs were arranged in the front left corner.

In the middle of the room was a fairly large kitchen. Its walls and counters were composed of fired red clay. An enormous open-fire oven dominated the center.

In the back were two sleeping rooms, partitioned off from one another by richly embroidered yellow and green curtains. In the front right corner was a work area. Ponderous shelves constructed of acacia wood were affixed to the walls. A massive desk of the same wood, adorned with the intricate carvings of Sadikis, was covered with scrolls and thick leather-bound books.

"What is this place?" asked Sheef, obviously astonished by the subterranean five-star accommodations.

"I told you. It's my home."

"I know that, but how? All the way out here in the middle of a desert wasteland? Did you build this?"

"It's been in my family for hundreds of years, so there's been plenty of time to make it comfortable. It was likely the private burial chamber of an ancient royal family."

Harvey looked around the room, a tinge of paranoia coloring his face.

"Oh, don't worry," continued Madora, "there's no evidence that the tomb was ever actually used. It appears that not long after its construction, a massive sandstorm swept over the land, burying the tomb and its entrance under multiple feet of sand. I'm certain that its existence was soon forgotten, and it would have remained so, too, if not for a powerful earthquake that struck this area about five hundred years ago.

"The quake uplifted the section of land upon which the tomb was built, and though there was substantial damage to the tunnel and rooms, the entrance was exposed to human eyes and discovery.

"My ancestors, also 'keepers', were tent-dwelling nomads at the time. They were the ones to first discover it and claim it as their home. It turned out to be the perfect location for people who wish to attract little outside attention."

"Has anyone ever tried to take it away?" asked Sheef.

"There have been attempts," Madora said as she pulled out a razor-sharp dagger and proceeded to trim one of her nails, "but only that. Though there was a gentleman by the name of Carter who stumbled upon it in the early 1900's. He wanted to publish a series of articles regarding its discovery and history, believing that it would establish his name in the annals of archeology.

"In order to keep him quiet about it, I offered him a deal that only a fool would refuse. If he agreed to forget about the tomb and my home's existence, I would give him the details and burial location of a certain boy pharaoh."

"No way," said Harvey. "You're the one responsible for his most famous discovery? The Howard Carter?"

"I am. And obviously he took the deal. Subsequently, my home has remained hidden from the outside world to this day."

"Wait a minute," said Sheef. "You said that you offered him a deal. If what you said is true, that would make you well over one hundred years old, and if you don't mind my saying so, you don't look a day over thirty."

"Well, we 'keepers' have always kept well," she said with a coy smile, and in such a way that indicated that the topic was over and closed to further discussion.

Changing the subject, she gave an appraising look at both Harvey and Sheef and said, "You two look and smell as though you're in dire need of a bath. The room next to my quarters is the bathing room. An artesian spring waters the pool. It's very refreshing, though I must warn you that the invigorating water temperature takes a little getting used to.

"There are towels and robes hanging on wall hooks. We'll do something about your clothing later, but for now, use the robes and return here after your bath. You can rest in the beds in the back of the room. I'm sure you're exhausted after sleeping on a pyramid. Afterwards, I'll prepare us a quick meal, and then you'll have all the time required to tell me the details of your adventures."

Harvey and Sheef didn't have to be asked twice. They were both crusted with a gritty layer of sand and sweat. A bath was exactly what they needed.

The pool filled practically the entire room. Madora told them later on that a fissure was created directly under the room during the earthquake, forming an open cavity between the granite floor of the room and a deep, spring-fed subterranean river. The water filled the entire cavity, and over the subsequent years, eroded away the floor of the room to the point that it eventually caved in, forming the pool.

The walls and ceiling of the room were covered with a stark white limestone, significantly increasing the brightness of the room. This in turn had the effect of coloring the water a lighter and more vibrant shade of blue.

"It looks like a tropical lagoon," remarked Harvey.

"Yeah, but I promise you, it'll feel more like the Artic. You know, the worst way's the slow way," shouted Sheef while shedding his shirt, pants, and shoes, and then cannon-balling in.

Fromp, who had trotted into the room with Akeila, splashed in a second later. As soon as Sheef surfaced, he was rapidly treading water in order to generate body heat. Fromp dog-paddled around him like a circling shark, periodically snapping at the water.

Harvey was quick to follow, but Akeila remained dry-pawed on the edge of the pool, sitting down with a dignified air about her as if she was above the uncouth antics of the boisterous warp-hound.

They spent an hour in the pool. Even so, they never even flirted with becoming acclimated to the water's temperature. They exited the pool and dried themselves. After donning the robes, they returned to Madora's living quarters and were soon sound asleep in the curtained areas at the back of the room. They awoke hours later to the enticing odors of dinner cooking. A meal of roasted chicken, wild grains, and pomegranate seeds awaited them on a low table made from a slab of the same dark granite as that of the floor.

Madora said nothing while everyone ate, but immediately after Harvey placed his napkin on his plate, signaling that he had eaten his fill, Madora broke the silence.

"Let me first apologize for my initial curtness. I hope that you understand that when something appears in this part of the world via an unconventional means of conveyance, such as warping, it usually bodes evil intent. This area of the world is heavily saturated with supernatural power, and through the millennia, many unsavory characters have sought to exploit it."

Harvey and Sheef communicated their tacit understanding and acceptance of her apology with slight nods.

"Now please tell me . . ." Madora suddenly stopped speaking. "I need to apologize yet again for my rudeness. I'm embarrassed to admit that I don't even know your names."

"I'm Sheef. The young teenager is Harvey, and our faithful, though at times overly exuberant, warp-hound is Fromp."

"Well, it's a pleasure to meet all of you. And now, Harvey, if you would, please share with me all that you've been through since the moment you first encountered the warp-hound."

Harvey spent the next two hours retelling in vivid detail all that had occurred, finally bringing the story to the present.

"And that's why we warped to the pyramids," was how Harvey finished his lengthy narrative.

"Chosen by the Unseen, passed through the green veil, and defeated Nezraut, and all of this at just thirteen years of age. It appears, young Harvey, that there is much more behind, above, and within you than anyone would ever imagine."

"There have been," she continued, "signs amongst the celestial bodies. By them I knew that heightened activity was occurring in the other realms. The heavenly bodies are very trustworthy. The problem, however, is that they lack specificity. But now, by the will and power of the Unseen, He has ushered you here with details that the stars and planets were unable to provide."

Madora paused to pour herself a cup of strong Arabica coffee. After savoring the first sip, commenting on the exquisite roast, and offering Sheef and Harvey a cup, she continued to speak.

"My friends, only a select few have ever fallen into and become entangled in Nezraut's webs of deceit, and then escaped with their minds and wills still intact."

"I guess this means that you've had more than one run in with the Vapid Lord," interjected Sheef.

"More than I care to remember, and I have the scars as mementos of our paths crossing. Not physical, though. Nezraut has always sought to subdue and enslave humanity, but rarely does he resort to actual physical force. He understands, like every great despot or tyrant throughout history, that physical violence is an ineffective means by which to control a populace.

"Propaganda, deceit, a coloring of the truth, a slight twisting of the facts, a tug on the heart strings, an empty promise to give the people what they want instead of what they need, and a dividing of the masses, convincing them that the other group is the enemy. Such are the deceptive, manipulative stratagems of all successful dictators, most especially Nezraut. And it is all achieved through the mind."

"And he's been active in this part of the world, too?" asked Harvey.

"Markedly so. He, his Vapid Lords, and those infernal Insips were thick as gnats in this region when it was the epicenter of the ancient civilized world. Many of the most powerful pharaohs, for example, didn't rule autonomously."

"Nezraut was controlling them?" asked Sheef surprised.

"He was, but they were ignorant of his influence and existence. He led the pharaohs to believe that they were endued with supernatural powers from a minor deity who did their bidding. Never once did they suspect that there was a power behind the throne pulling the wires with the skill of a master puppeteer. Yet such is the folly of an over-inflated self. Nothing quite blinds one's sight like pride."

"That's crazy," remarked Harvey. "Nezraut, the one I fought, controlling ancient Egypt."

"Trust me, Harvey, his reach wasn't only confined to Egypt. Wherever and whenever people have been oppressed and exploited by a single leader in whom all power is vested, there is good reason to suspect that Nezraut's skeletal fingers were in the shadows and working the wires. And now it seems that he's found a way to expand his manipulative oppression to every other world in every other dimension."

"That's why we have to go back in time," said Harvey, panic beginning to edge itself into his voice. "It's the only way to stop him and save everybody."

"And you both believe this is the only way? You're certain that there's no way to save Ecclon at this point?"

"The light of Ecclon's clouds were all but extinguished when we last warped from the planet."

"I'm amazed," said Madora, "but shouldn't be surprised by Nezraut's success in turning away so much human thought from the Unseen. And it is human thought, oriented to the Unseen, which illuminates the clouds of Ecclon and sustains all of the planet's life?"

"It is," answered Sheef. "And going back is the only way to undo what is occurring."

"Because by going back in time, you believe you will be able to destroy the root cause of so many turning their thoughts away from the Unseen: the Narciss Glass. And the only way back is through the Phantasian."

"I think my father was trying to do the same thing," said Harvey.

"He was."

"My father came here?"

"He did," said Madora, who stood up and retrieved a second carafe of hot coffee from the kitchen counter and refilled everyone's cups. After she sat down, she resumed. "He came here ten years ago seeking my help in traveling back to the 1930's. I still have no idea how he learned about me or the Phantasian. He had extensive knowledge about the realm. Not only that, he also knew that there was only one way to access it."

"The Sadiki," said Sheef.

"Obviously, that's why he sought my help."

"And did you?" asked Harvey. "Help him, I mean?"

"Only after a considerable amount of persuasion on his part. I finally relented and agreed to lend him Kafele, Akeila's sister. And that was the last I saw of either of them."

"Sheef, then it's true. My dad did go back, which means we definitely have to." A mixture of worry, hope, excitement, and dread shaped the tone of Harvey's words.

"It's good news, Harvey, but let's try to remain calm and keep our wits about us. We can't afford to get ahead of ourselves. The last thing we want to do is rush into things and make a careless mistake along the way."

"I suppose," continued Sheef, "this means that we need to make the same request that Harvey's father did."

"Absolutely not!" said Madora emphatically. "I can't risk losing another Sadiki. There are only seven, including Akeila, left."

"I don't mean to be rude," remarked Sheef, "but it seems to me that if we don't go back and change things, and stop Nezraut from enslaving every world in existence, it won't matter one way or the other how many Sadikis are left."

"I agree with you, Sheef. You're absolutely right. But since I refuse to lend you one of my dogs, that leaves us with only one option. It looks like I'll be going with you."

"You'll be doing what?"

"You heard me. I'm going with you. The only way you get to use a Sadiki is if I accompany you. I'm your ticket to the past. You can take it or leave it."

"Well, kid," said Sheef trying to look annoyed but inwardly pleased, "looks like she's got us right where she wants us. So, Madora, when do we warp?"

"One step at a time. It's not that easy. You go off and warp without first carefully planning, and you'll end up stuck in a fictional world. The Phantasian is not only a place of human dreams; it's also one of human nightmares. It's a dangerous realm, and if you don't know what you're doing, you'll get yourself and everyone around you killed. So let's get one thing straight before we go any further. You'll both do precisely what I tell you to do. Do we understand each other? Am I being clear?"

"Crystal," said Sheef with a grin that Harvey perceived as being lightly salted with flirtation.

"Wipe that stupid grin off your face," snapped Madora. "We've no time for any such nonsense."

Sheef flushed red all the way down to his earlobes. "Yes, Ma'am," he said as he stood up and cleared his plate and glass from the table. "You're the boss."

"That's right, and please, whatever you do, until we make it through the Phantasian, don't forget it."

Harvey, who was still seated, looked down at his shoes, doing his best to hide his smile and suppress the urge to burst out laughing.

22

Harvey's mother, Thurngood, Gnarl, the wounded Jules, and Joust warped to Egypt an hour or so after Fromp dropped Harvey and Sheef atop the pyramid.

Joust, unable to track Fromp's warp trail to its exact destination, had warped the group to an area just in front of a smaller, adjacent pyramid. Unfortunately, the group was unaware of how close Harvey and Sheef were at the time.

Harvey did observe a flash of light from the direction of the smaller pyramid, but the notion of it being caused by a warp hole opening never crossed his mind. He dismissed it as lightning from a distant storm and didn't give it a second thought.

When Joust had recuperated enough to open another warp hole, Gnarl returned to Ecclon as planned. Thurngood, meanwhile, searched the perimeter of the smaller pyramid, closely scrutinizing the ground with a flashlight for any sign of Harvey and Sheef.

When he found no evidence of their arrival, he returned to where Harvey's mother was propped up against the base of the pyramid and decided to wait until daybreak when he would expand the search area.

Thurngood spent the entire morning combing the desert sands. Disappointingly, he found no clues indicating that two humans and a warp-hound had been in the area. He did, however, witness something rather bizarre.

About two hours after sunup, a rider on a motorcycle suddenly appeared, seemingly out of nowhere, and rode along the side of a larger pyramid nearby. Whoever it was, quickly disappeared behind the back of the enormous structure, completely out of Thurngood's line of sight.

Not long after, though, he saw a small dust cloud rising from the desert floor, possibly the sandy wake of the motorcycle and its rider receding into the distant wilderness.

"I didn't find any sign of them," Thurngood informed Harvey's mother after his morning search.

"Is it possible that Joust warped us to the wrong location?"

"It's possible but not likely. Warp-hounds are highly skilled at tracking a warp trail, and Fromp's was still very fresh, no more than an hour old. No, they're somewhere around here ... or were."

"Thurngood," said Harvey's mother fretfully. "We have to find them. I have to warn Harvey that he's being followed and that Nezraut now knows of the Narciss Glass."

"We'll find them, Dwen. You have my word," said Thurngood. He then finished his thought, speaking under his breath as he turned away. "I just hope it's not too late when we do."

***

"Based on what you told me, Harvey," said Madora, "it appears that you understand the basic workings of the Phantasian."

"It's made up of fictitious worlds formed by the creative imaginations of humans."

"That's correct, and there are millions of these worlds. Every famous oral tale, novel, and movie exists as an actual three dimensional world in which you can interact, converse, and even be harmed by its characters."

"Madora, we were told that the Phantasian was used by ancient civilizations," said Sheef.

"It was. Have you ever noticed the frequency of dog's depicted in the artwork of some of these ancient cultures? Take the Egyptians, for example. Anubis, the jackal-headed god, was believed by the Egyptians to be a guide and protector for the spirits of the dead. However, if you look carefully at the depiction of the jackal head in the ancient paintings and etchings, you should notice a striking similarity with another type of dog."

Madora led Harvey and Sheef over to the living room area and pointed to a framed print of Anubis hanging on the wall.

"It's a Sadiki head. Isn't it?" asked Harvey.

"Very close resemblance," replied Madora. "The mythological Anubis was inspired by the very real Sadiki: a protector and guide, not for the underworld, but the Phantasian."

"And remember," she continued, "time is irrelevant in the Phantasian. The first oral tale to the last filmed movie, and everything in between, all exist there simultaneously."

"And that's what aided the ancient world in making so many significant leaps in such a short duration of time," commented Sheef.

"Exactly," said Madora complimentary. "Engineering, technology, architecture, science, the list goes on and on, and the mystery of how these cultures accomplished so much, which to modern study seems impossible due to their rudimentary knowledge of science and technology, is suddenly solved. What was learned from the Phantasian, though, didn't end with science and technology. Ideas such as democracy and the structure of the Polis or city-state, did not originate with the Greeks. They borrowed it."

"Speaking of the Greeks," asked Harvey, "does this mean that their myths . . . ?"

"Are in the Phantasian," answered Madora. "The heroes, villains, monsters, and gods of Homer's *Iliad* and *Odyssey* move and have their being there. Mt. Olympus, Achilles, Medussa, Zeus, have height, width, and depth."

"And the Romans?" asked Sheef.

"Learned much of their road building and military strategy from visits to the realm."

"Are you serious?" asked Harvey.

"One hundred percent. But it was the Egyptians who frequented the Phantasian most often, which explains why they cherished and worshipped the Sadiki so much that it eventually inspired the creation of one of their gods: Anubis."

"But what about Nezraut?" asked Sheef. "If he was as involved in Egyptian rule as you said he was, he must have been aware of the Phantasian."

"Trust me, Sheef, he was. He coveted the realm, desiring to exploit it. He knew that if he had access to the Phantasian, he could easily control every culture on Earth. This is precisely why he hunted down the Sadiki. He killed hundreds of the dogs, from the tip of Africa to the farthest reaches of northern Siberia. His strategy was to allow only a handful to remain alive, which he alone would possess, allowing only him access to the realm."

"He obviously didn't succeed," commented Sheef.

"He nearly did. Using his Vapid Lords and Insips, he searched far and wide. It was during this time of the Sadiki decimation that the Guild of Keepers was formed. He wiped out over ninety percent of these intelligent and gentle creatures. We hid those we were able to rescue before he found them. Luckily, Nezraut was never able to breed any of the animals. Males are much rarer than females, and they'll not breed with one another in a threatening environment. Fortunately for us, Nezraut never figured this out. Thus, when those he had enslaved eventually died, he wrongly assumed that the breed had gone extinct."

"So he has no idea that there are Sadiki still alive?" asked Sheef.

"No, but if he were to track you here, it wouldn't be very difficult for him to uncover the truth. I assume you covered your tracks well?"

Harvey and Sheef exchanged looks: Sheef's questioning, Harvey's guilty.

"I believe so," responded Sheef.

"Good, because we certainly have enough to worry about as it is."

A rumble shook the ceramic coffee cups on the table. Lines of fear raced across Harvey's face like wind upon the water.

"That sound is nothing to fear," said Madora. "It's only my brother Yuya returning. He's a Sadiki trainer, and basically my right hand in all things. I couldn't possibly manage the dogs without him. He can be pleasant once you get to know him, but whatever you do, don't react to his name. He's very sensitive about it. It's a powerful Egyptian name from a bygone era, but to modern and foreign ears, it doesn't really have the same ring."

"Don't worry about me saying anything. When you're known by the name 'Sheef', the last thing you're going to do is poke fun at someone else's name."

"Where's he returning from?" asked Harvey.

"Each Sadiki needs continual outings to maintain its skill, as well as frequent exercise. Yuya and I accomplish both by warping with each of the seven Sadiki separately to the Phantasian, and we do this every week. And though we alternate days, it's still exhausting work. There's just no possible way I could to it all by myself. Going every single day with no break would kill me. These excursions enable us to keep an eye on the realm, specifically to ensure that no one has made an unauthorized visit."

"But I thought you were the only ones with any Sadiki?" asked Harvey.

"It's not a certainty."

Just then, a tall, deeply bronzed, sinewy man, with short cropped black hair and a neatly trimmed beard, filled the doorway. He was wearing chocolate brown cotton twill pants and shirt. He held a sweat-stained, wide-brimmed hat in his left hand.

Yuya seemed more irritated than startled when he realized that his sister wasn't alone. "Pardon me, Madora, I didn't realize you were entertaining guests this evening. Apparently, you failed to mention it to me last night," he said sarcastically.

"I didn't mention anything, brother," Madora said shortly, "because I had no idea that they were coming until this morning.

Their arrival was quite unexpected, to say the least. And don't just stand there like a piece of furniture. Come in and join us for a cup of coffee."

"I must be about the tending of the dogs."

"The dogs can wait. I need you sit down and listen to what I have to say."

With a sigh and a look of defeated resignation, Yuya walked over to the kitchen table and took a seat next to his sister.

"Do you recall," began Madora, "the gentleman who paid us a visit a little over a decade ago."

"How could I forget. We lent him Kafele, my best trained Sadiki at the time, and that was the last I ever saw of her."

"Well, this is Harvey, the man's son and his friend Sheef. They've requested my help in following the same path that Harvey's father took."

"I'm not in the habit of being rude in front of people I've just met," said Yuya as he shoved his chair back and abruptly stood up, "but I hope my sister has already informed you that there is no possible way that we would even think of letting another Sadiki out of our possession!"

"Yuya," said Madora, placing a hand on his chest, "Nezraut is involved! The gateway planet of Ecclon has fallen into his clutches, and it's just a matter of time before he invades other worlds! The only ones who have a chance of reversing these dark events are Harvey and Sheef, but they can't do it without our help."

"But, Madora, you know as well as I do that we can ill afford to give up another Sadiki."

"I agree, and that's why Akeila and I will be going with them."

"You'll be doing what?" asked Yuya angrily.

Yuya, we have no choice in the matter. You must see the logic in my decision."

Yuya slowly sat back down and looked up at the ceiling. "I do," he said in a much calmer voice, "but I don't like it. Maybe I should accompany you."

"No, you need to stay here and protect the other dogs. If Nezruat finds out that they're not extinct, you know what he'll do. And lose that worried look of yours. I'm a big girl and can take care of myself. Besides, I'll have a thirteen-year-old warrior at my side."

Harvey flushed red with embarrassment. He was attempting to formulate a response which would lessen the redness in his cheeks, when a pain-soaked yelp echoed through the tunnel.

"Nubia!" Yuya shouted. "It sounds like she's topside!"

Yuya bolted from the room with Madora and Akeila clipping his heels. Fromp immediately followed. Harvey and Sheef quickly changed out of their robes and put back on their dirty, sweat-stained clothing before joining the others.

They ran up the tunnel, through the A-frame opening, and into the desert night air where Madora and Yuya were standing. The night sky was glowing brightly from the multitudes of stars, enabling everyone to see far into the desert.

Close to the entrance, two sets of paw prints were observed. The smaller prints, created by smaller paws, emerged from the tunnel and suddenly stopped. The sand indentions of the prints were shallow, created by a light-footed footfall: cautious and suspicious. The prints were obviously Nubia's, who likely halted her tentative emergence in order to scent a foreign odor on the breeze.

The second set of prints was deeper, the backs flayed out as if the heels had suddenly exploded. They intersected with Nubia's at a right angle. Yuya bent down and closely examined the prints.

Without looking up at the others, he said, "The pattern suggests a surprise attack. Whatever hit her was large and moving fast. Poor girl, likely had no idea of her attacker's presence until the moment her flank was struck. But it makes no sense. There's no predator around here with paws that size, at least none that I'm aware of."

"I might have an idea of what did it," said Harvey hesitantly.

Yuya stood up and turned to face Harvey.

"What do you mean by that, young man?"

"Sheef, I didn't tell you. I'm sorry. I know I should've, but I was hoping that it was nothing more than my imagination."

"What are you taking about?" asked Sheef.

"Last night on the top of the pyramid, right before I nodded off to sleep, I thought I saw a set of eyes in the desert."

"Eyes?"

"Glowing green eyes."

"A Volkin Wolf?"

"That's what I didn't want to believe. I should've said something. And, Sheef, there's only one wolf that could fill those paw prints. Sköll's been trailing us."

"And now he's captured a Sadiki," sighed Sheef, cradling his face in his hands.

"Excuse me," interrupted Madora, "but would someone please inform me who Sköll is, and why Sheef has his face in his hands?"

"Sköll," said Sheef looking up from his hands, "is the leader of the Volkin Wolves, Nezraut's twisted version of a warp-hound."

Harvey and Sheef braced themselves for an enraged burst of anger from Madora. Instead, she walked a few steps away from the group, stopping to stare pensively in the direction of the pyramids.

Everyone looked at her in silence. Finally she spoke. "What we have endeavored for so long to conceal has now been exposed. As if the Phantasian didn't have enough perils and pitfalls already, we will now have the enemy to contend with."

"But the enemy may not pursue us there. He still doesn't know what we're after," offered Harvey

"It doesn't' matter, Harvey," said Madora gently. "If he tracked you here, he can track you anywhere. And let's not be naïve. Nezraut's quite clever. He's been around long enough to figure out, with only a few clues at his disposal, what we're up to. Rather than hoping that he or one of his lackeys won't pursue us into the Phantasian, it would be wise to anticipate our eventual crossing of paths."

Another yelp of pain shattered the night air. The source was the same as before, but this time distance had muffled the sound. As the group turned towards the direction of the Sadiki cry, they glimpsed the silhouette of an enormous wolf, dragging a smaller dog by the scruff of its neck. Seconds later there was a flash of green light, and both the wolf and his prey were gone.

23

Nezraut sat brooding over his young enemy's elusiveness. Three times the boy had slipped through his talons. Three times he had been humiliated. The powerful Vapid Lord fumed in the dimly lit cavern where Harvey had defeated him and destroyed voluminous copies of the book which had turned so many humans from the thoughts of the Unseen

The dim lighting of the cavern emanated from a weakly glowing fire sphere that Nezraut was slowly manipulating with his bony, elongated fingers. Sharpened shards from the roughly hewn wooden throne upon which he sat pierced his body whenever he adjusted his position. He enjoyed the pain. It helped him focus in plotting his next move.

The rock ceiling above was thickly covered with thousands of Insips, hanging inverted like a colony of bats. They were impatiently awaiting their next assignment from their master, passing the time by jostling and biting one another, as well as mumbling curses and spewing vitriol into the atmosphere.

A blinding green flash interrupted Nezraut's brooding. When the light faded and dimness once again clung to the walls and ceiling, Sköll stood growling before Nezraut's throne. A limp animal hung from his mouth.

A pale, semi-transparent Insip detached from the ceiling and flapped to a hover at Nezraut's side.

"Your majesty," the flying sycophant said with a deferential hiss, "the intrepid Sköll has returned with a prize. Might we Insips toy with it after you are through with whatever brilliant designs you have in store for the creature? A few lines of deception, a manipulative warping of truth upon its malleable mind would satiate our hunger. It has been days since we have implanted our lies and feasted upon an unsuspecting mind. Oh please, Sire, allow us to scratch the itch."

Nezraut, without turning his head in the direction of the Insip, replied, "I do not recall granting you permission to fly about my personal space, and most especially, to pollute the air with your infernal babbling."

The fire sphere in Nezraut's hands suddenly glowed white hot, and in the same instant, the Vapid Lord flung it into the body of the unsuspecting Insip. The creature's torso, arms, and legs were instantly vaporized. The sphere then returned to Nezruat, resting in the palm of his right hand, while his left reached out in order to catch the falling Insip head.

Nezraut tossed it to Sköll. "A new ball for your amusement, my pet. Now come closer and show your master what you have brought home."

Sköll lowered his head in submission as he approached his master's throne and laid the unconscious Sadiki at his feet.

Nezraut peered down at the animal, tilting his head from side to side while scenting the air with his two opened mouths. Double grins appeared like bent parallel lines. Reflected flames from the sphere's fire danced in each of his eyes.

"Well now, Sköll, this is quite a prize you have retrieved for me today. So the Sadiki are not extinct after all. Do you know what this means, my pet?" asked Nezraut excitedly as he stepped off his throne. He tossed the flaming sphere upward, where it burst like exploding napalm into a cluster of Insips. The charred ashes from their bodies slowly sifted downward.

"It means that not only Ecclon and the other worlds are mine, but also the dreams and fictions of men!"

His insidious laughter violently shook the entire cavern, dislodging hundreds of Insips from the ceiling, most of which were so tangled up that they had no time to unfurl their wings and flap before hitting the ground. A cacophony of pitiful moaning, vehement cursing, and excited squealing echoed loudly off the caverns walls.

"Silence!" Nezraut shouted. "Yes, there is good reason for your excitement, but I need you to listen carefully for your next assignment.

"Slink, before me, now!"

A large dark green Insip, with long fangs that protruded upward from its lower lip, was soon hovering with bowed head in front of Nezraut.

"Take a legion of your best deceivers and go to where Sköll apprehended the Sadiki. Find the boy and work his mind to our advantage. I feel that his defenses are currently not as formidable as they once were."

"As you wish, my master," hissed Slink as he led a shrieking horde of Insips through the cavern's entrance.

"Grauncrock, your presence!" commanded Nezruat.

A Vapid Lord, whose face and body were hidden by a dark gray cloak, materialized within feet of Nezraut.

"Nurse the Sadiki back to health, and then prepare to warp to the Phantasian. If Slink and his legion fail to turn young Harvey, be prepared to follow the group into the realm. Either way, we shall be victorious."

"Yes, my master," replied Grauncrock with an exaggerated bow. "The boy will not escape our clutches again." He picked up the still unconscious Sadiki and was soon gone.

24

ack in the Egyptian desert, Akeila was lying in the spot where Nubia had been attacked, pawing at the sand and making pitiful whining sounds.

"Yuya, how much longer do you think she'll be out here grieving for her sister?" asked Madora.

"I doubt that she will let us take her below. She feels compelled to do something to help Nubia. If she were to go in right now, it would be like giving up, but since she doesn't know what to do, she remains rooted to the same spot and whines. It's been nearly two hours since Nubia was taken, and Akeila hasn't budged."

"Neither has Fromp," said Sheef.

Fromp was lying down next to Akeila with his paws crossed over one another. He was doing his best to express his concern for Akeila without being annoyingly present. He attempted to maintain this balance by licking her head periodically, and then pulling back to allow her room to grieve.

"I hope for all our sakes that she's ready to warp by morning," said Madora. "Now that Nezraut knows where you are, Harvey, you can rest assured that it won't be long until he or one of his henchmen pays us a visit. And if Nubia's still alive, our old nemesis will have a ticket into the Phantasian."

"Can't we just take one of the other Sadiki and go now?" asked Sheef.

"We could, but none of the others are as well trained as Akeila. She's the best and doesn't make mistakes," replied Madora.

"Perhaps," offered Harvey, "we should reconsider using the Phantasian at all."

"What do you mean?" asked Sheef, somewhat surprised. "You know it's our only chance to save Ecclon and stop Nezraut."

"You're right, you're right. Sorry, Sheef. I don't know why I said that. It's the only way. Just feeling a bit dizzy and confused. I guess I'm worn out from all the stress. Would you remind me of the plan once again?"

"Remind you of the plan? Harvey, are you kidding me? You helped come up with it." Sheef passed his hand through his hair and then dropped it to his side in surrender.

"Okay, but I still can't believe you need reminding," Sheef said after a pronounced sigh. "We're accessing the Phantasian to go back in time in order to locate and destroy the Narciss Glass that Millud stole from Ecclon and took to Earth. Remember, he placed it in a movie? And those who watch it become consumed with themselves and begin turning away from the Unse . . ."

Sheef suddenly stopped speaking, his flesh tones momentarily muted. He surreptitiously reached into his pants' pocket and retrieved the small bottle of Kreen nectar.

"Sheef, what's wrong?" asked Harvey. "Why did you stop in the middle of your explanation?"

"Sorry, kid, something seems to have blown in my eye. Sand I think. Hold on a minute while I try to flush it out."

Sheef turned away from Harvey and unscrewed the eyedropper top of the bottle. He tilted his head back and deftly placed a drop of Kreen nectar in each eye. The familiar sting caused him to squint, but once the annoyance had passed, he turned back around and looked directly at Harvey, and saw what he was hoping he wouldn't: dozens of Insips were swarming like a hive of bees around Harvey's head.

Because he hadn't placed any drops in his ears, Sheef wasn't able to hear what the Insips were saying, but he could clearly observe their tiny fanged mouths rapidly moving as they infected Harvey's mind with their deceptive venom.

"Harvey," said Sheef as calmly as possible given the situation. "I need you to focus on what I'm about to tell you."

"Sheef," said Harvey, a faraway glaze dulling his eyes, "why are you looking at me that way? There's nothing wrong. I simply want to be reminded of the particular elements of our strategy and its anticipated efficacy."

"'Elements of strategy?' 'Anticipated efficacy?' I don't think so. Listen to those words coming out of your mouth, Harvey. You don't speak like that."

"Whatever do you mean, Sheef?"

"Harvey, listen to me! You're being controlled and deceived. Right now, a turban of Insips is writhing about on top of your head, so listen to me carefully. I know the real you is in there and can hear me. I need you to fight back. Remember your training at the cabin. Just begin declaring truth and the Insips will loosen their grip."

"Sheef," said Harvey laughing, "apparently you're even more exhausted than I am. You're imagining things. There's nothing atop my head. See," said Harvey as he passed his hands over his head, "nothing but air."

Sheef nodded and smiled. He didn't, however, respond to Harvey's last statement. Instead, he walked over to where Yuya and his sister were standing. Both were wearing dumbfounded expressions. Sheef leaned in and whispered something in Yuya's ear, and though his expression didn't change, Yuya nodded in response.

Sheef walked back towards Harvey, stopping a couple of feet from the writhing mass of Insips and said, "Listen, kid, you're right. I must be hallucinating. Crazy, isn't it? Thinking that there was anything really – "

The distraction worked. Harvey gave his full attention to Sheef's words, rendering him blind to the movements of Yuya who grabbed him from behind. He wrapped both of his muscular arms around Harvey's arms and chest while pulling him backwards. Yuya hit the sand hard but still held tightly to Harvey.

Sheef was immediately atop Harvey, the end of the dropper poised and ready above his right eye. Sheef pried open Harvey's eyelids and squeezed the dropper, then repeated the action in his other eye.

During the sequence of events, Harvey was screaming hysterically. When Sheef finished, Yuya released Harvey, who stood up, furiously rubbing his eyes and yelling.

"Sheef, what do you think you're doing? You could've killed me!"

Harvey froze. Images of leathery, membranous wings, sharp talons, and snarling, hissing mouths were weaving in and out of his field of vision. An Insip's tail found its way into Harvey's mouth, its tip dipping down into his esophagus. The sight jolted him out of his Insip-induced stupor.

"SHEEF, I'M COVERED WITH INSIPS!" Harvey shouted as he wildly swung his arms and hands over his head. "HELP ME GET THEM OFF!"

"Calm down. Like I said before, remember your training. Just begin declaring truth. Why don't you start by declaring things about the Unseen."

"Okay," panted Harvey, trying to ignore the tail which was still slithering in his mouth. In the loudest and most authoritative voice he could muster, he declared, "THE UNSEEN IS TRUTH! BY HIM ALL THINGS WERE FORMED! I HAVE BEEN CHOSEN BY HIM, AND BY HIS POWERFUL PRESENCE, I ORDER YOU TO FLEE!"

The Insips shrieked and lifted off of Harvey's head. The tail retracted from his mouth. The freedom, though, was short-lived. Within seconds, the entire horde of Insips returned and landed once again on Harvey's head.

"WHAT'S HAPPENING HERE, SHEEF? WHY DID THEY COME RIGHT BACK?"

"Try to settle down, Harvey. I don't know what's going on. Why don't you declare something else and maybe shout louder this time."

"SHOUT LOUDER! I'M SHOUTING AS LOUD AS I CAN!

"Just do it!"

"All right. Here it goes. I AM PROTECTED BY THE GOODNESS OF THE UNSEEN. HIS POWER KNOWS NO EQUAL, AND BY IT, I COMMAND YOU TO LEAVE THIS VERY MOMENT.

As before, the Insips briefly took flight before quickly returning.

"This shouldn't be happening," a panicked Sheef mumbled to himself.

"SHEEF, HELP ME! I CAN'T BREATHE"

"Okay, just hang on a minute and let me try."

Sheef approached within inches of the swarming mass and loudly declared the exact same words that Harvey had just uttered. Immediately, the Insips screeched in pain, scattering away from Harvey in all directions.

Harvey fell to his knees, while Madora, who was still wearing a perplexed expression, practically shouting herself, asked, "Sheef, would you mind explaining to me what just happened?"

"He was attacked by a swarm of Insips. There must have been close to a hundred."

"You can't be serious, Sheef," Madora replied. "Trust me, I've had more experience with Insips then I care to recall. Definitely enough to recognize them when they appear, and I clearly saw nothing."

"What?" asked Sheef. "If you've had any experience with Insips, then you know that they can't be seen with the natural eye. Kreen nectar must be used to see them."

"Hey you two," moaned Harvey, "don't worry about me. I'm fine. I'll just lie here and recover while you argue about whether something was really poisoning my brain."

"Sorry, kid. Are you okay?"

"Better than I was, but I think I would be a whole lot better if I had a swig of Kreen."

"Coming right up," said Sheef as he tossed the bottle to Harvey.

Harvey sat up and caught the bottle. He took a respectable swig before lying back down on the sand.

"Sheef," said Madora, returning to their conversation, "when this area was Nezrauts' playground, Insips could be seen. They were out in the open. No nectar was needed to see what they were up to."

"And how long ago was this?"

"Centuries. The time period of the Great Pharaohs."

"And you were there? If you don't mind me asking, exactly how old are you?"

"Inappropriate and untimely question, Sheef. Now, why don't you explain to me why I can't see the Insips without putting that alien fruit juice in my eyes?"

"I'm not really sure. My best guess is that they determined at some point that concealing themselves from human sight – hiding behind a dimensional curtain, if you will – was more effective in deceiving humans than appearing out in the open. I assume that the people back then believed in a spiritual world, and that creatures such as Insips, could actually exist."

"Of course. The cultures of the ancient world were saturated by the spiritual realm," said Madora. It was as real to those people as the trees and oceans are to people today."

"Well then, that probably explains it. When people embraced a spiritual reality, the Insips took advantage of it and directly appeared to them. By offering their services or by frightening the people, the Insips were able to manipulate and deceive. It was an out-in-the-open frontal attack."

"However," Sheef continued, "when humans began to doubt the existence of a spiritual world, and increasingly put more and more of their trust in only what could be perceived by their senses, the Insips, and I'm sure the Vapid, too, must have reasoned that the best place to deceive humans was from a place that humans believed didn't exist. The most thoroughly deceived people tend to be those who have no idea that there is something trying to deceive them. So when the Insips began hiding in the shadows, they could deceive all day long, without people ever having the slightest clue as to what was really occurring."

"So, you're telling me," said Madora, "if I were to place that nectar in my eyes, I could see them right here and now?'

"Well actually, no. They're gone after the words I said."

"Speaking of that," said Harvey, who had stood up weakly and slowly walked over to where Sheef and Madora were speaking, "do you have any idea why it didn't work for me?"

"I've no earthly idea what happened there. I mean the last time you tangled with Insips, they didn't stand a chance against your words. To be honest, I'm baffled. I really don't know what to say, but I suspect that you might."

"What are you talking about, Sheef?"

"Harvey, something led Sköll and the Insips to our doorstep and also weakened the power of your words. And I think it's about time you let me know what that is."

25

Madora was walking to the entrance of her underground quarters when she said, "I'm going to leave you two here to talk, while I go below and conduct a little research on this Millud of yours. Hopefully, we'll be able to use one of the movies he acted in order to access the past."

Surprisingly, Akeila followed her, but not before pawing at the sand a few more times. Fromp dutifully did his job as her escort below. With Yuya's primary concern no longer exposed to the elements, and feeling out of sorts around people he didn't know, he went down as well.

The desert temperature had already fallen by fifty degrees from its afternoon high. Harvey shoved his hands into his front pockets. A shiver quivered through his body in an attempt to ward of the evening chill. Sheef, meanwhile, vigorously rubbed his exposed forearms and then exhaled into cupped hands.

"Whenever you're ready, kid. The time's come for you to lay whatever it is out in the open."

"That's the problem, Sheef. I'm not really sure what 'it' is."

"Harvey, it's been my experience that we often know the root of our problem, but we don't want to admit it, talk about it, and most importantly, deal with it. Either we fear how others will react, or we have this distorted notion that if we reveal what's been locked up inside, it will somehow become more 'real', having even greater power over our lives."

Tears began to gather in Harvey's eyes.

"I hope you see that both of these reasons for holding back are nothing but lies we spin ourselves, lies which Insips have a field day with. You know, things that are kept in the dark can't be accurately perceived or judged. Their size and shape is often enlarged and made more frightening in the shadows of our hearts and minds. It's similar to what goes on in the imagination of a child in a darkened room at night. Speculation runs wild concerning what dwells beneath the bed, and as long as it remains dark in the room and the child doesn't look underneath, all manner of hideous, slimy creatures continue to lurk.

"But, Harvey, what happens when a parent comes in and checks on the child? The light is turned on and the imagined monsters beneath the bed disappear. Telling me what's going on inside that heart of yours is like opening the door and turning on the lights. And if we don't flip them on soon, those Insips will be back and in even greater numbers. Whatever is festering inside of you is giving off an enticing odor, and remember what I taught you, Insips are continually hungry, always on the prowl for a delectable morsel of negative thought."

"You really think I've been giving off some sort of odor trail for the enemy to follow?"

"You have something that makes more sense?"

"I guess not," said Harvey as he shifted uncomfortably. He looked down at the ground and began making circles in the sand with his shoe. After a few moments of awkward silence, he continued, "It's my mom and dad, Sheef. I mean my real dad, and I guess Thurngood, too."

"What about them?"

"I understand why everyone kept the truth from me. I really do. It makes complete sense, not telling me who I really am and where I'm from. But the thing is, Sheef, it was all one big lie. Thurngood's not even my real father. And my real, biological one, he basically abandoned me when I was still in diapers. Do you have any idea how many times I felt like I was a disappointment to the man I thought was my dad? I believed he didn't want to be around me and was grateful for a job that kept him on the road and away from home. And my mom . . . she could've told me the truth at any time."

"Come on, Harvey, would you have believed her?"

"I don't know. Probably not, but should that have made a difference? You just don't lie like that to your children."

"But they didn't have any other choice. Telling you the truth would've endangered everyone involved."

"I get that, Sheef, and I think that's why this is so difficult for me. I know that I need to forgive them. They were just doing what was best for me, but it doesn't change the fact that they lied. It hurts."

"You're absolutely right, and you have a legitimate right to feel hurt, but at some point, you're going to have to forgive them and let it go."

"I know. Believe me, I know. It's the right thing to do, but to be honest, I don't feel like letting go."

"I hear you, kid, but sometime really soon, you'll have to make a decision that transcends your feelings. In fact, I think this is one of those instances in which feelings will follow action, and if you want the honest truth, if you sit around and wait on your feelings to change . . . well, we don't have that time to waste.

"Harvey, we've all been hurt and offended. Welcome to life. Being hurt is common ground for every man and woman, but what's rare is being able to forgive and release the hurt."

"But what if I can't?"

"The hard truth is that if you can't, then you'll continue to expose yourself and everyone else to attack, not to mention how your ability to fight will diminish. In time, you'll lose the will to fight because you'll no longer be aware that a fight is even occurring."

"Sheef, that's crazy. I would never let that happen."

"That's exactly what I once thought, until I was so deceived that I found myself in the service of Nezraut. Arrogance was my Kryptonite; don't let unforgiveness be yours."

"But what if it's not in me? Seriously, I don't think I can forgive and let it go."

"Well-spoken truth. It's not and you can't. Not really, I mean. To really forgive and let go, you'll need something outside of yourself, something much larger than your hurt."

"The Unseen?"

"Just as we need Him to reveal what's actually occurring in and around us, so too, do we need Him to free us from our wounds. Forgiveness, you see, is not a human trait, but it is one of His."

Harvey quietly nodded.

"Tell you what. Why don't I leave you out here by yourself. Talk it over with the Unseen. I'll head below and help Madora. Come down when you're ready, but ..."

"But what?"

"Don't make it too long. The sand in the hour glass is quickly slipping away."

Sheef disappeared through the entrance, but returned a few minutes later with Harvey's Lignum shirt.

"Probably a good idea to keep this thing on from here on out," Sheef said as he tossed Harvey the shirt.

Harvey nodded. He slipped off the shirt he was wearing and put on the Lignum shirt. As before, the fabric fused with his skin, and it wasn't long before the night chill was warmed away from his body.

Harvey was quiet, standing statuesque under the glow of the starry host above. He was thinking over what to say to the Unseen when the desert scene before him suddenly changed. The image that replaced it was a large cage with thick iron bars, resting on jagged lava rock. The locked door on the opposite side faced a lush mountain valley, divided in half by a crystal clear stream. Inside the cage were Harvey's mother, Thurngood, and a man with an indistinguishable face. They were all staring at Harvey with questioning expressions, as if waiting for him to make a decision.

The lava rock around his feet cracked, releasing pools of molten lava, from which rivulets began to flow toward his shoes. He tried to move, but something was anchoring him to where he stood. The lava, closing in from all directions, was mere inches away. Harvey could feel the rubber soles of his shoes soften.

Intense heat radiated through the fabric of his shoes and pants. Beads of sweat formed on his brow as the heat singed his arm hair.

A voice whispered on the air. "Speak and release."

"'Speak and release?'" What in the world does that mean?" thought Harvey.

And just as quickly as the image had appeared, it was gone. The scene of the desert night returned.

Both frightened and frustrated, Harvey spoke into the darkness. "What was that? Why were they in the cage? What exactly am I supposed to speak and release?"

The howl of the desert wind was all he heard.

26

arvey stayed outside for thirty minutes more trying to solve the riddle of the image and the words. Finally, he gave up in frustration and headed in to join the others. He found them gathered around Madora, who was sitting at the kitchen table with a laptop computer.

When Sheef saw Harvey, he mouthed, "What?" Harvey responded with a shrug of his shoulders and mouthed back, "I'll tell you later." Sheef nodded and turned his attention back to the computer screen.

"What are we doing?" asked Harvey.

"Discussing where we go from here," responded Madora. Pointing to the computer screen, Madora continued, "We need to access the past by using one of the three movies that I discovered Millud acted in."

"How exactly does that work?"

It's tricky, Harvey, and doesn't always work. Let's just hope that a character Millud played in one of these three movies was very similar to his real-life personality. If not, then locating a doorway to the past will be next to impossible."

"Characters and doorways? I have no idea what you're talking about," interrupted Sheef.

"I don't expect you to yet. Now if you'll let me finish, everything will soon make sense," Madora shot back with the hint of a smile. "If you have a properly trained Sadiki," she resumed, "you can access any of the Phantasian worlds. But stepping out of one of these worlds and into a different time period on Earth is only accomplished by leaving a world that was created from a movie. When an actor in a particular film plays a character whose personality in the film is nearly identical to the actual personality of the actor, the fictional Phantasian world can merge with the actor's real world and time period, creating a warp hole or doorway between the two."

"And entering the warp hole would take one to the actor's actual life?" asked Harvey.

"Not only that, but the time period when the movie was filmed."

"So if Millud played a character in one of the movies that was nearly identical to his real self," said Harvey, "then a warp hole would be opened between that Phantasian world and his actual life."

"And stepping through it would take us back to the 1930's when the movie was made," concluded Sheef.

"That about sums it up," said Madora.

"Okay then, but how do we get back to our own time?" asked Sheef.

"This is where we have to be careful and watch our time. A type of trail will be left behind when we move through the

Phantasian, and if we return to the realm within a week or so, the trail will still be strong enough for Akeila to retrace. However, if we stay much longer, we risk losing the trail."

"What happens then?"

"We'll never get back to our lives. But then again, if our mission fails, there'll be nothing worth getting back to anyway."

"So this very well might be a one-way ticket," commented Sheef. "But getting back to the characters Millud played in the three films, if we can't find one that reflects his real-life personality, then there's no chance of a warp hole opening, and thus, no way back to the 1930's."

"Precisely."

"Then why don't we just have Akeila take us to 1930's movies featuring talented, famous actors?" asked Harvey. "It seems like we would have a better chance of finding a warp hole in one of those movies instead of one of Millud's."

"We likely would, Harvey, but if we want to find and destroy the Narciss Glass, it will be much easier if we access the past through a Millud-created warp hole."

"But why? What's the difference? The past is the past, right? What difference does it make how we get there?"

"Trust me, it makes a tremendous difference, but it's a bit tricky to explain. To begin with, you need to understand that humans are all moving through time at a set speed, but the thing is, the exact speed is never the same for any two humans. Just as all humans have unique DNA signatures, so too, do they have their own unique speed signatures. Now granted, the difference is extremely small, only a fraction of a millisecond, but in the strange world of physics, this tiny variance makes a world of difference."

"How so?" asked Harvey.

"It allows one person to see, hear, and touch another person."

"So what happens if you have exactly the same speed signature as someone else?"

"That's impossible, unless, of course, you access the real world from the Phantasian by traveling through an actor's warp hole. Then you would enter the time period when the movie was filmed, and your speed signature would be exactly the same as the actor's. Now this is where it gets really bizarre. You would be able to see and hear the actor, but to him or her, you'd be invisible, a veritable ghost. The other people from the time period, however, would be able to see you. To them, you'd be as real as the next person."

"It makes sense then," said Harvey. "If we hope to locate the Narciss Glass, it will be much easier to pull off if Millud has no idea that we exist."

"And now you understand why it would be better to access the past through one of his warp holes," said Madora. "If we can find one, that is."

"I suppose then," said Sheef, "there's only one way to find out. And the way I figure it, we might have to visit all three of the movie worlds Millud acted in. Am I right?"

"Unfortunately, yes. I say unfortunately because all three will be fraught with danger, and I'm not merely talking about getting injured."

Harvey audibly gulped. "So what happens if you die in one of those worlds?"

"If you die there, then you die everywhere."

"I'll tell you what, this adventure just keeps getting better and better by the minute," said Sheef with a chuckle. "So those are the three movies he acted in?" asked Sheef, pointing to the computer screen.

"Yes. *The Phone Rang Twice,* a gangster tale; *The Barnacle Buccaneers,* a comical pirate adventure; and *The Kaleidoscope,* a sci-fi thriller."

"So, which one do we begin with?" asked Sheef.

"Great question," replied Madora. "Why don't we let the leader of our little adventure choose."

Every eye in the room turned to Harvey.

27

"**B**ut I don't know anything about the Phantasian," cried Harvey. My choosing doesn't make sense. Madora, you know the most about where we're going. Shouldn't you be the one to decide?"

"When it comes to selecting which of the three movie worlds to warp to first, I have no advantage over you, Harvey, and since the Unseen obviously has been guiding your steps, the wisest course of action is to let you decide."

Harvey still didn't want to shoulder the responsibility of choosing, but Madora's logic was too sound for him to argue with.

"Looks like I don't have a choice." Harvey paused to take a deep breath before continuing. "Okay then, here it goes. Since I've had more than enough stranger-than-science fiction experiences over the last month, I say we don't begin with *The Kaleidoscope*. And if it's true that we can be maimed or even killed in one these worlds, being on a ship with a motley crew of pirates, even comedic ones, seems like a place I would rather avoid. Besides, Millud doesn't strike me as a very funny person.

I can't imagine a warp hole opening from that world. So the *Barnacle Buccaneers* is out. That leaves us with *The Phone Rang Twice*. I realize that it has gangsters, but at least we won't be trapped on a boat with them."

"Great, decision made," said Sheef. So now what?"

"I'll need to show Akeila as many images from the three movies as possible," said Madora. "If I can locate some film clips online, all the better. It's imperative that the character's faces and the settings of each of the films are deeply imprinted in her memory. Any vagueness in her thinking, and we'll find ourselves warped to a completely different movie world."

"How long will it take?" asked Sheef.

"About three hours. Why don't the two of you try to get some sleep? There's really nothing you can do to help me, and to be honest, you'd probably just get in my way. I'll wake you up at dawn. We'll have a quick bit to eat and then be off."

Harvey and Sheef didn't need to be told twice. They were both beyond exhaustion, even after their earlier naps. They walked back to the sleeping area. Fromp, however, elected to stay behind with Akeila, who was seated next to Madora.

Surprisingly, Harvey was soon hundreds of feet below surface consciousness. His deep sleep meant that Madora had to practically push him out of bed and onto the floor in order to rouse him. His return to consciousness was accompanied by a prolonged groan, which easily woke Sheef.

"It's already sunup?" asked Harvey groggily. Feels like I just fell asleep."

"Not quite sunup. It's about 5:00 a.m. Yuya's been topside all night keeping watch. He sprinted into my quarters only seconds ago in a state of panic, informing me that he observed at least fifty green flashes less than five miles away!"

"Volkin Wolf warp holes," said Sheef, fully awakened by the news, "which means Vapid Lords and Insips will be here very shortly."

"Yuya's setting a charge at the entrance. He plans on blowing it whenever they arrive. Hopefully, the explosion will take out some of their numbers, but even if it doesn't, it should buy us some extra time. It will take them a while to get through all that rock."

"Let's hope those Volkin Wolves need to recuperate like warp-hounds and can't immediately open another warp hole, because if they can, we're done for," said Sheef.

"Then let's quit the chatter and get out of here as quickly as possible," said Madora. And, Yuya, once you blow the entrance, you'll need to get out quickly."

"Don't worry," he replied. "There's no way I'm staying here. Once I set off the charge, I'll have one of the girls warp me and the remaining Sadiki out of here."

"Good. That's settled then."

Madora called to Akeila. The Sadiki made unblinking eye contact with her. Madora thought of the faces and settings from *The Phone Rang Twice* and then transmitted them to Akeila, who barked enthusiastically, letting her know that the thought had been successfully received.

Harvey expected Akeila to begin rapidly chasing her tail as Fromp did whenever he opened a warp hole. She did nothing of the sort, however. Instead, she remained perfectly still except for her tail. While she was receiving the thought message from Madora, her tail was relaxed, drooping downward, but seconds after her bark, it curled up and over itself, creating a perfectly formed circle, no more than a foot wide.

The space within the circle drew Harvey and Sheef's attention. Looking through it, they could see the couch and wall on the opposite side of the room. The image appeared as a photograph framed by a furry border. As they continued to stare, though, the circular image began to bend and twist. This distortion was followed by the image bubbling outward and then collapsing inward, like a giant lens, alternating between convex and concave. This out and in undulation continued, growing larger and larger until the image could be stretched no more.

"Is it going to burst?" asked Harvey while turning away and squinting.

Madora didn't have time to respond, for right after Harvey asked the question, the burst occurred with a pressure-releasing pop. A shower of tinkling fragments spread throughout the room.

The image within the curved tail immediately changed to black and white. A man stood to the right of a street lamp in the pouring rain. His face was hidden by the shadow of his umbrella, but the tiny light of a cigarette flickering on and off was clearly seen.

An explosion shook the room. Rock pieces from the ceiling crashed down.

"Sounds like our guests have arrived," said Madora. "That's our cue. Time to make the jump!"

"Jump where? Through there?" asked Harvey, pointing at the image inside Akeila's curled tail. "We'll never fit through."

"Yes you will. All you have to do is stretch out your arms in front of you and put your head down like you're about to dive into a pool. Once your fingertips make contact with the image, you will be pulled through, becoming part of the world within the tail."

"Harvey, you first. I'm not chancing leaving you behind," Sheef ordered. Harvey nodded and positioned his body as Madora had instructed. With only a hair of hesitation, he placed his flattened hands in the space. His entire body was immediately stretched thin and pulled through. A split second later, Sheef could see him standing on the other side of the street lamp in the pouring rain.

Sheef dove in next, followed by Fromp, and then by Madora and Akeila. Soon, all five were standing just to the left of the street lamp and the man with the umbrella. The black and white of the movie world slowly awoke to living color. Already soaked and shivering, their expedition through the Phantasian had only just begun.

PHANTASIAN

28

The umbrella man took one more drag on his cigarette before exhausting a stream of smoke into the cold, damp air and flicking the butt into a street puddle. He looked suspiciously at the drenched group and then back out into the street.

While continuing to look straight ahead, and with a raspy, no-nonsense tone, he said, "Ain't healthy for anyone to sneak up on me like you just did from behind the street lamp. If you gave me the scare, which you didn't, you might all be lying in colored puddles right now. So, where's Marlow?"

Harvey, Sheef, and Madora looked at one another, hoping that someone had a split-second answer to the question. Not knowing what else to do, Sheef stepped in and bought some time with a question of his own.

Trying to match the man's tone and tenor, Sheef improvised, "Who wants to know?"

"Listen, you mug, and get this straight, see," said the man threateningly, "I ain't no canary. I ask the questions and never answer 'em. So unless you want to be Swiss-cheesed, I suggest you answer my question."

The man then turned in their direction and walked over to the group. As he drew to stop, he tilted back the umbrella, revealing his face for the first time. He had a square jaw and an enormous forehead, reminiscent of Frankenstein's. But even more jarring was the mealy red scar, which began at his chin, climbed upward through his right eye, crossed his expansive forehead, and vanished in a widow's peak.

"Sheef," Harvey whispered, "what does he mean by 'Swiss-cheesed'?"

Sheef pantomimed the firing of a machine gun.

"Oh," Harvey replied, thankful that he had followed Sheef's advice and kept the Lignum shirt on.

"So," said the man even more menacingly, "you gonna tell me where he is, or do I need to ventilate you?" He pulled back his jacket, revealing two guns hanging in a leather shoulder harness.

Not being able to think of any other way out of the situation, Sheef answered, "Marlow said he couldn't make it. He sent me instead."

"Oh yeah, and who might you be?"

Sheef replied with the first name that popped into his head. "Alphonso, and that's all you need to know."

"What's he doing?" whispered Madora to Harvey.

Harvey shrugged his shoulders.

"The drugstore man sent someone who's got a little spine, huh? Didn't know the little squeaker had it in him. So, Alphonso, I trust he gave you the merchandise?"

"Tell me about the girl first." Sheef guessed that a girl was somehow mixed up in the plot. In every gangster film he had ever seen, a girl was always involved.

"She's safe. No need to worry about that. You just give me the goods, and Marlow will get her back, all in one piece."

Sheef's palpitations increased. He did his best to keep his voice from breaking as he responded. "No deal, you monster-faced lug. You'll get the merchandise only when I get the girl."

It was a dangerous move to insult the man, but Sheef thought it even more dangerous to be perceived as weak. Thugs like the umbrella man respected cowardice far less than insults. If he sensed weakness, he would likely exploit it.

The ploy seemed to work. "Watch your mouth there, or I'll cut off them flapping lips of yours. That ain't the deal we made."

"Well I'm dealing new cards. No girl, no merchandise."

The man smiled grotesquely. His large scar seemed to darken. "You got some real moxie there, Alphonso. Might be able to use someone like you once you're done runnin' errands for the squeaker. Tell you what, you meet me and the boys at Dogwood Street and Fourth Avenue in an hour. There's an old warehouse there. You can't miss it. Bring the goods, and you can trade 'em for the dame, but I'm warnin' you, if you're one second late, or there's any funny business, I'll make Swiss cheese of the lady."

"We'll be there. You just make sure that there ain't a scratch on her. If there is, I destroy the merchandise."

"Yeah, and how you gonna destroy them rocks?"

"Rocks?" Sheef asked, looking momentarily confused.

The umbrella man held up his right hand and menacingly pointed his ring finger at Sheef. "The diamonds, smart guy. Don't play dumb with me."

"Yeah, that's right, the diamonds." Sheef paused, taking a few seconds to fabricate the next falsehood in his narrative. "Dynamite's how. You lay one finger on her, and I bring down the entire warehouse and everyone in it."

"Including yourself?"

"Life wouldn't be worth living without her."

The umbrella man's face recoiled in disgust. "Marlow's sister? You gotta be nuts! She's got the face of an orangutan! To each his own I guess," the man said with a snicker. "Beauty be in the eye of the beholder they say, but I ain't got no idea what you be beholdin'. An hour then, and by the way, what's with the others? This a family picnic or something?"

"I never work alone. You know how it is with people in our line of work, family's everything. Nothing ever gets between us."

"I can respect that, but what's with the hounds?"

"Protection," Sheef said, trying his best to appear aggressive and unafraid. "They're part of the family. What's it to you? You got a problem with them?"

The man pulled out another cigarette and lit it as he eyed Harvey and Madora, his facial scar coloring darker. After a deep drag on the smoke, he nodded to Sheef, "Just make sure you're there. One hour." He then turned around and walked down the block before ducking into an alleyway on his left.

Harvey, who didn't know if he should be hysterically laughing or fearfully shaking at Sheef's antics, said, "Sheef, what was that? Are you insane? I mean, you were great and all, but remember what Madora said, we can be killed here, as in really killed! And we don't have any diamonds. What's he going to do to us and that girl when we show up empty handed?"

"Don't worry, kid. I've got no intention whatsoever of showing up at that warehouse. I needed to buy us some time. Believe me, it wasn't my aim to get all mixed up in the movie's plot, but I didn't have much time to think."

"But, Sheef, if we're not there in an hour with those diamonds, he's going to hurt that girl."

"Harvey, none of this is real. It's a completely made-up world. We can't waste time worrying about the welfare of some fictional character."

"That's where you're wrong," said Madora. "This world is just as real to these characters as ours is to us. Sheef, you really shouldn't have inserted yourself into the plot like that."

"Well what was I supposed to do? I didn't see anyone else stepping forward," said Sheef, clearly agitated.

"I don't know, but trust me, this isn't good. In the Phantasian, it's always better to blend into the background and just observe."

"I'm sorry, Madora, but I didn't ask to be dumped right into the middle of a question from a gangster with two guns!"

Madora responded apologetically. "I know you didn't. I'm sorry, Sheef. Here I am criticizing you for actions that saved our lives, and I haven't even thanked you yet. It really was good thinking. Thank you."

Calming down, Sheef replied in a softer voice, "Don't mention it. Sorry, too, for snapping at you the way I did."

"But what about the girl, Sheef? She's real. We can't just leave her behind," said Harvey.

"You're right." Sheef raked his fingers through his wet hair. "Okay, here's what we're going to do. The umbrella man planned a rendezvous with Marlow here, so why don't we wait for the real Marlow to show up. Then we'll give the message about the diamonds and the warehouse directly to him. Then, hopefully we're out of the picture and the plot is back on track."

"But what if the girl is actually supposed to die in the movie?"

"Come on, Harvey, the dame always makes it out alive in these films. Now, let's get out of this rain and find someplace dry where we can watch."

Across the street was a small drugstore. Hanging in one of the windows was a sign advertising hot coffee and donuts for a dime.

"How about over there," Sheef said as he pointed across the street. "Coffee and something to snack on will do us all good, not to mention getting us out of this rain."

The clinking of the door's bell announced the group's entrance. The store was long and narrow. In the middle was a rectangular bar, surrounded by cushioned stools. Only a few of the stools were occupied, and not one of the patrons glanced up at the sound of the bell. Three small tables were situated in the space between the front door and the bar.

Behind the counter stood a sour-faced man wearing a white apron who was in the process of refilling the coffee cup of an older gentleman.

On the other side of the bar was the grocery section of the store, with shelves filled with a kitchen pantry's basic odds and ends. Spanning the left wall were bins of bulk candy, and in the very back of the store was a small pharmacy, run by a skinny, frail man wearing wire rimmed glasses. The man was nervously pacing behind the pharmacy counter.

Sheef led the dripping group to the table closest to the window.

"Can't you read, son," snapped the sour-faced man behind the counter. He pointed to a hand-drawn, faded sign pinned to the wall. "No pets allowed," he read. "Now get those dirty mutts out of here before I have to do it for you." He picked up a wooden broom and brandished it threateningly.

"Oh, I apologize, sir. We didn't see the sign," said Madora. She momentarily stared at Akeila, who responded with a quick scampering to the door. Harvey opened it for her, and she exited with Fromp close on her tail. Both animals lay down on the wet sidewalk, firmly pressing their bodies against the brick building to stay out of the rain.

"So, what can I get for you fine folks who've decided to flood my floor?" asked the man sarcastically.

"I'm sorry about that," said Sheef. "Rain kind of caught us off guard. Coffee and donuts all around would be wonderful, sir."

The man grunted in response as Harvey, Sheef, and Madora took their seats at the table.

"If Marlow shows up, we certainly can't miss him from here," Harvey said.

"If it's in the plot of the story, he has to," replied Madora.

Their conversation was interrupted by the man slinging down empty coffee cups and a plate of donuts on the table. He haphazardly filled each cup from a pot of steaming coffee, behaving the entire time as if serving the group was the greatest inconvenience.

"What's eating that guy?" Harvey whispered after the man had returned to his place behind the counter.

"Beats me," said Sheef. "Probably suspicious of us. I would be. Look at the way we're dressed, not exactly period clothing, and don't forget that we left a trail of puddles behind us. Besides, were not locals, not to this area of town, this time period, or for that matter, this world. Let's just try to play it cool and not draw any more attention to ourselves."

They each grabbed a donut and spent a few minutes sipping and snacking before Sheef asked the question which chaotic circumstances had yet to permit.

"We've got some time to kill here, Harvey, so why don't you share the specifics of your time with the Unseen."

"Here? In front of Madora?"

"Considering the precarious position we're in and everything that's on the line, I don't think there's really any margin for keeping secrets. Plus, she might be able to help; she's certainly been around long enough to have plenty of wisdom and insight."

Madora swung the toe of her right boot into Sheef's shin.

"Ow! What was that for?"

"Implying that I'm old."

"What are you so upset for. It's true, isn't it?"

"Yes, but it's still not polite to say it," Madora said with mock annoyance.

"Sorryyyy," Sheef replied, putting both hands up.

"It was really strange, Sheef," Harvey began. "It happened so quickly. I was in the process of organizing my thoughts when the desert disappeared."

"Disappeared?" asked Madora.

"Not literally. I guess it was a vision. Anyway, instead of a desert, there was suddenly a large iron cage in front of me. My mom, Thurngood, and another man, whose face I couldn't make out, were all trapped inside. All three of them were staring at me like I had a key or something."

"Did you?" asked Madora.

"No. I don't even know if there was a lock on the door. It was on the other side of the cage, so I never even got a look at it. But then, all this lava started coming out of these cracks in the ground, melting my shoes. That's when I began to panic. I know it was only a vision, but I swear, it felt like my legs were about to catch fire."

"And what happened next?" asked Sheef.

"A voice, not very loud, though, more like a whisper, said just three words: 'Speak and release'. And then it all vanished and the desert returned."

"That's it? No other words or anything?"

"Nothing. Do you have any idea what it means?"

"Perhaps," said Sheef as he grabbed a second donut from the plate. "Based on what you told me before, I'd say that the people in the cage are those you need to – "

"Well then who's the guy with the face I couldn't recognize?" asked Harvey, interrupting Sheef before he could complete his sentence.

"Most likely your real father. He left when you were still a baby, so it would make sense that you wouldn't remember his face. Did you speak anything?"

"No. I didn't know what to say. Actually, I did try, but the words wouldn't come out. It was like they were weighed down by something."

"Weighed down by something? Like what?" asked Madora.

"Unforgiveness," said Harvey after more than a minute of silence. He turned to stare out the window.

"That would do it, wouldn't it?" asked Madora rhetorically. "Leave a nice trail for the enemy to follow. Someone like you, Harvey, with extraordinarily powerful thoughts, would definitely emit a foul odor if those thoughts turned negative. Unforgiveness would certainly do the trick."

"Yeah, I know that now. The problem is I have no idea how to get rid of it."

Before Harvey could say anything else, the pharmacist sat down at a table next to them. He ordered a cup of coffee and then began nervously drumming his fingers on the table. He briefly glanced over at the group before fixing his attention on the window.

"Sheef," whispered Harvey. "It's him. It has to be."

"Who?" asked Sheef, turning his head for a better look."

"Millud. He played – is playing – the pharmacist role."

Sure enough, when Sheef looked closely, he easily recognized the face he had seen on Madora's computer.

"He looks awfully nervous," whispered Harvey, "and he keeps glancing out the window. Do you think Millud is Marlow? You know, the guy with the diamonds who was supposed to meet the umbrella man?"

"It has to be, but we don't want to scare him away. We need to hear what he's thinking. What he's planning on doing and where he's going to go after the rendezvous. We need to follow him everywhere he goes. If a warp hole opens to his real life back on Earth, we can't miss it."

"But how is Harvey going to read the man's thoughts?" asked Madora.

"Kreen nectar. Harvey, here, take a swallow from the bottle," said Sheef as he pulled it out of his pocket and handed it to Harvey. "I'm going to walk over to the counter and ask for some cream for my coffee. On the way back to the table, I'll put less than a drop of Kreen into Millud's coffee. This little bit will increase the power of his thoughts enough for you to hear them, but not enough for Millud to hear yours. He's panicked enough as it is."

"And Harvey will actually be able to hear his thoughts?" asked Madora.

"Like Marlow was talking directly to him."

29

Sheef was as smooth getting the Kreen nectar into Marlow's cof-fee as he was speaking to the umbrella man. As he walked by, he convincingly spilled some of the cream he was carrying onto Marlow's left shoe.

Sheef apologized profusely while gathering a wad of napkins from the silver dispenser on the table and shoving them directly into Marlow's hand. Marlow now had no choice but to bend over and mop up the cream. While he was bent over, Sheef slyly reached his arm around Marlow's back and quickly released a tiny amount of Kreen nectar into his coffee. As Sheef sat down at his own table, he winked at both Harvey and Madora.

"A few sips is all it'll take," said Sheef.

They didn't have to wait long. Marlow, still extremely tense, was searching for something to occupy his hands. Picking up the cup, bringing it to his mouth, and returning it to the table filled the need. It wasn't long until he had drained the cup and was working on a second.

"Madora," Harvey whispered, "does Millud have any idea that he's not really a pharmacist, and that he's only playing the role of Marlow?"

"Not at all," she whispered back. "The man sitting at the table has never heard of Millud. He is the actual Marlow. Remember, what was fictional on Earth is not so here. The pharmacist character created by the writer – a fidgeting, nervous wreck of a man who gets mixed up in with some very seedy individuals – is a real person in this world. There's no acting going on."

"Harvey, let's quiet down," interjected Sheef. You should be able to hear Marlow's thoughts by now."

Harvey nodded. He bit his lip, closed his eyes, and tried to turn down the volume of his own thoughts. A high-pitched, annoying voice began rapidly speaking.

"I'm hearing his thoughts now," Harvey whispered. At first it was difficult for Harvey to understand what Marlow was thinking. His thoughts weren't very loud or clear, but like tuning in a radio station, the more Harvey concentrated on Marlow's face, the louder and clearer his thoughts became, and it wasn't long before Harvey was able to comprehend every one of his thoughts.

"Where is that man? Oh my, but this isn't good. He should be at the streetlight by now. This is certainly a pickle I'm in, a very sour one at that. I should've never gotten involved, but what choice did I have? None whatsoever! Those thugs breaking into my house and waiting for me to come home from work! A warning is what they said it was. And if I didn't play along, they'd visit me again, and it wouldn't be very pleasant for me or my family. I still have the bruises and the pain to remind me. A warning, that was a warning?

Sticking me in a metal trash can and rolling me down Baker's Hill. I don't know how I survived. The speed, the bouncing and banging, it was dreadful. Two fractured ribs, a sprained wrist, and a concussion, not to mention almost drowning when the can flew off the pier and into that icy water. I hate to think what could be worse than that, but they said it would be, and not just for me, my wife, too. Martha is so frail as it is! I didn't want to play along, but I was left with no choice, and now the man's a no-show."

"Sheef," said Harvey, "this guy's in serious trouble."

"Okay, you can tell us all about it later. For now, get back to his thoughts. I don't want you to miss anything."

Harvey nodded and closed his eyes again.

"And it didn't work like they said it would, now did it? They said it would be a simple job and definitely worth my while. All I had to do was dig at the old concrete wall at the back of the pharmacy after hours. The wall was hidden from view by all the medicine shelves. No more than an hour a day is what they said, and in thirty days there would be a hole, large enough for me to crawl through, leading directly into the jewelry store on the other side. Well, yesterday was day thirty, and I haven't even made it halfway through the wall!"

"Sheef," whispered Harvey, "Marlow doesn't have any diamonds."

"Okay, later. Listen."

Marlow's thoughts continued. *"And last night, a monster of a man was waiting in my car. Said he was giving me a little incentive for delivering the merchandise today. An insurance policy for them. My kid sister, Myrtle Mae, she's the incentive and insurance. I only get her back when I deliver the diamonds. I didn't make it through the wall, though, so no diamonds. What was I to do? I had to come up with something, didn't I? Oh, we're all done for. It'll never work. Even if the man does show up, he's never going to buy it."*

Harvey quickly shared Marlow's latest thoughts with Sheef and Madora, but when Harvey focused his mind to listen in on any additional thoughts, Marlow pushed back his chair, stood up, scurried to the front door, and walked out onto the sidewalk. Fromp and Akeila, who were still leaning against the building, stood up and walked around Marlow to the glass door. Fromp, whose back hair had once again stood vertical, looked through the door at Harvey.

"Something's wrong. Fromp's picking up on something."

"We should get the dogs inside then. If we lose Akeila, we'll never get out of gangster world," said Sheef.

Sheef got up and immediately opened the door for the two dogs to enter. The man behind the counter had gone back to the storeroom to get a box of napkins, so that by the time he returned to his counter, Fromp and Akeila were already lying down on the floor on the other side of the table, out of eyesight of the crotchety old man.

"We're in the wrong world," said Harvey.

"What do you mean?" asked Madora.

"This guy Marlow is nothing like the real Millud. From what I was told about Millud, he was completely self-absorbed. He couldn't care less about what happened to others. He was only in it for himself, willing to cheat, lie, and harm people to get his way. Marlow's not like that at all. He's only going along with the gangsters because they threatened to hurt his wife and have kidnapped his sister. Marlow wants to do the right thing. If a warp hole only opens up when a movie character's personality matches up with the actor's real personality, it's not going to happen from this place. Marlow and Millud are complete opposites." "If what you're saying is true," said Madora, "we shouldn't waste another second in this world."

"We haven't been here that long," said Sheef. "Do you think Akeila's recovered enough energy to open another warp hole so soon?"

"There's only one way to find out"

A large barge of an automobile roared up the street. The driver slammed on the brakes, and the car came to a screeching halt right in front of the drugstore. Marlow, who was standing on the sidewalk, desperately searching for the pick-up man, froze in place.

From out of the open windows emerged five machine gun barrels. The faces of the men holding the weapons were shadowed by wide-brimmed hats.

"I've got the merchandise right – " were the last squeaky words that Marlow ever uttered. He didn't stand a chance against the shower of machine gun bullets that sprayed the front of the building, shattering the windows and pockmarking the brick.

Harvey was the only one who got a glimpse of the car and its gun-toting thugs before he and the others threw themselves flat against the floor. Madora flipped the table back to shield them from the storm of hot lead.

There were eruptions of wooden splinters, plaster, and groceries throughout the drugstore. When the guns finally stopped and the car sped away, splatterings of tomato soup dripped down the walls. A faint cloud of all-purpose flour hung in the air.

One of the customers, who was seated at the counter, was lying on the floor, moaning and grabbing his right shoulder. Blood oozed between his fingers.

"A drive-by hit," said Madora as she shakily stood to her feet. She dusted herself off and walked over to the broken window. Peering through the hole, she yelled, "Sheef, Harvey! It's Marlow!"

The three of them bolted through the doorway and onto the sidewalk. In the words of the umbrella man, Marlow had been "Swiss-cheesed".

Madora knelt down, placing two of her fingers on his neck. She shook her head.

"I don't get it," said Sheef. "This makes absolutely no sense whatsoever. Why would they gun down Marlow? They had no idea that he didn't have the diamonds. Why were they even here? Shouldn't they all be waiting at the warehouse for me to deliver the goods."

"Sheef, I got a quick look at the car. Couldn't make out the faces, but I saw something else."

"Saw what?"

"Glowing green eyes."

"But why would a 1930's gangster have glowing green . . . You don't think it was one of those do you?"

"Yeah, I do," said Harvey.

"Are you saying that there was a Volkin Wolf in that car?" asked Madora in disbelief. "But if that were true, that would mean that those weren't gangsters."

"But Vapid Lords," said Sheef. "Which means two things: they're here, and they're tracking us. Marlow wasn't the target, we were."

"What's this?" asked Madora, pulling something from Marlow's clenched hand. It was a small velvet bag.

Madora untied the drawstring at the top and poured some of the contents into her hand."

"Diamonds," said Harvey.

"If so, they're very low quality." Madora held one up closely to her eye. "No, just as I thought, there's nothing 'diamond' about these. Might fool you from a distance, though."

"Then what are they?" asked Sheef.

Madora scratched one of the larger pieces on the sidewalk. It was extremely soft and left behind a white mark. She then touched the piece to her tongue and smiled.

"You've got to be kidding me," she said.

"What? Why are you smiling?" asked Sheef.

"You're not going to believe this," said Madora laughing to herself, "but Marlow was about to give the umbrella man a bag of rock candy."

"What's that?" asked Harvey.

"Old time candy, and it's about as basic as it gets," replied Sheef. "You boil a bunch of sugar and then let it cool and crystalize on a stick or a piece of string. Did you see those candy bins on the wall when we walked into the drugstore? I guarantee you that one of them is filled with the stuff. And I've never really thought about it before, but these sugar crystals do kind of look like diamonds."

"From a distance," repeated Madora. "Or if you were dealing with an idiot. I suppose Marlow was hoping he could fool the umbrella man long enough to get his sister back, and after that . . . well, I guess we'll never know."

"That must've been what he meant by 'they'll never buy it'. He was referring to the rock candy," said Harvey.

"Madora," said Sheef. "Would you put those back in the bag and toss it to me. And, Harvey, on the way, remind me of every thought you received from Marlow."

"On the way? Where are we going?"

"To the warehouse of course. We've got a delivery to make and a girl to rescue."

Before leaving the drugstore, Sheef surveyed the damage and looked down at Marlow one last time.

"Harvey," Sheef said, "that was too close of a shave. We were lucky this time, but you keep leaving bread crumbs for the enemy to follow, and you're going to get us all killed. If you don't get that cage open soon, then we're all just living on borrowed time."

30

Sheef was pointed in the general direction of the intersection of Dogwood Street and Fourth Avenue by a police officer who arrived on the scene as the group was leaving. Harvey and Sheef were perplexed by the behavior of the officer. He didn't ask any questions about the shooting, and when Sheef asked him for directions, the officer silently pointed, never saying a word.

As they were leaving the drugstore, Harvey mentioned the bizarre apathy of the police officer. Sheef commented that it was probably the result of the officer having become desensitized to violence in this area of the city. Madora, however, was quick to contradict him.

"It's an understandable assumption, and back on Earth, it would likely be the cause for his seeming indifference, but it's not the reason here. He doesn't appear to care because the screenwriter didn't provide the officer with any depth, zero character development. The actor was probably given no more than a line or two to speak in the entire movie. The Phantasian worlds are filled with these background characters who have no real substance."

"Like zombies," said Harvey.

"I never thought of them like that, but I guess in a way they are."

As it turned out, the intersection was only a few blocks away, and in less than ten minutes after leaving the drugstore, the three of them, in addition to Akeila and Fromp, were kneeling down behind an abandoned newsstand across the street from the warehouse. Harvey adjusted his position and leaned back against the structure. Unfortunately, it offered no resistance, and Harvey, with a yelp of panic, fell through. Fromp's ears stood tall in alarm.

Madora reached into the newsstand and pulled him up and out.

"What's wrong with that thing?" asked Harvey, completely caught off guard and frightened. "I passed through it as if it wasn't even there!"

"It's okay, Harvey," said Madora. "It appears that we've wandered away from the main plot of the movie. I'd be surprised if the warehouse was originally even in one of the actual scenes. It was likely only mentioned by one of the gangsters. Similar to the police officer, this area of town, since it wasn't integral to the primary storyline, doesn't have much substance to it. Think of a Hollywood movie set. The warehouse, though, is likely becoming more solid since the umbrella man recently included it in a new, evolving plot."

Harvey looked uneasily down at the sidewalk. "Could we fall through the sidewalk?"

"It's possible, but for the most part, the grounds of these worlds are typically stable and trustworthy, but if you get too far away from the plot, you could fall through a section, like jungle quicksand."

"Fall through! Into what?" asked Harvey, now even more worked up.

"Through this world and into Phantasian space. Not really a place you want to visit. You'd just drift out there forever. Don't worry, though. Like I said, the grounds for the most part are trustworthy."

"Somehow that's not very reassuring," Harvey replied.

"Hey, can we focus on the plan?" asked Sheef. "I think our hour is about up."

"Plan? I didn't know you actually had one, Sheef." said Madora, feigning surprise.

"Honestly, I'm making it up as I go."

"Really? I didn't pick up on that," she said sarcastically.

"Well then, maybe you have something to contribute?"

"Oh no, 'Alphonso', since you're the one who got us into this mess, you'll be the one who gets us out."

"Gee, thanks for the encouragement."

"My pleasure."

"Listen up. The plan is," said Sheef, pausing to poke his head around the newsstand to catch a glimpse of the warehouse before turning back around and continuing, "we ask for the girl, Myrtle Mae, first. Once we've safely received her, I'll toss the diamonds over to the one running the show.

"During the exchange, Madora will instruct Akeila to open a warp hole to one of the other worlds we need to investigate. Once it's open, wait for me to give you the signal to make the dive. If all goes according to plan, we rescue the damsel in distress and warp from here without being Swiss-cheesed. Of course, this is all contingent on them agreeing to hand over the girl first and not looking at the rock candy too closely."

"And what if they don't agree to hand her over first?" asked Harvey. "Do you have backup plan?"

"Come on, kid, would it really be a true adventure if I did?"

"Sheef, you take the whole idea of flying by the seat of your pants to a new level," said Madora.

"Why thank you."

"Not a compliment."

"Well, I'll take it just the same, thank you very much," Sheef said with a sideways grin. Harvey, you still wearing your Lignum shirt?"

"Yeah, but the pants are still in the backpack."

"Don't have time to change now," said Sheef while glancing down at his watch. "We've got about two minutes left. Time to move out. And, Harvey, be ready to unsheathe that sword of yours if need be."

Harvey reached back and touched the sword which was hanging on the side of his backpack. Sheef then took a deep breath and walked directly through the middle of the newsstand and across the street. As he was crossing, he pulled off the shirt he was wearing and replaced it with his Lignum shirt. Harvey followed, as did Madora, but not before rolling her eyes at Sheef.

Akeila hopped right through, never even batting an eye. Fromp, the intrepid hound of Ecclon, however, was hesitatingly cautious. He whined puppy-like while pawing at the ghostly structure. Finally, though, he dug deep and pulled himself together, letting fly a fearless whoof before sprinting through the newsstand and after the others.

The solid, rusty warehouse door resisted being opened by emitting a metallic groan. In fact, it took all three of them to open it wide enough to pass through. The space inside was enormous. Sunlight struggled to penetrate the few dirty windows, unable to scatter the folds of dingy grey that hung heavily in the air.

There was no indication that the warehouse had ever been occupied or used. It was completely barren. Not even a wood fragment from an old crate or a rusty nail to be seen.

In the center space stood ten ogre-looking gangsters who were wearing pinstriped black suits and white velvet hats. And though the gangsters were at least forty feet away, Harvey was able to spot the facial scar of the umbrella man. To his left, was an even more sinister looking man who was tightly gripping a young woman's wrist.

She was gangly, standing bowlegged on noticeably large feet. Stringy, unkempt blonde hair fell upon a faded floral print dress, which appeared to swallow her bony frame.

"That must be Myrtle Mae," mumbled Sheef.

"Now I know why the umbrella man reacted the way he did when you said you couldn't live without her," snickered Harvey.

"Harvey, you of all people should know better than to judge a book by its cover. Besides, she can't help how she was written into the storyline."

At that moment, Harvey was grateful for the dim light that hid his reddening shame.

"Alphonso," the umbrella man shouted, "I was beginning to worry that you might miss your date with your lady friend."

"I made it didn't I?"

"You did, but I hope for all your sakes that you didn't come here empty-handed."

"Don't you worry your pretty little scar about that. I've got the rocks right here," said Sheef, holding up the velvet bag. Marlow gave them to me this morning."

"Oh yeah, so where is that little pipsqueak anyway? Why ain't he here?"

"Marlow's done. He finished the job and won't be doing anything else for you."

"Oh really," said the umbrella man as he turned and looked at his fellow gangsters. "We'll just see about that. He's done when I say he's done."

"All right," shouted Sheef, "let the girl go, and I'll toss you the rocks!"

"Hey boys," said the umbrella man looking around, "do I look especially stupid today?"

"Oh no, boss," they said in unison while reluctantly chuckling.

"I didn't think so, but I thought I'd make sure. Did you hear that, Alphonso? The boys said I don't look stupid, but apparently you think I do. Is that what you think?"

Madora pinched Sheef's arm and whispered, "Sheef, control that tongue of yours. Don't say anything that'll make the situation worse."

Sheef bit his tongue. "No, absolutely not."

"I didn't think so. Now here's what we're gonna do. You toss me the bag, and once I'm satisfied with the merchandise, I'll release the beauty queen."

"Good one, boss," guffawed one of the gorilla-headed goons. "Beauty queen, I get it."

"Sheef," whispered Madora, "what do we do now?"

"We don't have a choice. We do what he says and hope the Unseen's with us," Sheef whispered back. "And feel free to have Akeila open that warp hole anytime now."

Harvey reached over his shoulder and touched his sword handle.

"Everybody ready," Sheef whispered under his breath. "Remember, as soon as I have the girl and give you the signal, dive through the tail."

Harvey and Madora nodded.

Sheef walked cautiously towards the goon gathering in order to cut the distance between the umbrella man and himself. Eight machine gun barrels were aimed directly at him. Harvey, Madora, and the two dogs followed. When Sheef was about twenty feet away from the umbrella man, he stopped.

"Okay," Sheef said, "here come the rocks. I hope you've got a good glove. Hate to see all this merchandise scattered on the ground."

"And I hope you got an accurate arm, Alphonso, or you might find yourself – "

Sheef cut him off. "Yeah, I got it. You'll Swiss-cheese me, right?"

The umbrella man's scar bulged.

"That mouth of yours, Alphonso, is gonna get you some serious pain one of these days. I hope your girlfriend here can tame it some- how. If not, she's gonna be layin' flowers on your grave real soon."

Sheef had a zinger of a reply locked and loaded in his mouth but decided to keep the safety on. He simply smiled instead.

The toss was perfect, a high arc over the space between the two groups, right into the umbrella man's outstretched hand. He untied the drawstring and poured some of the rock candy crystals into his hand. He stared at the candy, looked up at Sheef, and then back down at the candy again.

"They seem legit," said the umbrella man. "All right then, let the dame go."

When the thug released his grip on Myrtle Mae, she was momentarily confused, unsure of what she should do next. Sheef motioned for her to walk toward him as he tenderly spoke to her. "Come on, Myrtle Mae, you're safe now. Your brother Marlow sent us to get you."

She looked nervously to the umbrella man.

"Go on now and get. Skedaddle, you ugly dame, before I change my mind!"

Myrtle Mae took a step towards safety when her large feet turned against her, one of them tripping over the other. She stumbled to her right, falling into the umbrella man.

Myrtle Mae's stumble into the umbrella man capsized his hand. The rock candy he was holding spilled onto the floor. He growled and mumbled to himself as he bent down to pick up the spilled goods. A slight shuffling of his right shoe was all it took to trap one of the candy crystals underfoot, and with hardly any pressure applied, the piece of rock candy was reduced to powder.

The faint crushing sound and sensation was enough to unnerve the man. He slowly slid back his shoe and was mocked by a short powder streak across the floor.

Myrtle Mae was five feet away from Sheef's outstretched hand when the umbrella man erupted. In one rapid movement, he was back on his feet with pistol drawn.

"We've been duped, boys!" he roared. "Swiss-cheese 'em all!"

Sheef lunged forward, grabbing onto Myrtle Mae's hand as Harvey ran past him and swung like a door around the back of Myrtle Mae, shielding her with his body from the shower of incoming bullets. Harvey felt the impact of dozens of bullets slamming into the back of his Lignum shirt.

Sheef, who was still holding onto Myrtle Mae's wrist, flung her and her teenage shield behind him to where Akeila was waiting with warp tail curled and open.

"Now!" Sheef screamed.

Myrtle Mae, who had no idea what was happening, was forcefully pushed head first into the warp hole. Harvey dove through next.

Sheef's chest had already been hit multiple times, and if not for the Lignum shirt, he would've been dead. Nothing, however, was protecting him above the neckline.

The velocity of the moving bullets was impossible to see with the human eye, so either Madora made a lucky guess at exactly the right split second, or she was something else altogether.

One of the machine bullets was on a trajectory to Sheef's head. Even if he was somehow able to see the rapidly flying bullet, he didn't have the reaction time to move more than an inch.

Matching the speed of the approaching bullet, Madora's dagger streaked through the air on a collision course. The violent meeting of dagger and bullet, only six inches from Sheef's forehead, sent sparks flying in all directions, a few of which singed Sheef's eyebrows.

Having saved Sheef, Madora dove through. Sheef prepared to make his own exit when the machine gun fire suddenly stopped. He looked over to the group of gangsters and saw the umbrella man sprinting towards him like a raging grizzly bear. Both of his automatic pistols were drawn but silent. He was waiting until he was close enough before emptying the clips. A few steps more and a pleased smirk of vengeance appeared on his face. His index fingers applied pressure to both triggers.

Amidst the echoing reports of multiple gun shots, no one had heard the shattering of glass when a pack of Volkin Wolves broke through the windows, and so consumed was he with malice towards Sheef, the umbrella man never saw the coming attack.

Five wolves slammed into his side, their barreling inertia lifting him off his feet. Sheef was momentarily stunned by the sight. A woman's hand suddenly reached out from the space within Akeila's curved tail and grabbed him by the shirt. He was jarringly yanked in and away.

Fromp, who had waited until the last possible moment to be with and protect Akeila, followed next. After he was gone, Akeila rapidly spun in pursuit of her own warp hole. When she finally caught up with it, she jumped through and disappeared.

As the hole closed, Volkin Wolves were latching onto the legs and arms of the frantic gangsters, and stepping into the snarling chaos was Grauncrock, Nezraut's hand-picked Vapid Lord, charged to track and destroy.

31

They tumbled out of the warp hole onto a cushion of thick grass. Madora was still clutching Sheef's shirt. Harvey initially thought they had accidently been warped back to Ecclon, but a cursory view of the sky revealed this to be impossible. A yellow sun, rather than orb clouds, provided light and warmth.

The group was standing on one in a series of rolling, grassy hills, rising and dipping like swells in a green sea. They stretched down a narrow valley flanked by majestic mountains.

It took the group several minutes to find their breath and mental equilibrium. When they eventually did, Myrtle Mae was the first to speak.

"Who are you people, and what have you done to me?" she frantically asked, pacing back and forth on the hilltop and yanking her stringy hair. "Where's my brother. Where's Marlow? I want to go home!" she screamed.

Sheef was in the process of standing up to help the poor girl when Madora waved him back down with her hand.

"Let me handle this one," Madora said. She walked over to Myrtle Mae, softly placing her hand upon the frightened girl's back. Myrtle Mae swung around with fist raised ready to defend herself, but as she looked into the compassionate eyes of Madora, she collapsed into her open arms.

The flood gate was thrown wide. The fear and anguish of being kidnapped, held captive, and nearly killed by a hail of machine gun bullets, not to mention the whole warping to another world thing, found release in the heavy flow of tears.

After holding her for a bit, Madora gently released the frightened girl, and even though Harvey and Sheef couldn't hear what Madora was saying, they could tell by her facial expressions and gestures that they were words of comfort. Madora walked Myrtle Mae away from the group, consoling her with every step. Akeila and Fromp, of course, were not far behind.

Sheef looked over at Harvey examining his shirt.

"That was too close for comfort, Sheef. I must've been hit with a dozen or more bullets. If it wasn't for the shirt, I'd be dead."

"Yeah, me, too. But it wasn't just the shirt that saved me. I would've been shot on two separate occasions if not for the actions of Madora and a pack of Volkin Wolves."

"Volkin Wolves, at the warehouse?"

"Hot on your trail. We can only cheat death so much, Harvey. I know you don't want to hear it again."

"I know, Sheef, I'm trying to figure it out! I still don't know what to do though."

Harvey picked a blade of grass and tossed it into the air. He looked down the valley and remained silent for many minutes.

When he finally broke the silence, what he said had nothing to do with the warehouse or Volkin Wolves.

Pointing to where Madora and Myrtle Mae were walking, Harvey asked, "What do you think she's saying to her?"

"Don't know, but I bet it's exactly what Myrtle Mae needs to hear right now. I'll tell you one thing, there's a whole lot more to Madora than we realize."

Harvey studied Sheef's face for a moment and saw an opportunity to change, not only the topic, but also the tension in the air. "You like her, don't you?"

"What? Me? Like her? That's ridiculous. You must've hit your head during that last warp." Sheef's response was hardly convincing.

"No, my head's just fine, but I suspect that yours may not be."

"Listen, I'm only saying that there's more to her than meets the eye. I mean, she was somehow able to see and intercept a moving bullet with a dagger, which incidentally, is humanly impossible." Sheef then diverged from the point he was making to explain in more detail what occurred after Harvey warped from the warehouse.

"And then there's her age." Sheef continued. "She has to be thousands of years old to have had first-hand experience with the pharaohs, but looking at her . . . she's still . . ."

"Beautiful is the word I believe you're looking for," Harvey said, smiling with eyebrows raised.

"Well-preserved is actually what I was thinking."

"Well-preserved, huh? Come on, Sheef, be honest. You're going to start attracting your own Insips if you refuse to tell the truth."

Sheef's facial muscles were madly twitching. "Harvey, this conversation is over because there's nothing to it, and it's going nowhere."

"Okay, whatever you say," said Harvey laughing to himself.

"So, which world do you think Akeila dropped us into this time?" asked Sheef, clearly desiring to change the subject.

Harvey didn't resist the change. "Well, we're obviously not on the sea, and I assume were not anywhere near one. And since there appear to be no pirates around, my guess is that we're in the sci-fi one."

"You mean *The Kaleidoscope.*"

Harvey nodded. "By the way, what's a kaleidoscope anyway?"

"It's a cylinder that you look into. The inside is covered with mirrors which reflect bits of colored glass that move around when you rotate the cylinder."

"Oh yeah, I've played with one of those at school. My science teacher has one on his desk. I just never knew what it was called. So why name a movie after one?"

"Great question. I'll bet if we stay here long enough, we'll figure out the answer, but then again, after our experience in *The Phone Rang Twice* world, we may not want to. Let's walk around a bit and see if there's any sign of people nearby, a village or something."

Harvey and Sheef walked in separate directions, disappearing into the grassy troughs and then reemerging atop other hills as if they were riding upon ocean swells. They wandered for about a mile from where they started. Over an hour later, they rejoined one another, both reporting that they had seen no sign of any people.

Madora and Myrtle Mae had returned from their walk. Madora was sitting quietly, watching Myrtle Mae pick wild flowers amongst the tall grass.

"How's she doing?" asked Sheef as he and Harvey sat down next to Madora.

"Take a look at her face and decide for yourself."

"That's amazing," remarked Harvey. "She looks completely at peace, and there's something else."

"Yeah, I see it too, kid, but that can't be right."

"What?" asked Madora knowingly.

"Nothing," replied Sheef. "So why the sudden look of serenity on young Myrtle Mae?"

"I had a talk with her."

"I know that," said Sheef with a hint of annoyance, "but what did you tell her?"

"At first I simply told her that she was now safe, and that everything was going to be okay. Then I didn't say anything else for quite a while. I just walked with her in silence, waiting for her memories and experiences to dissipate."

"Dissipate?" asked Sheef.

"Yes dissipate. If a movie character like Myrtle Mae leaves the Phantasian world that she was written into, she is no longer bound by the script of that particular world. The words written about her, determining her personality, appearance, temperament, preferences, and so on, are severed once she exits the world, basically rendering her a blank slate."

"Then what or who determines all of those things when she lands in another world?" asked Sheef.

"The environment of the new world in which she finds herself, primarily its inhabitants. They, in essence, become her writers."

"So that means in this world, we're her writers?" asked Harvey.

"As unbelievable as it sounds, that's precisely what we are. It's a heavy responsibility, and why I cautioned about us getting mixed up in the plot of the movie. But we can't do anything about that now, and I believe we're off to a good start."

"How so?" asked Sheef.

"Both of you put your lives on the line in order to rescue her, and though it happened in the other world, it was in the forefront of her memory when she arrived here. Those acts of selfless, sacrificial kindness have already begun shaping her. All you have to do is look at her to see that everything about her is changing."

"Then it is true," said Sheef.

"What is?" asked Harvey.

What you and I both noticed. Her appearance has changed. It's already so different." They both looked at Myrtle Mae who was only twenty feet or so away. "Her hair's not stringy anymore, and her body, it's not rail-thin. Her face, it's radiant. She's actually attractive."

"Behold the power of love and kindness expressed in word and deed," said Madora smiling. "Such positive effects, but I'm confident, Sheef, that this is something you're already well acquainted with."

"What's that?"

"Really, Sheef, I'm surprised that you don't know," Madora said playfully. "You see, as amazing as women already are, they become even more so when they are respected, honored, and most importantly, cherished by others. Myrtle Mae's internal and external beauty will continue to flourish as long as she is treated in a loving and kind manner."

"Whoa," said Sheef, not knowing what else to say and feeling the weight of his words and actions. "So how long will this writing of her new self take?"

"To be honest, it's never finished, but she'll be especially malleable for the next week or so. Don't worry, though. You and Harvey just continue to be your kind and gracious selves," Madora said as she winked at Harvey. "Although, you, Sheef, might need to be even more attentive than Harvey."

"And why's that?" Sheef said, eyeing Madora suspiciously.

"Because she thinks you're her father."

"What? And just who put that bizarre and completely false notion in that head of hers?"

"Why me, of course, but it's really not false. You were the first one to think and speak of her with compassion. I overheard what you said to Harvey in the warehouse. And you were the first one to reach out to her. So you see, Sheef, if truth be told, you're her primary writer, which, in essence, means that you're her daddy."

"Great, as if helping Harvey save the universe wasn't stressful enough, now, on top of that, I'm suddenly a father of the world's most impressionable daughter! I don't know how to be a dad. What do I say to her?"

"Oh, I doubt that coming up with something to say will be difficult for you, Alphonso. You're quick on your feet. And by the way, her name's no longer Myrtle Mae. It's Gwen."

"You changed her name?" asked Harvey.

"Take a good look at her, boys, and tell me she still looks like a Myrtle Mae to you. I didn't think so either."

Carrying a collection of wildflowers in her hands, the emerging Gwen walked over and joined the group.

32

"**A**ren't they beautiful? The colors are so vibrant, and the aroma's simply heavenly," said Gwen, sitting down next to Sheef.

Akeila and Fromp trotted over to her, wagging their hind-quarters in greeting. They both sat down and were soon being scratched under chin and around ears.

"Oh, what lovely dogs, and so affectionate," Gwen said while giggling under the slobbering of Fromp's tongue. "Are these your dogs, Daddy?"

"Um . . . no, not exactly . . . daughter."

"Daughter? That sounds so formal." Gwen giggled with a puzzled expression and leaned into Sheef's side, wrapping her arms around one of his and snuggling closer.

"I guess it does sound a bit funny . . . Gwen."

She looked up at Sheef's face and said, "I do so adore my name. 'Gwen', to me it sounds like elegance. Don't you think so?"

"Uh . . . yes, of course. Definitely. Elegance . . . exactly, Gwen."

"Madora told me that we're all on a quest to find a treasure. Isn't that exciting?"

"It is, honey . . . very exciting, and . . . I'm glad you're here with us." With each word he spoke, Sheef felt more comfortable in his new role.

"Oh, thank you, Daddy," said Gwen as her skin lost its last imperfections, becoming creamily smooth. "That's such a sweet thing to say. I wouldn't want to be anywhere else in the world but here with you and my little brother Harvey."

"Brother?" asked Harvey, surprised and sitting up straight.

"Yes, son, apparently our good friend Madora didn't tell us everything that was said during her little walk with Gwen."

Gwen looked momentarily confused, but it quickly passed, replaced by bright eyes and giggles. "Harvey, you and Daddy are just playing with me again, aren't you?"

"Well . . . yeah . . . I mean, you know how we love to joke around."

"Welcome to the family, kid," Sheef whispered under his breath.

"Daddy, where are we?"

"In a place known as Kaleidoscope."

"Kaleidoscope. What a strange name for a place. But where are all the people? Are we the only ones in Kaleidoscope?"

Sheef, feeling uncomfortable answering questions he had no idea how to answer himself, and needing time to process everything that had occurred in the last five minutes, said, "Gwen, I bet Akeila and Fromp would enjoy a walk right about now. Would you mind taking them on a short one for me?"

"Really? Oh, I would love to. Thank you, and don't worry, I'll keep a close eye on them." Gwen stood up and then bent over to give Sheef a kiss on the cheek."

"You're welcome. Just don't go too far." Sheef's smile was genuine, as was the warmth he was feeling in his heart.

Once Gwen and the dogs were gone, Harvey said, "Wow, Sheef, I mean 'Dad', you're actually beginning to sound like a father."

"That will be enough out of you, son," said Sheef jokingly.

"Okay, okay, no need to ground me."

After a few minutes of silence, the expression on Harvey's face turned serious.

"What is it? What's eating at you?" asked Sheef.

"I don't know. I guess I feel guilty lying to her. Truth is supposed to be our greatest weapon against the enemy, and here we are spinning lies."

"I understand what you're feeling," said Madora, "but what we're doing is not at all the same thing as lying. We're no more lying than writers of fiction. We're creating something completely new from the words of our imaginations and the actions of our hearts. Like it or not, we're now her family, and becoming her brother is more than appropriate; it's a perfect fit."

"I hadn't thought about it like that," said Harvey.

"The Phantasian's a very strange place. When you're here, you can't approach things as you would on Earth."

"You can say that again."

Changing the subject, Sheef asked, "Madora, why do you think Akeila dropped us here, away from any of the movie's characters?"

"Because this was the only image of the movie I could find. It was on a promotional poster for the film. When I searched online, this image kept coming up."

"Then it's possible that we could be hundreds of miles from any other people, including Millud?"

"Could be, but I suspect that if the image was significant enough to put on the posters, then it must be important to the storyline. We might have to wait here for the main characters to arrive."

"I suppose," said Sheef. "I've got plenty of Kreen to take care of our physical needs, but I don't know how I feel about just sitting around and waiting for people who may never arrive."

"Do you have a better plan at the moment?"

"No, other than taking a bite of Kreen and lying down for a nap, I've got nothing."

"Well, in that case, why don't I leave you and Harvey to rest. I think I'm going to join Gwen and do a little character shaping."

"Madora, before you leave, would you explain to me what you did back at the warehouse?"

"Why, Sheef, whatever are you referring to?"

"You know exactly what I'm referring to. Deflecting a bullet that was destined for my head with a dagger?"

"Lucky toss."

"Please, luck had nothing to do with it."

"Then I'm sorry. That's the only explanation you'll get right now. But don't you think you owe me something?"

"Something?"

"A simple thank you for saving your life?"

"I'm sorry, Madora. Yes, thank you very much for saving my life, though I would still like to know how you did it."

"All things in due time, Sheef." As she said this, she tucked the hair on the left side of her head behind her ear. Up until this point, her thick, flowing locks had covered much of her ears, especially the backs. But with the tuck, the back of her ear was exposed, revealing two triangles of skin, each about a half inch in length.

Madora shook her hair, concealing the ear once again, and walked off to where Gwen was walking the dogs. Sheef was certain that she had done this on purpose, deepening the mystery and his frustration.

"Harvey, did you see that?"

"See what?"

"Madora's ear. It's different."

"Really? How so?"

"The back of it was . . . I don't know. Never mind," said Sheef shaking his head. "Probably just scar tissue from a battle wound or something."

"Harvey! Sheef!" screamed Madora while sprinting back to them. "Look! There, behind you!"

Harvey and Sheef turned around, and what they saw almost defied explanation. A circle, close to one hundred feet in height, was slowly rotating inches off the ground. Inside the moving shape were images of blue sky, grass, distant mountains, and birch trees. The problem was that all of these images had been broken into small fragments and were moving around each other, forming abstract unnatural configurations: a section of birch tree was moving above a triangular-shaped piece of blue sky, which was about to collide with a square of grass.

It was as if someone had painted the scenery on an enormous piece of thick glass, shattered it with a giant sledge hammer, and then picked up the glass shards and placed them inside a huge rotating glass drum.

Even though the shape was more than a mile away, the sound of the fragments jostling against each other could clearly be heard from where they were standing.

"Sheef," said Harvey, "Is that what I think it is?"

"It would explain the name of this place."

"What would?" asked Madora, panting from her sprint.

"A kaleidoscope. Take a good look at that," said Sheef as he pointed toward the object, "and tell me it doesn't remind you of one."

Madora studied the rotating images for a moment. "You're right, looks like the bottom of one, where all the broken pieces are. But where did it come from? I know it wasn't there before. Did it just appear out of thin air?"

"Seems to be the case. Did you hear anything before you saw it?" asked Sheef.

"Nothing at all."

"Not good. It means that one of those things could appear spontaneously with absolutely no warning."

"Imagine what would happen if you were caught inside one of those things," said Harvey.

"I'd rather not," replied Sheef.

"Your entire body would be shattered into pieces and rearranged."

"Thank you – that's exactly what I didn't want to imagine."

Another one of the shapes suddenly appeared to their right.

"Uh, guys," said Madora nervously, "that one's only about forty feet away."

"Harvey," said Sheef urgently, "we've got to get everyone out of here, now!"

"But what if this is the world that will take us back?"

"It might be, but if we stay here much longer, we'll end up as mosaics." Sheef looked over to Madora. "The sooner the better."

"I hope Akeila's had enough time to recover."

"If she hasn't, there may be no place for us to hide."

Madora knelt down in front of Akeila and thought her images from *The Barnacle Buccaneers.* Although Akeila wasn't fully recuperated, she was still able to open the warp hole; it just took her twice as long to do so.

Gwen, who had been standing on the periphery of the group, quickly walked to the others after Sheef urgently waved her over.

"Gwen," said Madora, "it's time for the quest to continue. You'll have to take the same ride as you did before. All you have to do is put your hands out in front of you and duck your head, like you're about to dive into pool. As soon as your fingertips touch the space within Akeila's curved tail, you'll be transported to our next stop."

Gwen clapped her hands together and did a little jump. "Oh, the quest is continuing. What fun! Where are we going next?"

"Telling you now would take away some of the fun," Sheef said anxiously, shifting his gaze between her and the approaching shape.

"You're right," she said, jumping for a second time. "Keep it a surprise!"

But as she positioned herself to make the dive, she realized that she'd left her wild flowers on the grass when she set them down to walk the dogs.

"Wait! My flowers. I don't want to leave without them."

"Gwen," said Madora, doing her best to maintain a calm and kind tone, "we really need to be going. We don't have much time."

"But they're right over there. It will only take a minute."

"Let me get them for you," Madora said while gently touching Gwen's arm. "You just stay here."

"Oh thank you, Madora," she replied, oblivious to the impending danger.

Madora ran the twenty feet or so to where the flowers were lying on the grass. But the very moment she reached out to pick up the flowers, a rotating circle suddenly appeared in front of her, trapping her extended right forearm.

Harvey had never heard a scream like the one Madora let out, which was soon drowned out by the noisy chaos of fragments being tossed about. Sheef sprinted to her as fast as his feet would carry him. When he arrived, Madora had already pulled her arm out of the circle and was lying back on the grass, wailing in pain.

Sheef knelt down without any idea of how to render aid or comfort. What was once Madora's forearm had been replaced a by a glob of randomly arranged three dimensional pieces of arm, sky, grass, clouds, and leaves, which were all moving about one another.

"SHEEF!" Madora yelled.

"I'm here, but I don't . . ." said Sheef breathlessly.

"SHUT UP AND LISTEN! You need to do exactly what I say."

"Okay, anything, just tell me what to do."

"Help me up." The words were difficult for Madora to get out. She had to pause every few words to allow a grimace of pain to pass. "Then I need you to . . . take your sword and cut it off."

"WHAT?" No, I can't do that. It's your arm!"

"DO IT, SHEEF! It's spreading. I can feel it. Before it's too late."

Sheef scooped up Madora and hurriedly carried her back to the others. Madora was still moaning in pain when he set her down on the ground. Panic and concern for Madora had tensed the features of Akeila's face. She whined pitifully and took a step towards Madora, who gave her a curt command to stay. The faithful Sadiki let out another heart-wrenching whine but obeyed.

"Harvey, you and Gwen, go now!" yelled Sheef.

"But what about Madora?"

"She'll be alright, but I need you to get Gwen safely out of here, and make sure Fromp goes with you!"

"All right," Harvey said. He motioned for Gwen to place her hands in front of her and to assume a diving position. Within seconds after her fingertips touched the warp hole, she, Harvey, and Fromp were gone.

"I hope the blade's as razor-sharp as Thurngood said it was," Sheef thought to himself as he unsheathed his sword from the scabbard attached to his backpack.

"Madora, I need you to lie flat on your back and extend your arm as straight as you can."

Though the intense pain was contorting her facial muscles, she was still able to manage a nod. Sheef could see that the disarrangement had already spread above her elbow.

"I'll have to take it off in the middle of your upper arm."

"FINE! JUST GET IT OVER WITH!"

Doing his best to suppress his revulsion, and at the same moment to muster the courage for what he was about to do, Sheef drew a deep breath before swinging with all his might. Fortunately, for both parties, the blade was as Thurngood described it.

Tears were streaming down Sheef's cheeks as he knelt down beside Madora. He was in the process of taking off his shirt to use as a tourniquet for what remained of her arm when Madora screamed again.

"NO TIME! JUST GET ME IN THE WARP HOLE!"

As Sheef picked up her quivering body, he recalled Harvey's words and realized just how accurate they had been. At some point, he would have to face the truth. And with that thought, he jumped out of the kaleidoscope and into the sea.

33

Harvey and Gwen hit the slippery wooden boards stomach first, sliding fifteen feet before slamming into a large mast. Fromp came next, on his side and spinning across the deck towards the others. Madora and Sheef landed in a tangled mess and slid into Harvey, Gwen, and Fromp, who had not even begun to get their bearings. Finally, it was Akeila's turn. She touched down gracefully, lightly kissing the deck and then gliding on her nails to a safe, impact-free stop.

Sheef went immediately to Madora who was still on her stomach but trying to push herself up.

"Madora, don't try getting up. Let me help you."

"Thank you for the offer, Sheef, but I'm perfectly capable. It's not like I have only one arm," she said calmly.

"Madora . . . but how? I cut your arm off. You were screaming in a pain, and I was trying to . . ."

"I know you were. You were trying to help. Sheef, thank you for not fighting with me and doing what I know must have violated every part of your good nature. You saved my arm and my life."

"How? I cut it off, and the thing that I cut off no longer resembled a human arm, but now it looks perfectly normal. I don't even see a scratch."

"Amazing isn't it," said Madora as she examined her lower arm and hand. "Just like new."

"But how?"

"Remember where we are, Sheef. In the Phantasian, you play by a completely different set of rules. One of them is that if you receive a nonfatal wound in one of its worlds and warp off that world soon after, the wound doesn't convey."

"Doesn't convey? I don't follow."

"It doesn't go with you, provided, as I said, that you leave quickly enough before the wound has time to set: before it becomes a permanent part of that world's reality."

"But how's that possible? Once you've been wounded, how can it be reversed?"

"It's not possible for the characters written into the Phantasian worlds, but it is for us. If Gwen, for example, had lost her arm, she would presently be bleeding all over the place, but for visitors like us, there's a lag time or delay between a physical change, such as a wound, and it becoming a permanent, immutable fixture."

"How long?"

"About three minutes."

"But that means . . ."

"You got me out with only a razor-thin margin to spare. In fact, if you had been a tad more hardheaded, you'd be tying on that tourniquet right about now, or worse, still back there."

"And you'd be?"

"If I was still back there, dead, without a doubt. A few seconds more and my major organs would have all been kaleidoscoped."

"Madora, I'm just really glad that you're . . . well, you know."

"Alive and in one piece? Me, too," she said, looking relieved. After taking a deep breath she continued, "Now, why don't we try to figure out where in *The Barnacle Buccaneers* Akeila has dropped us."

"But, Madora, what happened back there? What's Sheef talking about and what was cut?"

"Later, Harvey. I have a sneaking suspicion that our time would be better spent preparing."

"Preparing for what?"

"The crew," replied Madora. "We're obviously on a moving vessel at sea, and unless this is a ghost ship, it won't be long before we're welcomed aboard, and judging by the name of the movie and the flag on top of that mast, the greeting is unlikely to be one of Alohas and flowered leis.

Harvey's eyes followed the imaginary directional line created by Madora's pointing finger, all the way to where it stopped, at the dead center of a Jolly Roger flag.

"The skull and crossbones," mumbled Harvey. "Pirates."

"I'm glad we landed here at night," commented Sheef. "Even though *The Barnacle Buccaneers* is a comical pirate movie, we're still dealing with pirates.

"I agree," said Madora, "but the night watch and a handful of the crew should be up and about. I can't imagine that no one heard or saw us warp in. Sheef, why don't you take Fromp and I'll take Akeila, and we'll have a very quiet look around. Harvey, you and Gwen stay here at the mast."

The two reconnaissance teams began silently moving about the deck. An angry sea was unleashing on the hull, sending waves of frigid water over the gunnels or railings of the ship. The rolling of the boat and the wet deck made stable walking nearly impossible. Both Madora and Sheef slipped a half dozen times. Fromp, too, experienced his share of falls. The only one who seemed completely at ease, as if she was trotting about a bone-dry and level deck, was Akeila.

After looking over the gunnels and venturing only a few feet forward and aft, they returned to the mast and sat down.

"Looks like a brigantine," said Madora. "The double-mast brig was a favorite of pirates. Quick in getting into and away from trouble, good cargo space, and it can handle rough seas. I would say this one is at least eighty feet long, probably ten cannons on each side. Crew size is hard to tell, but there could be as many as a hundred, but I doubt that, pirate crews tend to be smaller. But then again, this pirate ship was created by a screen writer, so no telling."

"You really know your pirate history," said Sheef.

"When you've been around as long as I have, you really can't avoid learning a few things here and there. And, Sheef, don't even go there."

"Go where?" asked Sheef innocently.

"Good boy."

"This is so exciting!" squealed Gwen, much too loudly for everyone's comfort. "I've never been on a boat before! So, is the treasure we're searching for on our quest an actual real treasure with a map and an island?"

"Actually, Gwen," whispered Sheef, hoping that his drop in volume would inspire her to do likewise, "we don't believe that the treasure we seek is in this world, but we think that there might be a very important clue here that will help us find it."

"Oh, how wonderful! A clue! Then it's like a game."

"Sort of, but, Gwen, we need to keep our voices down. There might be people onboard the boat who don't like the game and could stop us from playing it altogether."

Gwen nodded and put her finger over her lips.

The chilly air and the continual dousing of sea water made the arrival of a sneeze inevitable. It arrived at Harvey's nasal passageways first, and snuck upon him so surreptitiously and quickly that he had no time to repress it or muffle its sound. Sheef later on said that it was, without a doubt, the loudest sneeze that he had ever heard. In the aftermath of the nasal explosion, all four of them looked at one another in stunned silence. Madora pointed to the back of the ship and whispered, "I hear voices."

"I'm tellin' ye, I heard me some voices," said a gravelly voice.

"You heard nothing but yer own drunkin' imagination," said a deeper, sluggish voice. "It's just the drink speakin' agin. Them voices in that head of yers, they be rummy voices."

"I'll have ye know, I've had not even a drop tonight, besides, since when did rum ever sneeze?"

"That don't make no sense. Not a drop, eh?"

"Look, Pauddles, I'm tellin' ye, ye lily-livered swine, there be voices and sneezin' at the forward mast, and all I'm askin' is that ye take a look with me. If ain't nothing there, me rum ration's yers on the morrow."

"All right then, Grimely, let's take a look then, shall we."

The tall lanky pirate, known as Grimely, drew a rusty sword from its scabbard, and then said to his very rotund partner, Pauddles, "Well?"

"Well what?"

"Are you plannin' on armin' yerself, or are ye just gonna use that fat belly of yers as a weapon."

"I thought we agreed on no more comments about me belly," said Pauddles as he drew his own sword. "Ye know I be sensitive about me weight. Runs in me family. We all big boned, especially me ma, can't be helped."

"Me apologies, Pauddles, but jist be ready."

"I'm ready, Grimely. No sneezin' bilge rat gonna get the jump on me," said Pauddles as his prodigious belly jiggled in time with his laughter.

Grimely momentarily pointed his sword at Pauddles and glared.

"Sheef," whispered Madora, "you and Harvey stay here. I'm going up. Madora briefly stared at Akeila and then scurried like a spider up the mast, with the blade of her dagger in her mouth.

"Sheef, what's she doing?" whispered Harvey.

"I'm not sure," Sheef whispered back, "but I think she might be taking advantage of the distraction."

"What distraction?"

"Us."

"Well now, Pauddles," said Grimely as he peered around the large mast, "what do we have here? To these seasoned eyes of mine, it looks like flesh and blood. Only rummy voices, eh? If ye wasn't stuffin' yer face with that hardtack ye stole, ye might have heard it as well."

"All right, Grimely, yer right, no need to rub salt in the wound," said Pauddles as he appeared on the opposite side of the mast.

The tips of both of their swords were pointed at the chests of Harvey and Sheef. Gwen was still seated, watching the unfolding events with the wonder and excitement of a five year old listening to an adventurous bedtime story.

"Looks here like we got us a sweet little family out on Sunday sail in their yacht," chuckled Grimely to himself.

"Sunday yacht, that's a good one, Grimely," said Pauddles.

"The only problem, it ain't Sunday, least me don't think so. Pauddles, what day it be?"

"How is I 'posed to know? Does I look like a calendar to ye?"

"Yer gonna be lookin' like a pin cushion ifin ye don't watch that mouth. Wells, whatever day it be, ye picked the wrong one to be on this ship here. And say, how'd ye get on the *Barnacle* to begin with?"

"Why through the tail of a Sadiki. However else," said a voice from above.

"Tail of a weweki. What's that, Grimely?" asked Pauddles.

"I don't know. Wasn't me who said nothin'."

"Well if not ye, than who?"

"The one who you're inquiring after is none other than myself."

Grimely and Pauddles looked up the mast, following the sound of the voice. Twenty feet above their heads, standing very casually on the ship's rigging, was the most beautiful woman Grimely and Pauddles had ever seen. Smiling broadly, Madora waved at them.

"Grimely," said Pauddles, "look, an enchanted woman of the sea. Must've been tossed by a wave and washed into the riggin'. She's a beaut ain't she? Been a hopin' to see me one for many a year. Heard the legends I did, but now, right before me very eyes. Strange, though, I don't see me no tail."

"Pauddles, you idiot, that's no mermaid. There's not a shell nor string of seaweed anywhere upon her body."

"All right then, Grimely, if she ain't a mermaid, then what?"

"Mine," said Grimely, smiling wickedly. "All mine."

"A pirate through and through," said Madora. "Always so possessive, a character flaw, by the way, which is destined to result in your personal pain."

"That so?" Grimely then turned to Pauddles. "She's got a sour mouth on her, Pauddles, which I aim to sweetin' straightaways."

"Do you now?" asked Madora.

"I do, and it will go much better on ye if ye come on down that mast before I haves to climb up and snatch ye meself."

"And how, may I ask, do you plan on managing such a climb and snatch while seeing double and with a splitting headache?"

"Grimely, how do she know you got a headache? Ye been belly achin' 'bout one all day. You sure she's not enchanted?" asked Pauddles.

"She be talkin' the jibberjabber. I'm seeing just fine, ye hear. Don't listen to her words. She's not right in the head."

"Actually, that would be you," said Madora as she dropped a sizeable iron pulley which she had cut from the rigging.

Still looking up at Madora, Grimely watched as the pulley made its descent toward his head, but because it was dropping so rapidly, his only reaction was to open his mouth wide. It's likely that a colorful pirate phrase might have been spoken if Grimely had a second or two more, but he didn't, and so the only sound that was heard was the dull thud of metal colliding with thick bone.

Grabbing his forehead with both hands, Grimely collapsed on the deck, howling in pain. Pauddles knelt down beside him, trying to render aid to his injured mate, which is precisely why he never saw Madora swinging by rope directly at his chest. The impact knocked Pauddles off his feet and into the side of the brig, where he slid down to the deck, stupefied and breathless.

"Are you kidding me? Seriously?" asked an astonished Sheef while looking wide-eyed at Madora.

"No time for gawking," said Madora. "You and Harvey secure our two friends before the others arrive. All this commotion has likely woken the entire crew."

"And that it has, me lassy," said a voice from the shadows.

34

Harvey and Sheef immediately drew their swords. The response from the shadows was the unsheathing of dozens of metal blades. From the dark briny mist, stepped forth a motley crew of sweat, scars, and rotting teeth.

Harvey and Sheef touched back to back, slowly rotating with their swords pointed outward as the pirate crew circled about them. The sound of wood tapping upon wood was heard. Two of the pirates stepped aside. An opening in the circle appeared, through which stepped a one-legged, one-armed, one-eyed pirate with a large, variegated parrot upon his shoulder.

"There you have it," mumbled Sheef to Harvey, "every pirate cliché rolled into one. A 'B' movie indeed."

"Well, it appears, lads," bellowed the one-eyed pirate, "that we have ourselves some stowaways who snuck topside for a bit of fresh air during the night watch."

"And one of them stowaways, Captain Smullet, is rum to me eye," said a hefty pirate with a piece of chain link dragging from his left ankle. The pirate took two steps in the direction of Gwen.

Harvey's move from where he was standing to the space between Gwen and the pirate occurred so rapidly that the pirate didn't have time to even set his hand to his sword grip.

"That there, laddie," said Link, the pirate with the chain, "is a fool of a move. Steppin' in the way of me and me treasure is a sure way to be feelin' the blade. I'll warn ye only once before I teach ye a lesson."

The quickness of Harvey's sword play was a whirling blur, and when it was over, Link's scabbard and sword had been loosed from his body and were securely in Harvey's left hand. Blood was dripping down from a fresh cut on the pirate's right cheek, the pain of which Link was only beginning to feel.

"Take one more step towards my sister and I'll do more than just shave that cheek of yours," said Harvey while slowing waving his sword.

"Now, now, laddie, there's no need for that," said Captian Smullet. "Why don't ye batten down the hatches on that blade of yers and haul in your jib sail."

Captain Smullet's words didn't alter Harvey's offensive stance. There was something about the captain's tone that made him uneasy. Harvey had good reason to be suspicious, for just after the captain finished speaking, he winked at the pirate immediately to his right.

Four rough-cut scalawags rushed Harvey from behind. The swords of the first two attackers made contact with Harvey's back, but their impact with the Lignum shirt snapped their blades like twigs.

Harvey ducked to avoid the second pair of attackers, and then sent them tumbling with a quick leg sweep.

"What sorcery this be?" asked one of the attackers looking down at his broken sword.

Harvey turned around and took a threatening step toward the pirate. Reaching out his hand with fingers spread wide, he said, "Stand back now, unless you really want to know the answer to that question."

The pirate dropped the broken weapon and cowered back to the safety of the other scalawags. His three fellow attackers followed suit, leaving Harvey standing alone before Gwen. Sheef and Madora, who still had sword and dagger drawn, slowly walked over and joined Harvey.

"Impressive sword play, I must say. Ye disarmed and humiliated four of me finest. Nimbleness with hand and blade, though, is still no match for a bullet."

Captain Smullet lifted up a long flintlock pistol, aiming the barrel directly at Harvey's head. A smile of missing and rotten teeth, framed by tobacco-stained gums, appeared on the captain's face as he set his finger to the trigger.

The flash of light was so intense that everyone was momentarily blinded. Harvey and Sheef both fell back on the deck. Madora, who was standing closest to the mast, was able to use it as a brace to keep from falling.

Harvey felt all over his body, frantically searching for a bullet wound. When he could find nothing, he assumed that the bullet had struck the Lignum shirt, but he hadn't felt any pressure as he did when the shirt was strafed with machine gun bullets.

The pirate crew stumbled about on the deck, impatiently waiting for the echo of blinding light to fade. When they were finally able to see again, they were astonished to see their captain flat on his back, with an enormous indigo dog sitting atop him and growling.

The captain was gasping for air under the ponderous weight of Fromp. He turned his head to the left in an attempt to protect his face from the snarling, teeth-bared snout of Akeila, which was only inches from his right ear.

"Those two make quite a great team," Sheef said to Madora, "but how exactly did they managae that?"

"Before I climbed the mast," said Madora, "I sent a thought to Akeila, telling her and Fromp to wait at the bow of the ship until there was trouble. I didn't suggest opening a warp hole and blinding everyone in the process. That must've been Fromp's idea."

"Like I said, they make a great team."

"Me apologies, mates," choked out the captain. "Had no idea that we was engagin' worthy fighters. Call off your hounds, and I promise no more trickery."

"And what's the worth of a pirate's word?" asked Sheef.

"You've got a point there, mate, but the promise of Captain Smullet be a safe harbor to moor yer sloop in."

Sheef and Madora called Fromp and Akeila off. The two animals walked backwards to where they were standing, keeping their eyes and growls on the captain the entire way. When Fromp sat down next to them, Sheef noticed that something colorful was sticking out of the warp-hound's mouth.

"Feathers. So much for the cliché parrot," Sheef thought to himself.

The captain slowly stood, adjusting his belt and scabbard. "That's quite a hound ye got there. Never saw it coming. Struck me like lightnin' it did. Took me by complete surprise, which no pirate, landlubber, or critter's ever done."

Captain Smullet's eyes narrowed suspiciously. "Just who are ye anyway?"

Taking inspiration from Sheef's performance as "Alphonso", Harvey said, "I'm the leader of this small crew, and I'm known as 'The Kid'."

"Ain't never heard of any 'Kid'," replied the captain with a sneer, "and I know every scalawag on these seas."

"Then listen up you marauding cyclops because I'm only going to say it once. Only a select few know me. Those who cross my path typically don't live long enough to tell anyone about their encounter."

"Not bad, not bad at all," Sheef whispered to Madora. "Pretty convincing. Marauding cyclops, nice touch. Very creative."

"Don't live long enough? Is that so, laddie?" asked the captain still sneering.

At that moment Madora decided to make her own contribution to Harvey's performance by throwing her dagger across the deck and into the captain's wooden peg leg. The dagger struck with a dull thud, vibrating quickly into inertness.

"It is," replied Harvey with a self-confident smirk.

Captain Smullet stared at Madora, malice briefly burning in his eyes before being chased away by a good-natured belly laugh.

"Beauty and skill. I could use a lass like ye," the captain said as he yanked out the dagger and tossed it back to Madora.

Catching it by the handle in midair, Madora replied, "Tempting offer, but I'll have to pass. I fight with The Kid and him only."

"Ah yes, 'The Kid' once again," said the captain as his words suddenly edged with anger. "If ye don't mind, Captain Kid, would ye please explain why ye and yer crew be trespassin' on me ship!"

Harvey was in the process of formulating a clever response when he heard the loud flapping of fabric above his head. The fore and aft sails of the main mast came crashing down, trapping The Kid and his crew, including Fromp and Akeila, underneath.

It was all but impossible to move under the heavy canvas sails. Harvey's sword was knocked free from his hand, and as he frantically searched for it, he accidentally collided heads with Sheef. The collision was so hard that the hollow thudding sound of two skulls meeting could be heard the entire length of the ship.

Harvey and Sheef crumbled to the deck, each cradling their heads in their hands. Meanwhile, Madora was quickly pushing aside the canvas cloth as if swimming through viscous fluid. She was trying to locate the edge of the sail. When she finally did and poked her head out, she was greeted by the sharp tip of Captain Smullet's blade.

Disoriented, winded, and surprised, Madora was unable to mount much of a fight. She slowly rose to her feet under the gleam of dozens of pirate swords and joined Gwen who had already been captured by the crew.

"Well now, me laddie," Captain Smullet shouted out to Harvey. "It appears that the winds have come about and changed directions. Ye see, I have the lovely lasses with me, and I would hate for ye to force me hand in marring their beautiful faces, but force me ye will if ye don't surrender yerselves straightaway."

Harvey, who was still caressing his forehead, whispered, "Sheef, what do we do?"

"We're pinned down, and they've got the girls. The deck's stacked against us. We don't have much of a choice."

Harvey and Sheef crawled out from under the sail where they were dragged to their feet and immediately bound with ropes. And there, standing before them and next to Captain Smullet, was the key to accessing the past. This time, however, he wasn't playing the part of a pharmacist, but rather, something much closer to his true nature.

35

Harvey, Sheef, and Madora were tied to the large wooden mast. Gwen was standing next to the captain, unbound and bewildered. Fromp and Akeila were chained to the deck and unconscious.

The capture of the dogs occurred while they were still under the heavy canvas sail. The warp-hound and the Sadiki were viciously snapping at the canvas, attempting to tear their way out. Since the crew hadn't the slightest inclination of getting anywhere near the snapping jaws, one of the pirates suggested "rumming' the animals down a bit.

Shortly thereafter, three members of the crew cleaned two fish and stuffed their insides with rum-saturated hardtack. It was common for seafaring men to soften their rock-hard biscuits with water or rum to make them edible, but no one had ever heard of placing four pounds of crushed hardtack in a bucket and dosing it with two large bottles of high-octane rum. A little stirring with a large wooden spoon, and soon there was ample stuffing to fill a dozen fish.

To ensure that the fish would be irresistible to the dogs, they were dipped in a barrel of pork discards. When the fish were pulled out, they were coated with pork grease, repulsive to humans, but irresistible to all canines, of this world and beyond.

The entire operation took less than two minutes. Fromp and Akeila were still trying to gnaw their way through the sail when the edge was lifted up and the loaded fish were tossed under.

After the first whiff, Fromp and Akeila should have bolted in the opposite direction, placing as much distance and fabric possible between their noses and the pungent fish. Fromp knew better. He understood that there would likely be negative consequences if he partook of such a tempting delicacy offered by disreputable men, and the truth is, he never intended to take an actual bite. He wanted just one more sniff before he fled.

As pungently powerful as the first whiff was, the second was even more so. Fromp's salivary glands, and then his mouth, were thrown wide. Soon the entire fish was gone, and with no peer support to help her fight the temptation, Akeila jettisoned acquired wisdom and succumbed to primal instinct.

Within minutes, the rummy stuffing began to do its work, rendering both animals too dizzy and bewildered to even walk, much less mount any type of resistance

Tightly bound to the mast, Harvey leaned over to Sheef who was next to him and whispered, "It's him, isn't it? Standing next to the captain."

"It's definitely Millud. It took me a second to recognize him with a beard and pirate garb on. I overheard one of the pirates refer to him as 'Splinter'."

"Sheef, this has to be the right world. I don't know what I was thinking before. It makes total sense now. We should've come here first. If a warp hole opens up between the Phantasian to real life when an actor's role and his actual personality are indistinguishable, then this has to be it."

Sheef nodded.

"From what we learned about Millud, we already know that he was a thief, a liar, and willing to do anything, even hurt others, to satisfy his selfish ambitions, which is an excellent description of a pirate."

"You nailed it, kid. If he was ever to open a door, it would definitely be from here."

"Splinter," the captain said, "two extra rations of rum for ye this evenin' for quick thinkin' and bringin' the sails down on the heads of the trespassers."

In an oily tone, Splinter replied, "Rum, though I do covet it so, is no needed payment for me, Captain Smullet. The pleasure and satisfaction of bein' able to serve ye, the greatest buccaneer to sail upon these seven seas, is payment enough for me."

"Aye, much obliged there, Splinter," said the captain, hoping that the statement would put a period to Splinter's annoying flattery. Unfortunately for the captain's ears, Splinter continued.

"Even a chest overflowin' with gold from a Spanish Galleon would be dull to me eye, compared to the value of serving under such a fine commander as ye, captain, and – "

"That's quite enough for now, Splinter," said the captain while raising his hand.

"It's hard to believe," said Sheef to Harvey. "It's as though the screenwriter wrote the role of a sniveling, groveling toady for none other than Millud. Perfect casting choice. Apart from the pirate lingo and accent, he really wasn't acting in the movie. He was being his own disreputable, traitorous self."

"True, but where's the warp hole linking this world to 1930's Hollywood?"

"That's the question of the day. We'll have to keep our eyes peeled and be ready, but before we do anything else, we need to figure out a way to get these ropes off while not getting killed in the process."

Sheef didn't realize that he was no longer whispering and that the captain and his entire crew had gone silent and were listening intently to everything he had just shared with Harvey.

"So, ye be desirin' to get free of them ropes do ye?" asked Captain Smullet. "Well, boys, do you think that the *Creaker* might be able to help the mate out with his desire?"

The pirates looked at each other with puzzled expressions until the light bulb of one of them flickered a bit.

"I think the captain's tallkin' 'bout the longboat."

"Oh," said the rest of the crew nodding, not because they had the slightest ideas as to what the captain had in mind, but because they all recognized the name of the rotted and less-than-seaworthy rowboat, appropriately named *"Creaker"*.

"Captain Smullet, what do ye have in mind for them and the *Creaker*," asked Grimely, who was now displaying a large lump in the middle of his forehead from the pulley incident.

"I aim to put 'em out to sea in it."

"But the *Creaker's* not seaworthy. It leaks somethin' awful," said a puzzled Pauddles.

"Aye, it certainly does that, Mr. Pauddles," chuckled the captain. "The rot in her timber welcomes the seawater to enter. The way I figure it, with the weight of these trespassers and their mutts, they'll have no more than a third of me hourglass before they're swallowed by the waters. We'll attach a rope to *Creaker*, though, and pull everyone back to safety here on the *Barnacle* if someone loosens their lips and tells me why they be on me ship and what they be after."

"Captain, I'm confident that ye already thought of this, considerin' the sizeable intellect of yours," said Splinter, "but might I suggest that ye put 'em to sleep before untyin' them ropes. They be a shifty lot and not to be trusted."

"Of course me thought of it," he said unconvincingly, "but much obliged that ye reminded me."

"Hey, kid, what do you think Splinter means by putting us to sleep?" asked Sheef.

"Don't know, but I'm really beginning to not like this guy."

Sheef's question was soon answered by the hard application of a small wooden club to the back of their heads. Sleep, apparently, was synonymous with unconsciousness. There was no need to do anything else to Fromp and Akeila who were still immobilized from the spiked stuffing.

Harvey was the first to regain consciousness. He awoke to the blistering heat of a tropical sun, flaring itself on his nose and cheeks. The side-to-side rocking motion of the longboat already had him nauseated.

The leaking nature of the boat wasn't an exaggeration. Already, three inches of tepid seawater covered the bottom. If the seas hadn't died down considerably since the previous evening, the boat would've been swamped and sunk soon after entering the water.

The *Barnacle* was about one hundred feet in front of the *Creaker's* bow. A long, weather-worn rope tethered ship and boat together. Along the back railing of the brig, stood the entire crew, gawking at the morning's entertainment.

Harvey, who was seated in the stern of the boat, sloshed his way forward, stumbling twice as he roused Sheef and Madora. They both awoke groaning, rubbing the backs of their heads.

"Ohhhh . . . I'm sorry I asked what Splinter meant by putting us to sleep," moaned Sheef. "I never dreamed fiction could be so painful."

"Where's Gwen?" asked Madora.

"Was kept on the ship. Look for yourself," said Harvey pointing to the *Barnacle*. In the middle of the crew, gathered at the back railing, was the captain, and immediately to his left was Gwen, waving to everyone in the longboat.

"She looks okay, anyway. I think she believes this is all still a game," said Sheef. "That should keep her spirits up and safe for the time being."

Captain Smullet placed a bullhorn to his mouth and yelled out, "I hope ye had a restful slumber, mates." The pirate chuckles were loud enough to make it across the expanse of water to the longboat. "I'm bettin' that the *Creaker 's* already gettin' good and soggy. Are any of ye soggy enough to start tellin' me who ye really are and what ye be about? I give ye me word that ye will be pulled to safety when there's a loosenin' of lips."

"What should we tell him?" asked Madora.

"He'll never believe the truth. I hardly believe it myself," said Harvey.

"Should we make something up then?"

"We could," replied Sheef, "but it's not likely to change our situation. They're pirates, and as such, they're not to be trusted, ever. You can rest assured, once they get what they want, that promise won't be worth anything."

"We'd better think of something fast," said Madora. The water's close to a foot deep and filling quickly. If we sink much lower, the swells are going to swamp us."

The conversation was interrupted by the captain's bellowing through the bullhorn again. "Durin' me time as captain of this brig, I found ways to increase me crew's motivation when I needed somethin' done right and quick. I'm beginnin' to think that ye might be in need of such motivation."

Captain Smullet motioned to a half dozen pirates who were holding three wooden barrels. At his signal, the pirates dumped the contents of the barrels overboard.

"Just a few odds and ends from the galley and the slop bins. Nothin' very appetizing to even a pirate, but there be some creatures of the sea which find them tasty!"

"He's chumming the water," said Sheef.

"He's what?" asked Madora.

"Chumming. Attracting sharks. They typically follow ships like the *Barnacle,* waiting for dumps like the one we just saw."

In the water between the longboat and the brig, multiple dorsal fins surfaced like rapidly moving submarine periscopes. Sheef observed them for a few seconds, and then looked down at the water level which now filled half the boat.

"Aye," shouted Captain Smullet, "yer increased motivation is here already! I figure ye got about ten minutes before becomin' a mornin' snack for them sharks there. That is unless ye begin speakin' "

"Somebody please tell me he has a plan," said Madora.

"I hope Harvey's got something, because I sure don't," replied Sheef.

"What does it matter anyway?" remarked Harvey in a monotone voice. "Even if we do figure out a way to escape drowning or being eaten, we'll never be able to stop him. Nezraut's too powerful. He's already won. Ecclon, the Flurn, everything, already dark and dead. The game is over. We just can't admit or accept it, but we need to. Resistance is pointless, so why not end our delusion. There's no need to waste any more time and energy trying to reverse the nonreversible."

"Oh, for crying out loud! Not now, kid! Of all the lousy times for them to show up. As if sinking ships and sharks weren't enough," said Sheef.

"What? Who's shown up?" asked Madora.

"The enemy's found us again, and they've taken hold of young Harvey's mind."

"You're absolutely correct, Sheef," said a glassy-eyed Harvey. "The enemy is here, as he will soon be everywhere now that he controls Ecclon, which is why he can't be defeated."

"Madora," cautioned Sheef, "don't listen to a word. That's not Harvey speaking."

"What do we do then? How do we help him?"

"First things first. All three of us need to open our eyes and ears to what's actually occurring right now."

Sheef pulled out his bottle of Kreen and instructed Madora to place drops in her eyes and ears. When she was finished, Sheef quickly did the same and then slogged through the water towards Harvey.

Harvey was in such a deep Insip-induced stupor that he did nothing to resist Sheef placing the drops in his eyes and ears. And as happened before, when the scales fell from Harvey's eyes and he was able to see and hear the nest of Insips covering his head and face, he panicked and began hyperventilating.

"SHEEF!" Harvey screamed. THEY'RE BACK! GET THEM OFF OF ME!"

Harvey declared every truth he could think of about himself and the Unseen. Other than a slight fluttering of their wings, however, the Insips were hardly affected by his words. And as the boat sank lower and the sharks swam closer, the image of the sea before Harvey's eyes vanished.

36

The vision returned. Once again, Harvey found himself standing upon steaming volcanic rock. Before him was the cage holding his mother, father, and Thurngood.

The words "speak and release" were carried on the air. Cracks emerged in the volcanic rock.

"WHAT DO YOU WANT ME TO SAY?" Harvey shouted in frustration.

Harvey's mother suddenly pressed her face between the bars. Her look was one of deep concern, not for own predicament, but for Harvey's. Tears of compassion and love pooled in her eyes, creating a chink in the armor of her son's heart.

"What have I been so angry about?" Harvey asked himself. "There's no one who cares more deeply about me than my mom. All those years of her not telling me who I really was, it was out of love. She was just trying to protect me."

Harvey heard the lock click.

"Speak and release" was spoken again.

"Mom," Harvey said out loud, "I . . . I forgive you. I release you. You're free to go."

Another click. Warmth radiated within Harvey's chest.

Emotions ascended from his heart to his mind, filling and animating his thoughts and words with love. As Harvey expressed the same sentiments and words to his father and Thurngood, the cage door began to rattle.

Molten lava oozed from the cracks in the volcanic rock, and just as before, Harvey could feel the soles of his shoes beginning to melt.

"What else do I say?" asked Harvey beginning to panic.

Cracks similar to those in the volcanic rock appeared in the sky above the cage. These, however, weren't meaningless, random fissures of nature, but intelligible inscriptions, scrawled in fiery letters. Before Harvey's eyes hovered a proverb of Gnarl the Deep.

"By spoken blessing, the viper's venom is now the honey nectar."

"What's that supposed to mean?" Harvey asked himself.

The words continued to hover and pulsate as if alive.

"I don't understand. How am I supposed to know what to do?"

Whether it was the Kreen, the influence of the Unseen, or a combination of the two, Harvey unexpectedly understood.

"Of course, how could I not have seen it sooner? My thoughts and words of forgiveness, they're just the beginning. In order to completely set them free, I need to think and speak the opposite. Blessing instead of cursing, life instead of death.

The vision suddenly changed. Harvey's mother, father, and Thurngood were no longer imprisoned. The cage which held them vanished, only to reappear around Harvey. He was the captive, as he had always been, imprisoned by his own thoughts and words.

"It was there all the time," he said to himself. "The cage never did hold them. They were always free. All along, I was the one trapped."

In a bold, commanding voice, Harvey began uttering words of release.

"Mom, I'm grateful that you're my mother, and for your care and protection all these years. I ask the Unseen that the health of Ecclon and that of your body would be restored and that . . ." Harvey continued speaking words of gratitude and blessing over his mother for many minutes before speaking to his father and Thurngood.

"Dad, though I don't remember you, I'm grateful for you sacrificing everything dear to you to save millions from the schemes of the enemy. May you be guided and shielded wherever you are and . . ."

By the time he was finished speaking over Thurngood, the bars of the cage were violently rattling. The sound of the shaking bars grew so wildly loud that Harvey was sure his eardrums would burst at any moment, but just when he thought he couldn't endure a decibel more, the rattling stopped. The bars disintegrated into gnat-sized particles before being whisked away by the breeze.

Harvey's mother, father, and Thurngood stood barefooted in the knee-high grass which had replaced the volcanic rock. They looked once more at Harvey, laughed, and then ran through the valley meadow like young children: free and lost in the joyous present. Their laughter trailed behind, inviting Harvey to join in their youthful romp.

He was about to take a step in pursuit when the ground he was standing on unexpectedly tilted to the right. A dousing of tepid salt water lashed his face. The knee-high grass which he was standing in became fluid in its movements, and with a second dousing of water, the vision disappeared altogether

Harvey was back in the longboat, which was only seconds from being completely submerged. The jolt of returning from the vision sent him stumbling backwards into the water-filled boat.

Though his head was still swarming with Insips, he didn't panic as he had done before the vision, for his thoughts were once again infused with power.

"THE UNSEEN IS TRUTH! HE HAS ALWAYS BEEN AND WILL ALWAYS BE! I AM HIS!" And with these simple declarations, Harvey set the Insips shrieking in terror. They were jettisoned away from his head, soaring into the atmosphere like rocketing fireworks, eventually exploding, leaving behind nothing but small puffs of brown smoke.

"Looks like Ecclon's favored son has returned," said Sheef. Both he and Madora were already out of the boat and treading water with Fromp and Akeila swimming circles around them.

"And now that you've taken care of those Insips, maybe you could think us out of drowning!" Sheef shouted.

"Or out of being eaten!" screamed Madora as a large dorsal fin surfaced less than four feet away.

By this time the longboat had gone completely under, and as Harvey looked down at his treading legs, he saw the weatherworn craft quickly receding into the blue abyss below.

A fifteen foot black tip torpedoed in from the right, moving so quickly that Harvey saw the shark and felt its exploratory bump simultaneously. Five additional sharks soon joined the game of weaving around the flailing legs of human and hound.

"They're investigating!" yelled Sheef. "Checking us out to see if anything looks appetizing enough to take a bite."

"How long will this phase last?" asked Madora.

"Long enough, I hope, for us to figure out how to get off the menu," replied Sheef.

"Sheef!" Harvey yelled. "Look, behind the brig!"

As Sheef turned around to look at the pirate ship, he paused in mid-tread, stupefied at the sight. Emerging from behind the brig, at a speed which was eerily outpacing the light breeze, was an enormous man-of-war. The length and height of the warship dwarfed the *Barnacle*. Moving as if before a storm gale, the ship suddenly came to a complete and silent stop, its port side parallel to Captain Smullet's starboard.

More than thirty hooded figures were gathered along the side of the man-of-war, their faces hidden in shadow. The tallest of the figures was cloaked in a familiar grey hood, and next to him, with monstrous front paws atop the gunnels of the ship, was a snarling, fang-toothed snout.

Sköll was viciously barking at the pirate ship. Grauncrock tilted his head backward, lifting the hood's shadow enough to reveal a fiendish grin of serrated teeth.

"And there I was thinking that things couldn't possibly get any worse," said Sheef as he reached out and punched an overly curious shark on the nose. The dazed animal changed directions and swam away from the group.

"I don't get it," said Harvey. "How could a detachment of Vapid Lords get hold of an 18th Century man-of-war?"

"Not the best time or place to explain it," said Madora as she kicked the back of a small shark.

"I know, but it might help."

"Really, Harvey! We're about to be eaten! What difference does it make now?"

"I might have an idea on how to save us, but I need to know!"

"Okay, but we better make this quick," replied Madora as she swam closer to Harvey. "Someone on board that man-of-war is familiar with the Phantasian. Probably been here hundreds of times. Takes experience in these worlds to do what he did, not to mention the powerful thinking required to pull it off."

"What exactly did he pull off?" asked Harvey.

"Rewriting parts of this world," sputtered Madora as a wave splashed her in the face, filling her mouth with seawater. "Think of what's happening to Gwen but on a much larger scale. It's rarely done. Not just because it's difficult to do, but because altering these worlds is dangerous. But it can be done if someone knows how and has thoughts powerful enough to make a rewrite."

"A Vapid Lord aboard that ship, maybe Nezraut himself, changed the details of this world and created a warship to attack us?" asked Harvey.

"Looks like it."

"Nezraut's not on that ship," said Sheef. "I can sense him if he's close. Must be one of his lackeys."

Madora suddenly shrieked out in pain. Sheef quickly swam to her side and dived under, ready to engage her attacker. The shark, however, had already gone, taking a nip of her calf in the process. Blood colored the surrounding water.

"Are you okay?" asked a panicking Sheef.

"I'm all right," moaned Madora, "It hurts, but it wasn't much of a bite. I'm lucky it was one of the smaller ones that only wanted a taste, but I think the investigative phase is over."

Sheef yelled to Harvey who was about ten feet away. "Madora's been bit and there's blood in the water! Won't be long until they're whipped into a frenzy. I'm going to swim her over to the brig."

"You'll never make it, and even if you do, you'll hand yourself over to the enemy."

"If you've got a better idea, you'd better let me know. The chances are slim, but I rather die trying than treading here waiting to be devoured."

Since the vision, Harvey could feel the Unseen's power increasingly infusing his thoughts. He wondered at the words Madora had spoken, wondered if it might possibly work. A soothing assurance let him know that it would. Rewrite. A rewrite would be their way of escape. While continuing to tread in the shark-infested waters, Harvey began to imagine.

"Sheef!" screamed Madora, pointing directly behind him. Sheef turned and saw a huge dorsal fin speeding through the water in his direction. The sharp blade was cutting through the water, tilling it in foam and spray.

Sheef raised his fist, hoping to get at least one hit on the shark's nose before it attacked. When the toothy torpedo was ten feet away, it opened its jaws wide. Because of its speed, size, and opened mouth, Sheef knew that he now had no chance of hitting the shark's sensitive snout to thwart the attack. He lowered his fist and squeezed his eyes shut, praying that the bite would be large and deadly enough to put a quick end to him.

Sheef couldn't believe, after everything he had endured, that it would end like this. Killed by a fictitious predator on a fictitious planet that was created on the typewriter of a Hollywood screen-writer decades ago. The writer never having the slightest notion that his imaginative thoughts would someday threaten the very non-fiction life of a fellow human being.

The tooth and fin encounter, though, never occurred. Instead of a searing pain ripping his flesh, Sheef felt large air bubbles buoyantly bouncing off his body, rising up from the abyss below.

The sharks were suddenly gone. Something from the deep had spooked them, and whatever was lurking in the darkness was stirring, its bubbles a prelude to its ascending emergence.

The temperature of the water dramatically dropped as a deep water isotherm was suddenly thrust upward. The rising water lifted everyone a few feet into the air.

The only one, including Fromp and Akeila, who didn't appear perplexed by what was happening, was Harvey. Casually tread-ing water, Harvey's countenance was one of tranquil fierceness. Sheef knew immediately that whatever was happening was being directed by Harvey. He had seen the very same look when Harvey saved him from plummeting to his death in the canyon near Nezraut's lair. Sheef grinned. The kid and his thoughts were back.

The one-hundred-foot behemoth appeared from below, rap-idly rising upward. When the blue whale broke the surface, the entire group was simultaneously lifted out of the water upon its back.

Standing and dripping upon the small island of drying whale skin, Sheef yelled out to Harvey. "It turns out that you did have a much better idea. I'm really glad I asked. You do know, Harvey, that you never cease to amaze me!"

"Harvey's responsible for this?" asked Madora, bewildered and attempting to process what had just occurred.

Smiling from ear to ear, and now resting comfortably on the back of the whale, Sheef nodded. "The Unseen's hand and power have been heavy upon the thoughts and destiny of young Harvey since I first met him."

"Seriously?" asked Madora, beginning to laugh. "First time to the Phantasian and he does a major rewrite! A blue whale to our rescue, brilliant writing is all I have to say! And my calf, there's no more pain," Madora said as she examined her leg. "There's no wound, not even a scratch from the shark bite. Harvey, you wrote away the wound, didn't you?"

"A true prince of Ecclon," said Sheef proudly.

The booming voice of Captain Smullet speaking through his bullhorn diverted their attention. The broadsides of the man-of-war and the pirate brig were no more than thirty feet apart. The hatches along the brig's starboard side were open, and protruding out of each was a large cannon barrel. The battery crew below had stuffed the muzzles with charge and shot, and each of the gunners was primed and ready for maritime combat.

The Vapid Lords, still standing along the port side of the ship, had cupped their hands together in front of them.

"Don't be recognizin' yer ship nor yer banners!" yelled Captain Smullet to the Vapid Lords. "And I don't look favorable on any ship, regardless of its size, sailin' into firin' range upon me. And since I can't see that yer moves could be in anyway peaceable, I'll be givin' ye just one chance of puttin' sail to that mast of yers and bein' off with ye."

The Vapid Lords remained motionless, their faces shadowed by their hoods. The captain dropped the bullhorn to his side and turned to Splinter who was standing next to him.

"I hate not bein' able to see me enemy's eyes," he said. "The eye being the window to a man's true intents, but when they be cloaked, many a time it means rough water ahead. Mr. Grimely, tell the boys to prepare to fire upon me signal."

The bullhorn went back to the captain's lips. "I won't be askin' for ye to weigh anchor again. This be yer last chance before I make splinters out of yer broadside!"

The captain's voice broke slightly in the middle of his threat, revealing that he was not nearly as bold and confident as his words would indicate and that he had no desire to open fire upon such a large warship.

Spheres of fire appeared in the cupped hands of the Vapid Lords.

Putting down the bullhorn, the captain said to the crew around him, "I don't be likin' the looks of this. Lightin' torches in the middle of the day be for only one reason: settin' flame to powder."

Captain Smullet turned around and addressed the crew. "Brace yerselves, boys. Seein' as this might be our last fight, let's make it one worthy of the name *Barnacle* and scalawags everywhere! Mr. Pauddles, take our guest below and put her somewhere safe."

Pauddles walked over to Gwen and attempted to escort her below deck. She, however, refused to go along. She didn't want to miss what she perceived to be the climax of the game.

The captain turned back around and once again faced the Vapid Lords. "Ye be givin' me no other choice," he mumbled to himself.

Raising the bullhorn to his lips for one final time, he yelled out, "FIRE!"

At precisely the same moment, the spheres of fire flew from the hands of the Vapid Lords, colliding with the cannonballs in midflight. Rather than destroying the cannonballs, though, the spheres halted their motion and then absorbed them. More than a dozen fire-covered cannonballs hovered in the air between the two ships.

"Well peg me other leg," said the captain gasping, "but what manner of sea sorcery be this?"

Grauncrock pulled his hood completely off, revealing his sharp, skeletal facial features. His yellow lifeless eyes bored in upon the captain's.

"The boy," the Vapid Lord hissed. "Hand him over to me now or die."

37

Thinking that Harvey had gone under with the sharks, the captain truthfully replied, "There be no boy here. Not even so much as a cabin boy to swab the deck."

"You lie," Grauncrock hissed again. "A foolish thing to do as you shall soon feel. Rest assured that you and your entire crew will die, but whether or not you are tortured before your death is entirely up to you. Now, tell me, where is the boy? Sköll tracked his foul trail here and his nose is never wrong."

"There *was* a lad here," the captain replied nervously, clearly shaken by the gruesome figure before him, "but he, bless his little heart, had an unfortunate accident. Lost his footin' while dumpin' the slop off the stern there. Straight into the drink he fell, right into a pack of trollin' sharks. Aye, it was sad sight to be sure. The truth is, the lad never had a chance."

"Is that so?" Grauncrock asked with narrowing eyes. "How interesting and ironic that a prince of Ecclon, who's proven his balance and poise in battle, would accidently fall overboard. No, that is not what occurred at all. Try again, but this time, Captain, tell me the truth or the pain you will – ”

Captain Smullet was momentarily saved by the interruption from another Vapid Lord. “My liege,” the Vapid Lord said to Grauncrock, “there is a tattered Insip that says he has seen the boy.”

Grauncrock invited the Insip to fly into his presence with a slow curling of his elongated finger. The leathery skin of the Insip was torn and mutilated. Hardly able to maintain flight, the injured creature landed on the gunnel and excitedly spewed forth its report.

“Oh, most malicious Grauncrock,” the Insip rapidly spewed out, “the boy which you seek is alive and well, too well, yes he is. He was, as I witnessed it all, set adrift with the others in a small craft. Done by the captain, yes, yes, the captain of the other ship. My companions and I were partaking of a lovely feast of the most toxic thoughts, delectable morsels they were, until everything abruptly changed.”

“Changed?” asked Grauncrock, his eyes narrowing to mere yellow slits.

“Yes, yes, changed for the worse. Food turned repulsive. The boy’s thoughts went completely to rot! Flavored with the One. Ruined the feast it did, and it was so lovely.”

Grauncrock grabbed the Insip tightly around the neck and lifted it up in the air. “Cease your interminable jabbering and explain what you mean by his thoughts flavored by the ‘one’.”

“Oh please, my lord, don’t make me say the name!”

“What name?” asked Grauncrock, squeezing the Insip’s throat even tighter.

"The Unseen," it choked out. "That's why, yes certainly why, we were flung into the air. The others tasted too much of Him. Couldn't take it. Burst into bits of scale and gut. Was the only one to survive, I was. And the boy and his friends are still there; you'll find them, yes. On the other side of the fool's ship they are."

Grauncrock tossed the gasping Insip aside as he said, "It appears, my fellow Vapid, that the captain's ship has been obscuring our view of young Harvey. Fortunately for us, it is a problem that can easily be remedied."

Grauncrock stretched out his arm towards the pirate brig and lightly flicked his skeletal fingers. The fire-covered cannonballs, which were still hovering in between the two ships, responded immediately, rocketing into the brig's broadside.

Fire engulfed the entire ship. The flames licked after the fleeing crew until all the men and Gwen fled overboard like leaping lemmings.

When the fire burned through the door of the powder magazine, the subsequent explosion created a plume of fire hundreds of feet into the air. Fragments of flaming sail, rope, and wood rained down upon the sea where the ship had been resting only seconds before. The men in the water dived under to avoid the falling debris.

The burning wreckage was billowing so much smoke that Grauncrock was unable to see through to Harvey and the others, who were still atop the whale on the other side.

Harvey directed the whale to swim within feet of the burning wreckage. He then conjured up a breeze strong enough to dissipate most of the smoke. As it cleared, Grauncrock was startled to see Harvey firmly planted upon the head of an enormous whale, a confident and grim determination etched upon his face.

Sheef and Madora, meanwhile, were helping Gwen and the men in the water climb out and onto the relative safety of the whale's back. And even though the petrified and disoriented men now posed no threat whatsoever, Fromp and Akeila still kept a close growl upon them. Gwen was smiling and giggling, thinking that her brush with death was simply all part of the ongoing game.

It was a rare occurrence for a Vapid Lord, such as Grauncrock, to be startled. In fact, to this point, only Nezraut and talk of the Unseen had ever instilled fear in him, and for this very reason, it took Grauncrock a moment or two to regain his aggressive posturing.

"Finally we meet, young Harvey," Grauncrock hissed. "Let me begin by thanking you for that most conspicuous trail you left for me to follow, though I do fear its pungency has weakened considerably."

"Not just weakened, gone entirely."

"Oh, how delightful for you. But it matters not at this point. I have located you, and as you will soon realize, stopped you from retrieving the Narciss Glass. Are you surprised, Harvey? Oh yes, Nezraut knows all about your little mission to destroy it. By the way, my master sends his apologies for not being present here himself, but he simply could not get away. So many preparations to be made for invading and ruling every world in existence."

"I'm sure I'll get over not seeing him again," Harvey said sarcastically.

"Now I must applaud your success at progressing this far. Nezraut spoke very highly of your abilities, Harvey, and coming so close to achieving your goal, certainly reinforces his high opinion of you. But alas, this is where your mission must end."

"Have you forgotten what was done to Nezraut during our first encounter?" Harvey asked defiantly.

"Not at all. To be ignorant or forgetful of such events is to be ill prepared. It is impressive to have gotten the upper hand in your first battle with my master. This time, however, the outcome shall be quite different. You see, Nezraut faced you the first time alone, without even one Vapid Lord to fight at his side. Additionally, he was not aware of your power, but as you can clearly see, I am not alone, and as for your power, it has faltered quite substantially."

"Past tense," Harvey shot back. "Had faltered. And it was never mine to begin with."

"Is that so? I am not sure I follow."

"The power did falter, but it was never mine to begin with. The power and strength of my thoughts and actions doesn't come from me, but from the unbounding omnipotence and goodness of the Unseen. All that I am and do is because I am His. And the thing that was dulling His power in me has been expelled."

"Has it now? Then we shall soon see, shall we not?"

"We shall."

"Harvey," said Sheef walking up from behind, "I hope you know what you're doing. You saw what they did to Smullet's ship, and that's a whole lot of Vapid to contend with."

Harvey turned and looked directly at Sheef, a confident smirk growing larger by the second. "Sheef, what was that proverb of

Gnarl's that Bellock shared with me? Something about the eyes of a giant being blinded?"

"I know, I know. 'Are blinded by the smallest grains of sand'. I just hope we have enough grains."

"Don't worry, Sheef, the Unseen has entire beaches full of the stuff."

Sheef smiled and patted Harvey on the shoulder. "That He does, kid. That He does."

Fire spheres once again appeared in the Vapid's hands. This time, however, the spheres were larger, and each was composed of a much hotter swirling blue flame.

"Now, Harvey," said Grauncrock, "before you and your friends are incinerated, are there any last words that you would like me to convey to Nezraut?"

"Yeah, tell him that the best laid plans of evil are often unraveled by noble acts of good."

"How quaint. I presume this is another adage from Ecclon's gnarled sage?"

"Nope, it's all mine, but you're going to find it difficult getting this message back to your master without a Sadiki and from the bottom of the ocean."

Grauncrock looked quizzically at Harvey for a second before snickering to himself. "I beg your pardon, Harvey, but I seem to have missed the intended meaning of your words."

"Are you sure about this," whispered Sheef, looking nervously over Harvey's shoulder.

"What do you think, Sheef," whispered Harvey, "is it time for our friend here to have a lesson in hydraulics?"

Sheef was just about to ask what Harvey was talking about when a towering ocean swell appeared on the horizon. As it raced closer to the Vapid's ship, its crest grew to a dizzying height, high enough to eclipse the mid-morning sun.

Grauncrock, unnerved by the spreading darkness, turned around and beheld the mountain of water, now hundreds upon hundreds of feet tall. The man-of-war was but a miniscule toy compared to the immensity of the approaching wave.

"Harvey," asked Sheef in disbelief, "you're doing that, aren't you?" Sheef tilted his head back and peered up at the enormous mountain of water. "That's amazing, kid . . . but just in case you didn't realize it, when that wave breaks on the Vapid's ship, it's going to take us out as well."

"Relax, Sheef, that'll only happen if we're still in the way," said Harvey as he turned around and smiled. "The thing I'm quickly learning about the Phantasian is that the only limits here are the limits of the imagination. But if you can imagine it, you can do it."

A tremor went through the whale's body, causing a number of its riders, including Sheef, to stumble off their feet and onto its back. When Sheef regained his footing and stood up, he realized that the man-of-war appeared to be growing smaller, as if the ship was somehow sinking down. It didn't take him long, though, to determine what was actually occurring. The ship wasn't sinking down, or for that matter, moving at all. Rather, it was the whale, and everyone on its back, that was moving. Rising up upon currents of air like a hot air balloon, the behemoth ascended heavenward.

Within seconds, the whale and its passengers were thousands of feet above the ocean. The man-of-war below appeared as a bath toy.

The wave broke less than fifty feet from the ship. The mushrooming mounds of turbulent white water swallowed the craft, the powerful hydraulics obliterating it into countless pieces and pushing them nearly a thousand feet below the surface.

Harvey was still standing on the head of the whale when Sheef said breathlessly from behind, "Harvey . . . I mean how . . . how did that . . . ?"

"I think I'm getting the hang of this whole rewriting thing," said Harvey, still looking straight ahead. "You know what I mean? Here, with just a little imagination, you can move an entire mountain."

"Or a whale," laughed Sheef in disbelief. "I think I'm inclined to agree with you, kid. You just might have a knack for this sort of thing," he said while playfully smacking Harvey's head with the back of his hand.

"Harvey!" yelled Madora, who was making her way forward from mid-whale. "Nubia, Akeila's sister, was on that ship. She had to be!"

"Not when the wave hit," replied Harvey. "Why don't you take a look behind you."

Madora turned around and saw Nubia being tended to by Fromp and Akeila.

"But how?" asked Madora. "Nubia had to be with the Vapid. There's no other way they could've traveled through the Phantasian."

"You're right, Madora. Nubia was on the ship, but I used the brig's explosion as the perfect distraction. The Vapid's attention was riveted on the burning brig, which kept them from seeing Fromp warp over there and snatch Nubia from under their noses. They were so pleased with the destruction they had inflicted on Captain Smullet and his crew that they were oblivious to what was happening on the deck behind their backs. By the time our whale began to rise, Nubia was already safely onboard."

"Prince of Ecclon indeed," said a stunned and elated Madora.

Harvey set the whale back down on the ocean once the sea had settled. There was not a shred of evidence that the man-of-war had ever existed.

When they were safely back on water, the pirates, who had tenaciously clung like barnacles to the back of the whale during its flight, began once again to move about.

Captain Smullet hesitantly approached Harvey. "Don't know what ye really be, but I ain't never seen the likes of ye or what ye done. It's as if some great myth come to life right before me very eyes. And I thank ye for savin' me life, especially in light of me tryin' to end yers. Much obliged."

Splinter slinked up from behind. No longer seeing the advantage in feigning loyalty to the captain, now that someone more powerful and potentially beneficial to the promotion of his selfish ambitions had emerged, Splinter turned on Captain Smullet.

Weaseling up to Harvey's side, Splinter said, "Mr. Kid, I hope you know that I was never in favor of seein' ye harmed in any way. Truth is, I tried with all me vigor to talk the captain out of tossin' ye overboard, but he wouldn't have any of it. There was bloody vengeance in his eyes for ye. Don't know why, but I be favorable of ye from the moment I saw ye on the deck of the *Barnacle*."

Here Splinter leaned in closer to Harvey as he lowered his voice. "And ye know I be privy to a secret. Know the location of Smullet's treasure. Aye, heavy it be with gold and jewel, and I'll gladly show ye the location if ye take me on as part of ye crew. Perhaps as your first mate, seeing as no man knows these waters better than old and faithful Splinter."

Sheef, who was close enough to Harvey to hear Splinter's words, turned to Madora and said, "I can't believe it. Splinter just sold the captain out. He must see Harvey as a better means to promote himself."

"No different than the actor who played Splinter's part," Madora remarked. "Schemers and scalawags through and through. This could very well be it. I need you to look very carefully for any peculiarities in the space around Splinter."

"What kind of peculiarities?"

"Not exactly sure. I've only seen it happen once before, and I don't think it always occurs in the same way. Maybe look for some type of optical distortion or something."

Sheef looked over at Splinter, suspiciously scrutinizing every inch of space above and around him. He saw nothing. He turned to Madora and shook his head. She motioned for him to move closer.

Sheef responded by walking behind Harvey and Splinter. Harvey turned and looked at Sheef, confused, but didn't say anything. Sheef still didn't observe anything abnormal. There was one place, however, that he had yet to check, the area around and under Splinter's feet. When he did look there, he saw what appeared to be a shimmering reflection on the whale's back.

Upon closer inspection, Sheef could tell that some image, other than the whale's back, was directly under Splinter's feet. It was distorted, so it took Sheef a few seconds to figure it out. When he finally did, he observed the image of a man standing alone in an office, appearing lost in contemplative thought. A smug expression was smarmily painted across the man's face, suggesting that he had recently figured out a way to exploit a person or situation. The man was rubbing his fingers together like a raccoon manipulating a treat it had just fished out of a trashcan.

The longer Sheef looked at the image, the more defined it became, and it wasn't' long before he recognized the face. It was Millud. A doorway to 1930's Hollywood had appeared.

Sheef quickly walked to the other side of Harvey, whispered in his ear, and stealthily poured a few drops of Kreen into his hand. Harvey very casually wiped his lips with his hand. He had no idea what was transpiring, but he knew that Sheef wanted to communicate without speaking.

"Sheef whispered to Madora about the portal and asked, "What now? How do we go through?"

"First we have to open it. Fromp and Akeila will have to do that, but we don't have much time. Splinter will have to be moved from atop the image. Once it's clear, Fromp and Akeila will grab hold of the reflection and pull it off, exposing the warp hole below."

"You mean the dogs are going to open a warp hole like they're going after a bone buried in the ground?"

"Don't look surprised, Sheef. We are in the Phantasian after all and just took a flight upon the back of a whale."

"Point taken."

"Once the portal's uncovered, we won't have very long to make the jump. We need to have everyone ready."

Sheef sent a thought to Harvey explaining everything. Harvey raised his eyebrows upon receiving it and then nodded. Sheef conveyed a similar message to Fromp, while Madora communicated with Akeila and Nubia.

Sheef then asked Gwen to join him. When she walked over, he reached out and took hold of her hand.

"Gwen, the game is about to get very interesting. Just do exactly what I do, but whatever happens, don't let go of my hand."

Gwen excitedly giggled and nodded her head.

Harvey then addressed Captain Smullet. "Captain, I will have this creature transport you to the nearest dry land, where I'm confident you'll find the means to resume your pirating, but as for my crew, the time for our departure has arrived."

The captain looked confused. "Depart? Depart how, laddie? I don't be seein' any way of ye leavin' other than swimmin', and I be sure that ye had more than enough of that today."

"Don't worry about that, Captain. And now for you, Splinter." Splinter smiled widely, confident that he was about to be asked to join Harvey and his crew. Harvey, instead, turned towards him and forcefully shoved him off his feet and over the side of the whale.

By the time droplets from the splash reached back up to the whale's head, Fromp and Akeila were already atop the reflection. Each latched on to a piece of the reflection with their teeth, and with a strong yank, flipped the image over like a manhole cover. Underneath was a deep black hole, and at its very bottom was what appeared to be a small blue and green marble.

Madora was already running to the opening. "EVERYONE, NOW! BEFORE IT CLOSES!" she yelled as she jumped through, falling down and back, to a planet below and a time before.

Harvey was the last to jump. As he descended through, he wondered if this mad-capped adventure to save Ecclon and all worlds could possibly get any more bizarre. Moments later, he entered the atmosphere of 1930's Earth, freefalling towards a small town in southern California, where he would soon learn the answer to his question.

38

ack in the Egyptian desert, Harvey's mother and Thurngood stood before the collapsed entrance of Madora's subterranean home. Joust had tracked Fromp's scent here and was now pawing in the sand around the large pieces of black granite.

Since there was no way for them to clear the large rocks from the entrance, it was impossible for Harvey's mother to know the fate of her son. But in her heart, she felt that he was still alive.

*****

Night had descended upon Ecclon for the first time in its long existence. The air was thick with smoke. The enemy had poured in like swarming locusts, setting fire to everything that was combustible. The smoke blocked any light from the stars above.

Gnarl the Deep stood amongst the charred remains of the Flurn Council. He was weak. Only one leaf remained on his limbs. Ecclon and her defenders were lost. Nothing could be done in the present nor the future to save them now. The only hope lay in the past.

A cold wind sliced through the darkness. Gnarl's remaining leaf trembled, loosed, and fluttered to the ground.

ABOUT THE AUTHOR

R Duncan Williams has been in the education field for over twenty years as a speaker, trainer, and teacher. Along the way, he has crafted numerous stories for use in and out of the classroom. Williams currently resides in Austin, Texas, with his wife and two sons. Be sure to read his first book in the Thinkwave series.

To learn more about R Duncan Williams, visit
his website at www.rduncanwilliams.com